Praise for

A LONELY GIRL IS A DANGEROUS THING

'This novel knocked me out. I read *A Lonely Girl is a Dangerous Thing* with escalating excitement, galvanised by the emergence of a powerful new voice. Tu's writing is fierce, bold and astonishingly controlled. The storytelling is deft and compelling.'

Christos Tsiolkas, author of *Damascus*

'Searing, unflinching and unapologetic, Jessie Tu is a fearless talent.'

Sophie Hardcastle, author of *Below Deck*

'I absolutely inhaled this book. Gutsy, bold and surprising, with a darkness that draws you in and keeps you hanging onto every word. This novel is both an adventure and an intelligent character study. It's a razor-sharp reflection of middle-class white patriarchy, but fun, too, somehow. I haven't read anything like this in a long while and especially not in a debut. I hope to see Tu's name on prize lists next year.'

Bri Lee, author of *Eggshell Skull*

A LONELY GIRL IS A DANGEROUS THING

A LONELY GIRL IS A DANGEROUS THING

JESSIE TU

ALLEN&UNWIN
SYDNEY • MELBOURNE • AUCKLAND • LONDON

Allen & Unwin
83 Alexander Street
Crows Nest NSW 2065
Australia
Phone: (61 2) 8425 0100
Email: info@allenandunwin.com
Web: www.allenandunwin.com

 A catalogue record for this
book is available from the
National Library of Australia

ISBN 978 1 76087 719 4

Set in 11.2/17 pt Aldus LT Std by Bookhouse, Sydney
Printed and bound in Australia by Griffin Press, part of Ovato

10 9 8 7 6 5 4 3 2

The paper in this book is FSC® certified.
FSC® promotes environmentally responsible,
socially beneficial and economically viable
management of the world's forests.

For M.L.

The panic of the female race comes
only after she falls for the other.

—THE NARRATOR

1

The ceremony lasts longer than anyone expected. We are gathered at the last minute to provide the music. The wife of the dead man had insisted on having the funeral at noon. Dragged from our Saturday morning sleep-ins by a text at 9 am. *We,* as in, the orchestra. His old students. It's a pop-up funeral. I suppose all funerals are pop-up. Nobody plans on dying.

Neither did I plan on being inside a chapel closet with a bassoon player, gripping his hair as he spread my legs apart. Pantyhose down. Donut rings around ankle. Cunt salivating. His tongue slips inside my mouth. We are upright, heaving our bodies against each other. Fingers struggling at his belt.

I'd known the boy from Young Performers Awards when we were both ten. He had braces, a scar over his left eye and bad breath that smelt like blue cheese. I felt sorry for him. The kind of pity that was entirely self-serving. I knew this yet felt no shame. He took pity on me, too, I think, because I was the only other Asian who made it to the final round of the comp, which was unusual. Usually, we dominate the podium. Now we were newly minted college graduates, reunited. Better hair. Better skin. Better sense.

Bassoon bends down to retrieve a condom from his pocket. Naked below our torsos. I kneel down. Give his cock a paddle-pop lick. He is smaller than I expected.

He tears at the aluminium wrapping.

'Here, let me.'

In the darkness, his hands trace my skull as I reach up and unpeel the rubber along his cock. His breath is heavy. I stand to meet his face. Open mouth fans the hair around my cheeks. He lifts me up, slides inside me. Thrusts. Groans. Marks each penetration with a short, muffled growl. The male is insertive. I am receptive. He grabs my wrist for balance. I flinch.

Tchaikovsky's Adagio Lamentoso floats through the speakers outside.

'Fuck! We're on.'

I push him off; leap out of the closet, pull on my panties, skirt, rummage for my shoes. He zips his trousers, pants frantically.

'I was so close to coming!'

'Where's my violin?' I scan the room.

He points to the corner where my Gabriel Strad lies on top of the piano. I slip on my shoes, pick up the violin. Bolt. Hand to the door. Pause. I still my shoulders. Composure.

On the stage, I arch my back. Violin gripped at the scroll. A large congregation of mourners blink in my direction like school children waiting for instruction. Eighteen musicians wait on me. Behind them, a row of twenty vocalists.

Suspended over our heads, a banner:

IN MEMORIUM

PHILIP RESLING

30 JANUARY 1948 – 10 JANUARY 2016

Bassoon shuffles into place next to the clarinets, his black hair standing up at weird angles. I glance at the leaders of each section and rest my eyes on the music. I guide the violin into my neck. Bow on the A string. Pull.

A low, sustained murmur trails through the chapel. We begin Mozart's Requiem in D minor.

He'd written it for his own funeral, supposedly. At university, Olivia and I wrote poems for our parents to read aloud at our funerals. We were stupid like that.

The choir enter on cue, dramatic and full of minor-key despair. My fingers drop like hammers on the fingerboard. I could play these lines half asleep. I glance at Bassoon whom I'd just let inside my body. His eyes are closed, brow creased. I return to the music in front of me. Long bows. Arms raised. We only play the Introitus; the opening. Sustain the final note. My eyes flick to the banner above, a photo of my former accompanist, who'd died suddenly last Sunday. A stroke in his sleep. In the picture, he is staring into the camera, daring us to look away. His wife and daughter are hunched in the front pew. They are silent. They are still. They are deflecting the pity being thrown at them. I look back at Bassoon. His eyes are still closed. What a loser.

The wife invites us to the wake at the family home. Other musicians exchange stories about the dead man. I hide in a corner with a glass of orange juice, staring at the plate of cut triangle sandwiches and assorted cream biscuits. There is nothing sadder than a plate of assorted cream biscuits arranged on a plastic plate.

Bassoon spots me from the doorway.

'Hey.'

'Oh, hi.'

'Good performance.'

I swallow some juice. 'I think so.'

'Olivia said you toured with him.'

'No. He toured with *me*.'

Just in time. My best friend pedals across the room, offering a plate of sliced melon and blueberries. I put an arm around her shoulder and take the plate.

'This is a dreary funeral. Why don't we get married?'

Bassoon glances between us. 'Very funny.'

Olivia pushes a palm into my face. 'You wish we were married. You're not my type. You're too thin.'

I roll my eyes. It's 2016. Anyone respectable is thin.

'You're also too pretty,' Olivia says.

'And you guys are both girls, so,' Bassoon chuckles.

'Are you serious?' I stop chewing midway through a piece of melon.

'Quieten down!' A man in a grey suit walks by and puts a finger to his lips.

'Fuck you.'

'Jena!' Olivia slaps my arm. 'That was Resling's brother. I have to go apologise.'

Bassoon and I watch her walk into the kitchen, where the man has disappeared into.

I am so ashamed. I'd just fucked a homophobic bassoon player.

'About before,' he begins. 'I don't think—'

'Don't worry.'

He smiles awkwardly. I want him to walk away.

What did I know about throwing my body at strangers?

A whole lot.

I was a child prodigy. I never learned to share the attention. I was always the only kid in the room. I was always the star.

My grandpapa was a child prodigy too. He believed talent chose people. He said it was his destiny to suffer. To pursue great art. He had needs. They were excessive. That's what he used to say. He used to say it all the time. Maybe I inherited his ferocity. It drove him mad. And wild. And to his death.

2

Home is Sydney. An old terrace house with cracked walls. Tasteful damp. I live on a quiet street in Newtown, a suburb in the inner west lined with milk crate cafes and bike stores owned by bearded white guys with sensible tattoos. Most practice takes place here, away from the chaos of the city. Away from my mother. Away from Banks.

A week after the funeral, Olivia and I find an evening to practise together. I'm in bed pushing a glass vibrator between my legs when I hear her arrive. I wipe myself clean and slip on a T-shirt and shorts before opening the door.

She wheels her bike onto the verandah as I step out, barefoot. Her hair bunched in a loose ponytail; violin case strapped to her back.

'Why did you cycle here? It's *dangerous* on King Street.'

She shrugs, unties her hair and whips it around like a dog shaking off its wet. She's clutching her helmet in one hand and extracting a Tupperware container from her shoulder bag. 'Brownies. I just baked them this morning.'

'These don't have hash in them, do they?'

I follow her into the kitchen. She pours herself a glass of water.

'Why would I want us to be stoned while practising?'

We're auditioning for a permanent place in the Sydney Symphony Orchestra; both of us have been casuals since the beginning of 2015 sustaining on sporadic incomes. The audition is a few months away. Only one position is opening. My best friend and I are vying for the same role. It's new terrain for us.

The orchestra performs four nights a week, beginning Wednesday. Most of the time, we're called on Friday or Saturday nights. The programs on those nights require larger numbers. Mahler. Brahms. Big romantic symphonies. The pay is decent. One concert is enough to cover a week's rent. I have a small amount of money left from my time as a soloist. Most of it I'd spent on books during university.

'Did you warm up already?' Olivia slips off her case and begins unzipping.

'Yep.'

We play chromatic scales. G, G sharp, A, A flat. All the way to F sharp. Then down again. We pick each other apart sonically. Whoever fumbles on intonation has to buy dinner. In the last two weeks, I've had to pick up the bill.

Olivia thinks I'm deliberately hitting the wrong notes because I pity her. We both know I am the better player.

The first five minutes, we play flawlessly, two violins in unison. We hit each note with the calibrated precision of a sniper. During a fast-descending passage of the F harmonic minor scale, her notes scatter off-key. I blast her.

She dips her chin in defeat. 'I can only afford Thai.'

After graduation, Olivia moved in with Noah. They'd met Theatre Sports one Tuesday afternoon when Olivia was in year ten at Barker College. Noah was in year twelve at Newington. They started fucking a few weeks later and haven't spent a weekend apart since. They have shared iTunes playlists containing Coldplay, Maroon 5 and Drake. They once played an entire Bruno Mars album on repeat at a party. I had to leave to find another party, one with better music. Their studio is on the ground floor of an apartment block in Enmore. They tell me they don't mind the forced physical intimacy.

Before Olivia, there was nobody else. I was one of those girls people saw coming and going, appearing too busy to socialise. I'd never known how to relax, how to 'hang out'. I had no idea how to 'be'. Recently, Olivia has been the one coming and going. Perhaps it's her job teaching violin at her old primary school in the Blue Mountains. Perhaps it's her mother, whose illness she has not yet named. Perhaps even she does not know what it is.

We finish the scales, arpeggios, bow exercises and move on to the excerpts. On my laptop, I bring up the third movement of Beethoven's 9th. We play along.

'Can we do it separately?' Olivia sighs through her nose.

'What's wrong?'

'You're playing too loud.'

'It's supposed to be loud—*fortissimo*.'

'I'm hungry.'

'Then order.'

It's past ten when the food arrives. A slim man stands at the door with a helmet on, holding a package at his chest. Olivia brings in the bag and I set up the plates in the kitchen. She scoops half the noodles into my bowl, the rest into hers.

'Let's put on some music.'

Silence makes Olivia nervous. When I first met her, she was always wearing earphones. She'd have them in even during class. One ear, usually the left. She was always distracted, in some other place.

'Beethoven? Mozart?'

'You pick.'

I settle on Ravel, the second movement of his Piano Concerto in G. Its sad waltz-like gentleness always soothes the bottomless need I feel to move, to do something. We eat, hum along, eat more. I look around the kitchen, stop at a small magnet in the shape of Royal Albert Hall on the fridge door. My mother had bought it when I debuted there in another life. Was I eight or nine?

Since I moved out of home, I have seen less of my mother. She was reluctant for me to leave the North Shore, but I'd grown weary of the stifling whiteness of the upper middle class. The casual wealth. The polite faces. The polished performance of adulthood. Pressed pants. Dark blazers. Straight hair. My mother didn't like the inner city and she didn't like my flatmates either. She thought I'd catch homosexuality.

As we're washing up, Mike and Jacob shuffle through the front door carrying a large canvas.

'What's that?' Olivia steps out to peek.

'The exhibition,' Jacob says.

They plant the picture against the back of the couch.

Mike's hair is damp with sweat, fringe clamped to his forehead. He stares at the canvas, picking at a loose thread on his denim jacket. 'Do you think it needs more, *grit*?'

Olivia and I look at each other, then back at the canvas. It is blank, a single shade of beige.

'I don't get it,' Olivia says.

'More grit, yes. Definitely,' Jacob says.

Mike disappears into the kitchen and returns with the pepper shaker. 'Let's do it now before it dries.'

Jacob lays the canvas on the floor and leans forward, twisting the shaker. Black flakes fall—ash on white sand. He looks to Mike, who is cupping his cheek with one hand and staring at the painting as though it is a text he cannot translate. 'Maybe.'

Olivia goes to her violin and begins packing up.

'I better go.'

I reach for her arm. 'We'll do this again?'

She shrugs, noncommittal. At the door, I wrap my arms around her shoulders. My ring catches the end of her ponytail. We spend a few seconds disentangling it.

I watch her ride away.

I am settling for a good orchestra. Something permanent. But Olivia. When have I ever wanted what Olivia wants? When did I settle for playing a melody with eight other violinists? I won't be alone in the spotlight anymore, like I used to be. Before I destroyed everything.

3

At the chemist, I am restocking on condoms. Banks calls. My teacher from another life.

'I've been busy.' He always begins by qualifying a call. 'Can you come around? I'd like to hear your excerpts.'

'Now?'

'Did you see the hand physio about your wrist?'

I make vague sounds.

Last week, I'd knocked my wrist against the station turnstiles while running to catch the train. I am always bumping into things. My body knows no boundaries.

With my free hand, I press my wrist to assess the pain.

'It's not bad today.'

'Your audition is only a few months away,' he says.

'Is that why you called? To remind me?'

'No. The orchestra needs you to step in for a concert tomorrow at noon. The soloist missed her flight from London.'

I stop in the middle of the aisle.

'What piece?'

'The Beethoven.'

The last time I played Beethoven's Violin Concerto, I was fifteen years old and standing on the stage of Carnegie Hall. I didn't finish the performance.

'I know it might bring up old memories,' Banks says. 'It's only one performance.'

I had a therapist once who gave me an exercise to do if I ever felt a panic attack coming on. I had to weigh up advantages and disadvantages. Of saying yes: good exposure, good venue, reputable orchestra. Of saying no: too much fame is not a good thing. Of saying yes: fame can be good, if used in the right way. Of saying no.

'Okay, I'll do it.'

We arrange to meet in a few hours. I go back to scanning the shelves. I can't find what I am looking for. Non-latex. Ribbed. Scented. Citrus. Large.

I find a salesperson nearby. 'Do you have those large, non-latex condoms?'

He looks at me as though I've asked him to take his penis out.

'They're in a sort . . . of reddish pink box.' The salesperson pretends to not be fazed, but he is fazed. I have fazed him.

'I'll ask my supervisor.'

He walks away, then doesn't return.

At the counter, I pay for two boxes of vegan condoms, three environmentally friendly lubes, a morning-after pill and a box of contraceptive pills. The pharmacist asks me to fill in a form for the morning-after. I count back the hours since I'd last had sex. The condom had broken while the man was inside me. Now, I am here, as if it is my job to clean up the mess.

On the train, I call my hand physio. She asks me to describe the pain.

I tell her I can't.

'What do you mean you can't?'

'I mean, I don't know what words to use.' She tells me she'll be available in the afternoon.

At the Opera House, I find her in the green room with bags of tapes and cream.

'It's pretty bad, Jena.'

She squeezes the side of my wrist like she is navigating the remote control of a game console.

'You'll need at least a week's rest.'

'A week? I've got a concert tomorrow.'

She shrugs.

'You can either rest it or damage it further.'

'What about the anti-inflammatory tablets?'

'They are not a cure.' She frowns and hands them to me anyway. 'No more than two in six hours or your muscles will spasm and you won't be able to play at all.'

I swallow two pills as soon as she leaves then go into the communal kitchen for some ice. Physical injuries never stopped me from playing when I was the world's best. Though back then, I didn't do anything likely to cause injury. I didn't do anything apart from play. My father wouldn't even let me use a knife in case I sliced my finger. He was protective like that. My fingers, he'd say, were the most valuable part of our family.

My mother wasn't so strict. When we were on tour, she would let me use a butter knife.

'Don't tell your father,' she'd say. My mother and I found communion through shared lies.

I press the muscles around my wrist to test the pain. It had flared up early this morning when I was in bed with a man. I met him last night at a recording session for Noah's band. A bass player. I invited him back to my place after and in the morning, I woke to his erection pressed against the small of my back. He slipped inside me without asking, moaning. At one point, I climbed on top of his body and put my hands on the headboard. A blunt pain shot through my wrist. In the climax of morning fucking, I held on, endured the pain. Gripped the wood tighter. Stayed silent. As he was getting dressed, he tried to make conversation.

'Noah says you're some hot shot violinist.'

He sat on the edge of the bed, pulling on his socks. I was sprawled on top of the covers.

'Not really.'

'He said you used to be, like, world-famous.'

I got up and reached for my shirt. 'That was another time.'

It troubles me—how little I care. As arranged, I visit Banks at the Conservatorium, but take my time. I will play for him again. I will forget the pain I caused him. It's cold inside his room. He never turns on the heating. It interrupts the sound. Damages the instruments.

'How's Monkey?' he asks.

I take out my plush toy from the case and squeeze its neck. 'Same.'

Banks slides the sheet music onto the stand and sits down. He smells of bacon and sweet milk.

'Let's hear the excerpts then. One by one.'

He does not look at me. His focus rests on the music.

'I thought you'd want to hear the Beethoven?'

He shakes his head. 'I trust you'll do well. The excerpts?'

I wait for him to pick up his violin. He played with the SSO for several years in the eighties, chiefly as the concertmaster. When he retired, they kept him on the board and sometimes he plays with us on special occasions, small ensemble stuff.

I reach for my metronome. He does not move.

'No metronome,' he says. 'I'll count you in.'

The tip of his thumb and forefinger join—a hoop. He draws circles in the air. He hums the opening flute line of the Brahms 4th. Nods his head for me to begin.

I take a breath. The hairs on my bow press into the steel strings.

'Too loud.'

My exhalation is pronounced.

'You're breathing too loud. You're part of a violin section. You're not a soloist. You can't breathe so loud.'

I begin again.

He raises a hand. 'Now you're playing too softly. Start again from the beginning, forte. But don't breathe so loudly. You're saying something with your breath, but don't be so frank.'

I stare at the dead skin peeling off the back of his hands. Twenty-five years of European sun had done damage, but it was the last few years in Australia that had brought out the sunspots.

I raise my violin to my neck and begin again, this time, holding my breath.

'Why are you doing that?'

'Experimenting.'

'Don't waste my time.' He stands.

There's a knock on the door. Another student.

'Come back when you're ready to take this seriously,' he says.

I slide the shoulder rest off the violin and begin packing in silence, stuffing Monkey back inside the small compartment in my case.

Before I leave, he raises a hand. 'What would you like from me?'

I wonder how he sees me now. If he hates me for what I did when I was his best student. His most famous student. His reputation had rested entirely on everything I did. Maybe he still loves me.

Part of me wants to erase him. Forget the years he spent teaching me. But there is hardly a memory of a sound that does not include him. Without him, I am rootless.

I turn to face him. 'I don't know.'

'I'm older. Less patient now. You need to clarify what it is you want. Otherwise I can't help you.'

'I think I want you to, I don't know—contribute, somehow.'

He frowns. 'Come back after the show. We can talk.'

'You won't be there?'

'No.'

Walking to the station, I wonder if he'd planned to re-enter my life as strategically as he'd planned to exit, all those years ago. Why did he make it seem as if I was the one wanting something from him? Yet, it was he who asked me to come. I'd forgotten that momentarily. When did I become so uncertain about myself?

The following day, I arrive at the Opera House an hour before the doors open. The concert hall. Musicians in their seats. That old familiar sight. The conductor shakes my hand at the podium. He introduces me to the orchestra. Formalities. They all know who I am. He makes them act as if I am someone I am not. Someone I used to be. The travelling soloist. The prodigy everyone talked about. A cellist on the first desk smiles at me; no teeth. Perhaps gritting them behind a closed mouth.

We run through the concerto. Standard play. I've memorised the music in my bones. The notes fly out. Under the surface of each phrase, my heart pounds in my throat, drumming a beat that distracts me from the rhythm of the third movement, its giddy eruption some form of pure joy. Optimism.

During the break, the cellist hangs back and watches me loosen my bow.

'What's that?' He points to Monkey, whose head is sticking out of the shoulder rest compartment in my case.

'Oh, him.'

'Your childhood doll or something?'

When I don't respond immediately, he says, 'Aren't you a bit old for that?'

I open the concert, just after 1 pm. I use more bow, tucking long phrases into one stroke. For the double stops, I am careful, hesitant about the intonation. Relax on the pressure. Later, the conductor tells me I was too soft. 'Fuck you.' If only I were bold enough.

I walk to the Conservatorium to see Banks.

I knock on his door and let myself in. He's sitting at the piano, marking a score with a pencil.

'It went well then?'

'As well as it could. I made it to the end, at least.'

'Tremendous.'

He has never used that word.

'I won't stay long,' I say. 'I need to work on those excerpts.'

'Why don't you play a little?'

'The excerpts?'

'Yes.'

'I'm not really ready with those yet.'

He smiles weakly. 'Never mind. I'll prepare for my next student then.'

He stands and gestures to the door.

Outside, I look back at him. But he has already turned around.

4

I miss Chinese New Year celebrations. My mother does not call to remind me. Intentionally or not, I tell her there is a concert on that evening. She doesn't ask more questions.

A week later, in mid-February, she visits me in Newtown carrying a jar of home-brewed jasmine tea, her signature brew. She inherited the recipe from her mother, a native Taiwanese farmer, who got it from her mother, who got it from her mother, and so on and so forth.

Sitting on the edge of my couch with her knitting, she's making a woollen cover for my violin, a new year's gift.

Mike and Jacob's pepper-sprinkled canvas rests on the wall beside her, unacknowledged. Warm blue sunlight. A rectangle of light on her forearm. Body erect, eyebrows drawn in dark coal, hair moulded and secured with hairspray. I wonder what she looked like at my age.

My mother doesn't know about my latest interaction with Banks. I don't tell her. Perhaps she wants to forget our history too.

I massage my wrist.

'What's wrong?'

'Nothing. It's just a bit sore again.'

It's been a long time since my mother sat in a practice session. When I was a child, she was always around, watching, her face fixed in permanent anxiety. I grew used to her uneasiness. She'd even make me wait while she went to the bathroom. Each note had weight and significance. Each note had to be interrogated. She would watch me closely as I played, as though in a trance. Every time she heard something she didn't like, she'd clap her hands, just once, and make me do it again. It annoyed my sister, Rebecca, who didn't play an instrument—but she was beautiful and that made all the difference. I got used to the sudden explosion of claps. *Do it again. Do it again.* Now, my mother sits still and does not make a sound.

Part of me wants her to go away. After what I did. After what she did. All those years.

Since I took up the violin again at the beginning of university, my mother has become more animated. She calls at least once a week. Without the violin, we had very little to talk about. Perhaps it was welcome news that her prodigy daughter was making a comeback.

I fumble a tricky chromatic ascend and take a pencil to mark in fingerings.

She sits up, rests the needles in her lap, a question hanging off her lip.

'Are you sure you'll be satisfied with an orchestral role?'

Christina Lin, formerly Christina Wang, loves to push people. It's a subtle form of emotional manipulation she inherited from her father. That's probably what she'd say if anyone asked.

I keep playing, ignoring her fixed gaze. I've learned, only recently, that just because a question is asked doesn't mean you have to answer it.

After a while, my attempt to perfect the Mozart ends in sheet-music-crumpling fury. I do it slow. Then at tempo. Then slow again.

I move on to the Brahms. Run through the high registers faster than the recommended tempo.

'Slow down. It's allegro, not presto.' My mother's hands are frozen on her lap.

'I'm just getting my fingers automated.'

'I thought you stopped doing that years ago. I never knew you to be so lazy.'

'Maybe I am lazy.'

She stands and grasps my hand, performs a detailed inspection. 'Are you using the cream?'

I pull my hand away and walk into the kitchen to pour some tea. She follows.

'What's all this mess?'

I'd forgotten to wash the dishes from last week's casserole dish, which cost me two hours of practice time to make. It was good though. Mike and Jacob said they'd pay me in artwork if I made it again.

My mother unbuttons her cuffs and folds her sleeves back.

Despite my protests, she puts on an apron, slips on gloves, and begins to wash up.

During the week, she volunteers at a soup kitchen and occasionally helps the local church with bookkeeping. Her life is filled with small tasks. Mine is filled with practise, rehearsals and performance. Banks had a theory that everyone is born with a special frequency we either find very early on and stay with or move away from the older we get. My tuning went off when I was fifteen and I've spent the last seven years trying to find it again.

'Do you think you'll get into the SSO?' my mother asks, wiping the floor with a tea towel.

'I don't know.'

When the floor is done, she walks out the front door and returns half an hour later with two bags of food. She spends the next hour chopping potatoes and apples. From the lounge room I can hear the thwack of knife on board. Her nasal humming of Mozart's *Jupiter Symphony*.

'Are you hungry?' she calls. 'It's almost done!'

I sit at the dining table. She serves me a bowl of barley soup, then a plate of her potato, egg and apple salad with mayonnaise.

I lean across the table and give her arm a squeeze.

She smiles. All those years we toured together, she didn't cook a single meal. She takes a seat next to me. 'Quick now, before the soup gets cold.'

5

On Sunday, Olivia hires a lecture hall at university to practise. We want to feel the sound of our violins in a large hall, to test the decisions we'd made about where to slide up the fingerboard and where to slide down, whether our bow changes are suitable. Ensure that the fingerings we'd marked out in the music are the most appropriate in a space similar to the concert hall where we will be auditioning.

It's the first time I am back since graduation. I studied English literature; four years of my life I don't remember well. I always knew I would return to the violin. Or, rather, I knew it would come back to me. It was unavoidable, like the rain. Before that happened, I wanted to escape the world of music and live among ordinary people. Ordinary, unambitious people. English literature majors are ordinary. Floaters. Wanderers. White. I wanted to surround myself with people to whom I could feel superior.

I met Olivia and Noah at orchestra auditions in the first week of semester in 2012. I spotted a girl with pale skin in a tangerine sweater from across the auditorium. The sweater was loud. Demanded attention. I knew I wanted to be her friend. When I approached her after the audition, I saw that she'd matched the sweater with jeans the colour of beetroot and R.M. Williams boots. I discovered she was an English major too.

As I walk into the theatre I look down at my faded black jeans. Ripped cotton shirt reflected in the sliding door.

Olivia is sitting in the front row, ankles crossed. She looks up from her phone.

'Hey.'

The double door cracks open and Noah enters as if on cue. He's carrying his clarinet and a plastic bag. I am relieved to see he's also casually dressed; baggy grey sweater, brown cargo pants, thongs. As he comes closer, I see he hasn't shaved in days.

'Hi, girls.'

Olivia tilts her face up to meet his. He is so tall.

'What's in the bag?'

He opens it. Shapes, Doritos, Mars bars and LCMs.

'Were we meant to bring something?' I ask.

His eyes lift quickly. 'I thought we might go see a movie if we finish early.'

'I've asked you to come play the clarinet,' Olivia says. 'Not distract us.'

He looks wounded.

He deposits his things on a seat and Olivia and I climb onto the stage. We align the stands, place the music on the metal plates, tune up.

She lifts her gaze. 'How's the practice going?'

I tell her I haven't been documenting sessions on Google Docs like we promised we'd do, but I am following the exercises in the order we planned.

'I can't seem to practise after five. I'm just so exhausted. The humidity is killing me.'

I am interested in Olivia. I really am. But my brain turns off each time she complains about playing. I don't understand her struggles. Instead, I give her my best sympathetic expression.

She clears her throat and rolls her shoulders.

We begin with Saint-Saëns' Symphony No. 3. A series of difficult passages in tenth position. I watch her lift the scroll of her violin as her fingers drop onto the E string, micro-millimetre shifts. Firm bow pressure, inching closer to the bridge.

Noah's voice cuts in.

'What?' I shout.

'I can't hear Olivia.' He looks at me, then down at the mouthpiece he is screwing onto his clarinet.

'I can hear myself,' Olivia says.

Noah walks up with sheet music clamped under his arm, clarinet in hand. 'From where I was sitting, it sounded like you were playing forte and you were playing piano.'

'There's no specific marking,' I say.

Noah points to the sheet music. 'Dolce.'

Sweetly. Loud sweet? Or soft sweet?

'I suppose maybe tone it down a little?' Olivia blinks at me.

I'm not a soloist anymore. Why do I keep forgetting?

For the rest of the hour, I play with a dulled, weak force. I feel bad for my Strad, lent to me by a mining investor in Germany. It deserves to be heard only on its own. The idea of it being part of an orchestra is like asking Oprah to join the *Today Show*. Noah plays with the usual compliance of a tutti clarinet, blowing with mild interest. There's a reason why all clarinet players are the same. No one who wants to stand out plays the clarinet.

'So, movie?' Noah asks me while Olivia is in the bathroom.

'I've got stuff on, sorry.'

My first lie to Noah. I feel bad that I don't feel bad.

6

I wasn't always a dishonest kid. Though, I certainly wasn't a typical kid either. I do recall the year or so I had a normal life.

Year one. I was Mrs R's favourite student. In the classroom, I sat on the carpet with my legs crossed, back straight. When Mrs R gave an instruction, I'd bolt straight to it. I was always eager to be loved, especially by my teachers.

Jenny Lee was the only other Asian in my class. She was much prettier than me, though I didn't know it back then. I just thought people preferred her because her skin was whiter than mine. I had darker skin back then. I was bark, dirt, milk chocolate. I didn't mind it though. Sometimes people thought I was Native American, which made me feel special because I loved Pocahontas. She was dark-skinned and beautiful. A white man with a plain name fell in love with her. After seeing that movie, I began to believe that it was possible for someone like me to be loved. Or at least to be noticed by a man; the right kind of man.

Before Jenny Lee, before Mrs R, there was the violin. My mother told me I'd begged for lessons after I saw someone playing on television in preschool. I don't remember.

By the time I started year two, I'd been playing for two and a half years and had competed in three competitions in Australia. My mother wanted me to stay in school, though she'd been told by her friends that a child with my talent should be sent away—'To America! To Germany!' Those places sounded like suburbs or towns I'd not yet visited because my parents didn't have time to take us anywhere. I'd only seen the city a handful of times when my mother took us to my father's dental surgery in Chinatown.

I forgot to eat sometimes, I was so consumed by practice. When it became really bad during the first year of touring—this was when I was eight—my mother kept a food diary to make sure I ate at regular hours. Her bag was full of muesli bars, tubs of nuts and dried fruit. I found toilet breaks distracting too. Every second away from the violin made me anxious. Later, they called me obsessive compulsive and tried to medicate me, but I refused to take anything in case it affected my playing. When I was six, I performed at a festival on an open stage. After my last note, the clapping started. I stayed and smiled and took several bows. But then my mother raced onto the stage and pulled me off. In the toilets, my stockings wet and warm, she asked why I hadn't gone offstage.

'The clapping was for me,' I said. I was only six but had already acquired the language of self-abuse.

Mrs R often asked me to bring my violin to class, usually on Fridays. I was a stand-in for the kids who forgot to bring in their show-and-tells. I remember playing with half my mind occupied by what my hands were doing, the other half on the kids sitting cross-legged in front of me, chins in hands, backs curved. Some of them dozed off; some of them looked intrigued at first then quickly lost interest. I hated seeing how easily I bored them. I wanted to be like Stacey Williams who was a gymnast and showed off tricks in the playground, bending in unusual places, making her body do magical, wonderful things. I wanted to be liked the way Stacey Williams was liked, but my violin never gave me much of a chance. The violin is the instrument of the highly strung, alpha types—hard-working, obsessively disciplined kids. No wonder string sections around the world are dominated by Asians.

In the playground I was called Stringer. Violin Nerd didn't have the same ring. Stringer followed me around that entire year. I was too scared to tell Mrs R about the name-calling. What if she told me to stop playing the violin? If I didn't have the violin, I would be no one.

I worked hard to be good. Even before I could write an entire sentence in English, I could play all the Mozart sonatas. With my eyes closed. While the kids in my class went to the oval on Saturdays to kick balls, I was practising in my room.

I missed out on camps, discos and sports carnivals; instead, doing competitions, recitals and solos. My sister, Rebecca, entered competitions too, but those were different; modelling contests and beauty pageants. Her talent was being beautiful, which I thought was bullshit, because being beautiful isn't something one works hard to get. She was just born with that face. What kind of talent is that? I was jealous of her face because it seemed to win people over straight away, while I had to work hard to get people to notice me. People only noticed me when I did something extraordinary which was only when I was the best.

7

The bass player arrives at my door after nine. Hair uncombed. Shirt collar flapped up.

For a moment, I am distracted by his height, which is impressive; he is almost as tall as Noah.

'Hey.'

'Hi.'

Although he's been here before, he is shy, like it is his first time.

We retreat to my bedroom and fuck the way most people fuck. Grope around the usual places. Undress. Missionary. We assume our positions like seasoned actors on stage. Hands here. Mouth there. Legs at this angle, neck twisting.

In the morning, he uses more tongue, less fingers. We devise a way of telling each other what we like by squeezing the other's hand when they're doing something that feels especially good. I feel an orgasm coming while he glides the tip of his tongue along the side of my clitoris, but then the sensation, like a sustained pinch, disappears when he stops and thrusts his penis inside me. I am reluctant to ask him to go back down.

•

The following weekend he comes over and we fuck for three whole minutes. He rolls off my body then falls asleep almost immediately. I feel that old disappointment cave over my chest, the loneliness trapping me in some state of unfulfilled despair. I listen to his muted snores and stare out the window at the grey sky. There's always a piece of steel in my chest. My life will never be enough. The hunger rises when things start to settle. And then I crave the attention of men. It feels more powerful to be desired than to desire. There's safety in being wanted. No risk in being the desired. The last time I wanted something, I blew up the lives of two other people.

At the next recording session for the band's album, I learn that the bass player has gone away on tour. He doesn't get in touch.

A new sound technician catches my eye. He tells me I have great vibrato.

Noah overhears this and smirks. 'Geordie, get a grip mate.'

He comes over and seizes my hand, tells me to stay clear.

'Stay clear of who?' I ask.

'Geordie. He's a serial fucker.'

'But so am I.'

A faint warmth swims up into my chest. Noah's warning feels strangely proprietorial.

'Just don't go there.'

My father used to express contempt for any boy who showed interest in me. The few times he showed interest in me.

I squeeze Noah's arm. 'I know how to look after myself.'

Geordie sends me a Facebook message the next day. His profile picture has him posing all smiles next to two black kids.

Two nights later, he takes me out for drinks and we return to my place.

Inside, he puts his hand on my waist as naturally as a hand to a wall.

'I need to use the bathroom,' I say, bolting down the hallway.

'Can I join you?'

'I need to do a shit.'

Perhaps it was a mistake to bring home a boy with a name like Geordie.

In the bathroom, I fix my hair and squirt coconut cream onto my legs.

On the couch, he is combing his moustache with a plastic comb. He brushes it three, four times. He makes me listen to his samples on his phone. I nod, pretend to care.

'You don't do this often, do you?' he asks.

In the bedroom, his skinny jeans are tight and hard to strip. When he takes his shirt off, I am disappointed. His shoulders had looked broader with layers on.

'Do you know what would make me come?' he whispers hoarsely, pushing me against the bedroom door.

'What?'

'Seeing *you* come.'

He moves his face down level with my opening, frames himself, ears cupped by my inner thighs. He breathes, inhale, exhale, puffs of air. He talks at my vagina.

'Am I driving you wild?'

I don't even ask myself if I'm enjoying it. I just move my body, the way I've learned to move it; choreography inherited from somebody else. I moan. I slither like a performer.

We fuck in a total of two positions. Afterwards, I hold my breath to hear his breathing. I want to conjure up these men whenever I need, to draw them to bed, even though I never really like what they do.

In the morning, I offer him breakfast. He declines. Relief explodes inside my head.

I see him again on the first weekend of March. The tracks for the album are put into place and everyone heads home in their cars. This time, he gets in his car with somebody else and waves as he drives by. At home, I pull out my laptop and watch a girl in a blue school uniform being thrashed by her stepfather. Then his four friends. They're large and old and white. They're circling her small body on a rug in the middle of a room. I last a few minutes before reaching that tired, empty euphoria. I need those images. Moving body parts on the screen. It has to be violent. It has to be quick. I can't separate the girl's suffering from her pleasure. I don't know if she's crying from pain or pleasure. I've always reached for violence. The more violent, the better. The man needs to be much older. He needs to be in control.

I take a shower. Clean again. I think about the stepfather and the old white men. The small female body. Abandonment. Complicity. Love.

8

There are six categories of men. Within each category lie subcategories. The categories are arranged according to race: white (the plainest, yet most desirable, the default); Asian; black; Hispanic; Jewish; other. Subcategories include: big; small; northern European; southern states; alpha; beta; borderline; chapstick.

I created this taxonomy of men when I was living in Wayne, New Jersey, a deadbeat suburb of fifty-five thousand, three and a half hours' drive from the centre of the universe.

In the two years my father and I lived there, he gave me all the relationship advice he thought I'd need: 'Find somebody who likes you more than you like them', and 'Don't be too easy. Men don't like easy girls.'

At the time, I was seventeen and sleeping with three different boys, none of whom knew about the others. My father knew nothing of them either. My mother would call once in a while from Sydney. I never told her about that part of my life, though I suspect she knew I was not innocent.

After my breakdown, I delighted in the assortment of penises available to me. Having spent time in cities like London, Berlin, New York and Amsterdam, I was surprised by what I found. A feast of flesh. Chalked-up sneakers. Spit on the pavements. In many ways, I was still a little girl, charting my progress with the same diligence and precociousness as I'd recorded my violin practice. In the absence of acclaim for my musicianship, getting a boy into bed was as fulfilling and joyful as any other accomplishment.

I kept a journal called *In the Land of Dicks* where I would record the date, time and location of each conquest. I gave each boy a score out of ten for the following:

Length (circumcised Y/N?)

Texture

Balls

Temperament

Tongue

Lips

Pain (good / bad)

Attention to nipples

Nose size

Tempo

Phrasing

I took pride in my journal. Someday, I thought, someone might publish it. I made a list of all the men. The Slovaks; the Germans; the Americans; the Dutch; the Italians; the Poles; the Dominicans; the French; the Ticos; the Filipinos; the Haitians; the Greeks; the Brazilians; the Portuguese. The Australians.

Bassoon was circumcised, with a Length score of 3, Texture 3, Balls 2, Temperament 8, Tongue 8 and Lips 6. He had a biblical name. Something dull. I haven't seen him since the closet incident—I mean, the funeral. I hear he's now dating a trombonist with a lisp.

In Wayne, I liked being told I was an animal. I liked the idea of being an animal because I knew I wasn't. I knew I was much more than an animal. I knew I was one of the best violinists in the world.

Sometimes, though, it felt good to be slapped by a boy I hardly knew. Have him call me obscene names. Horse. Dog. Sloth. Eel. It always made me laugh.

Everything I did with these men was an ode to myself. A contradiction between my public life and private life; a chasm between Jena Lin, darling Australian violinist, globally adored by lovers of classical music, and Jena Lin, raging sex addict. I was gifted in more ways than one, and I needed those in power to understand. I never saw my thirst for sex as anything wrong, much less a disability. But the therapist who my father made me see once a week began using that word when I told her how accomplished I'd begun to feel.

Being gifted and being disabled are the same thing. I was told this by a professor who used me as a research subject when I was ten years old. Other children are scared of you, he explained. Nobody quite knows how to treat you, so they isolate you. They just don't know how to be around you.

My mother preferred to think they were jealous.

They called me an aberration, even before I knew how to spell that word. And when they flirted with the label 'prodigy', my parents panicked. It happened right after my debut with the Sydney Symphony Orchestra. I was on the front page of every newspaper in Australia. They called me a wunderkind, a freak, a stolen creature from the future. Or the past. I wasn't sure what it all meant but I remember my parents' hesitation.

'I don't want you to be a circus freak,' my father said. 'You're not going to perform just because you can.'

'But I want to.'

My mother placed her hand on my shoulder. 'Don't worry. You'll perform.' There was something savage in her voice.

My father worried I'd be burned out by sixteen, which is what happened, more or less. Perhaps that's why at fifteen, I decided to move to that small suburb outside of New York City with my father. I needed to escape my mother. I needed to know what I could be without her. In her mind, she'd lost me. In my mind, I severed old wings.

Part of me wanted my mother to ask me to stay, but she was silent. Maybe there was some part of her that wanted to be freed of me. I wish she'd made a fuss. I wish she'd said something. Anything. She'd have been easier to love.

9

Olivia is late again. At the train station, Circular Quay, I fumble with my case to avoid crashing into the mass of bodies at peak hour. Suits and tourists.

Tuesdays are difficult for Olivia. She struggles to make rehearsals on time because the morning is spent with the carers who supervise her mother during the week. She rarely talks about her mother and I have learned not to ask.

'Thanks for waiting.' She gives me a quick hug.

'We'd better get going.'

Overnight, we received an email from the manager of the orchestra, Bryce. The chief conductor has pneumonia. A replacement has been found. They will take over for one season. The announcement will take place today.

As we hurry towards the Opera House we speculate on this sudden onset of pneumonia.

'There's probably a sketchier reason he's standing down,' Olivia says. 'He's been getting pretty close to some of the flautists.'

'How do you know?'

'People talk. I hope they'll choose a woman.'

'More likely they'll choose a turnip.'

Olivia goes on and on. Says that they must know diversity is important.

'They don't,' I say. 'That's why they've only ever chosen men.'

'They *must* know.'

'Olivia, when was the last time you saw a black person in the Opera House?'

In the green room, the players are stretched out on the floor, rubbing their knees, kneading their shoulders. Nobody looks up when we walk in.

We find two seats in the back corner. The concertmaster stands and makes introductory remarks. Then he introduces the new conductor.

It's a man and he's an American, a former professor at Curtis Institute of Music and assistant conductor of the New York Philharmonic. He gives a brief, genial speech and talks about the partnership between the two orchestras. He mentions a seasonal exchange for violinists; open to permanent members only. Golf claps settle across the room.

We go into the concert hall for a rehearsal.

He conducts the way most conductors do. Overemphasising the beat before the end of the bar. Moving their torsos too much. It's always too much. They seldom seem to understand that less is more. Even the slightest twitch of a muscle in the face can change the sound of an entire orchestra. I often watch the face more than the baton. But these men follow each other. Same faces. Same gestures. Same sounds.

Afterwards, the new conductor invites the orchestra to the Opera Bar. In the green room, he approaches me as we're packing our instruments. Long neck. Steely eyes. Forehead creased with lines. He's wearing a grey polo, suit pants and navy loafers on his feet. Like Leonard Bernstein, if Bernstein had lived to be one hundred.

'Jena Lin.'

'Yes, sir.' I stand to shake his hand. 'Nice to meet you.'

'We met when you were still a child in London.'

'We did?'

He pokes my arm like we're old friends, but I am sure I've never met him in my life.

'Are you coming for a drink?'

I look over to Olivia, who is zipping her case. I wave her over. 'This is Olivia.'

He glances at her. 'Yes, second violin. Good bow arm. So, the bar?'

I wait for Olivia's cue.

'Noah's working late so I'll have to make dinner.'

I pull on her shoulder straps. 'Come for one, please?'

'You guys go ahead.'

We perform an awkward three-person farewell. I watch her walk away looking down at her phone.

'Shall we?'

I turn. The conductor is looking at me. Untrimmed brows. Deep brackets around his mouth.

My body shivers with familiar anxiety. A need to smile without showing too many teeth. The faint narrowing of my eyes. Performing desirability. An involuntary response to a male gaze. I do it so well.

'Okay.'

As we walk across the forecourt to the bar, he asks about my playing, what I've been doing, America, my mother.

We join some musicians sitting at the outdoor bar and he pulls out a cigarette. I excuse myself and head to the ladies. I decide there's no reason for me to stay. There is no one in the orchestra I want to fuck. No one with anything interesting to say. Instead of going to the toilets I make my escape.

•

The following evening, the conductor makes his debut to a full house. He does not look at me once.

Afterwards, I ask Olivia if Noah is picking us up as he usually does on weeknights. She's loosening her bow and staring vacantly at the wall in front of her. She shakes her head.

'Everything okay?' I ask, pausing between sips of water from my water bottle.

'Yeah, I just told him not to. Let's get a drink.'

We head to the Australian Hotel in The Rocks to avoid the musicians at the Opera Bar. Inside, a young couple are seated at a table, a larger group near the back. A few suits in a booth, their table scattered with empty glasses and bottles, their faces smeared by an oblivious joviality. We sit on wooden stools drinking beers and crunching pistachio shells. As she talks, I stare at her face, which is always bare, no make-up.

We talk about the conductor and his forceful style. I make wild, flamboyant gestures and imitate his heavy breathing, the exaggerated movements of his torso. She laughs until she's bent over.

We try to decide whether he's gay or straight or something in between. We hear from other players that he has a reputation for trying to get young players into bed. It was rumoured that after last year's White Cocktails to which he'd been invited as an international guest, he took home two players from the woodwinds. The rumour is hazy on the gender of the players. The White Cocktails is a wank, we agree. An annual Sydney Symphony event held at Bennelong Restaurant in the Opera House to introduce new players to the orchestra's patrons and board members.

'You'd know all about it,' Olivia says. 'You've been in that world since you were a kid.'

I shake my head. 'I was a soloist. I hardly mixed with the orchestra. They were the lowly farm animals and I was the star lion.'

She drains her beer. 'Jesus.'

'It is a bore, come on. We know that, right?'

'Well I've never been, obviously, since they only invite permanent players, but apparently it's a pretty big deal. Monica said she spent over two thousand dollars on her gown last year. You need to really make an impression.'

I swirl my finger inside the bowl of pistachio shells and wait for her to look back at me.

'I bet the men don't have to buy an expensive suit.'

'They probably do.'

We switch from beer to wine, ordering from a bartender who looks like the bass player. They all look the same. Thick trimmed beard. John Mayer eyes. White T-shirt. Broad smile. I shift my gaze to the suits in the booth.

'You checking them out?' Olivia asks.

'Those guys?' I shake my head. 'Losers.'

'Losers who'll make more money this month than we will in our entire lives.'

'But do they have good sex?'

Olivia stares into her glass. 'Noah is withholding sex from me.'

I slap my hand on the table. 'What?'

'I've been spending more time with my mum lately, and he thinks I'm overcompensating.'

'Overcompensating for what?'

She lifts the wineglass to her lips and sighs into the pool of liquid. 'I don't know.'

As we get up to leave, one of the suits walks over.

'You girls interested in a game of chess back at my place?'

Olivia pushes past him. 'No thanks.'

He turns to me. 'You?'

Outside, the suit hails a taxi. He raises one arm in the air like he's asking a question.

In the taxi, he places a hand on my thigh, squeezing it as though testing the ripeness of an avocado. I ask him where he works and he mutters the name of a bank. Hyde Park whirs by in a blur of black and red, broken by strings of lampposts. The aircon blows straight into my eyes.

I'm curious to know what kind of bed this man owns. The colour of his sheets. If he has paintings on the wall, or just cheap pretend art for a pretend life. I'm not sure what compels me. An insatiable thirst for thrills? Danger? All I know is that I am desired in this one, particular way, this one, particular, familiar way, and it has nothing to do with what I can do on the violin. I don't want it to go to waste.

When the taxi pulls into a driveway, I peer out the window. Large birch tree. Bush out the front. Low metal gate, locked. Built-in letterbox in the wall. At the front door, he plants a kiss on my mouth. Dry, no tongue. I keep my eyes open. He moves a white piece of plastic in front of a black keypad. The door clicks open.

'No key!' he beams.

The light turns on slowly. Marble dining table. Bamboo lampshades hanging low above the sink. Large pot plants in each corner. The floors, grey pebble mosaics. A real estate agent's office.

I walk towards the huge windows.

Before I reach the view, I feel a tug on my leg. I look down to see a white rope around my calves. The rope tightens. I'm yanked off my feet. I fall and land on my bad wrist. I hear a small crack. The slap of flesh on tiles. It's violent, and then painful, and then—my hands are being tied behind me.

'Wait!' I scream, and he pauses, stepping back.

'What?'

'I just—I need to pee.'

He thinks for a moment, then releases my hands. 'On your right.'

As I step past him, I reach for my bag and bolt for the door. I don't stop running until I reach a main road. I stand under a streetlight and raise my arm, waiting for a taxi.

10

A postcard of a Barnett Newman painting is stuck on the fridge door as inspiration for Mike and Jacob's latest works. *Concord* was painted in 1949, during the artist's most prolific year. Sometimes, I'd get milk from the fridge, close the door and stand there staring at the image; its pair of golden bars like handles of a door into a fancy New York City loft. The colour always reminds me of the ocean. Mike and Jacob have spent months working on a show inspired by the American mid-century abstract expressionist. The pepper-dotted canvas that spent weeks on the floor of our lounge room will now be on display. Sometimes, as I'm practising modern pieces by Copland, Stravinsky or Glass, I think about Newman's paintings. The colours. The lines. The shadows. The suit from the other night had something like this on the wall. A single piece. Minimalist.

The opening of their exhibition falls on a Friday night, usually a concert evening, but the program is baroque so they don't need a full orchestra. It will be Mike and Jacob's first exhibition as a couple. I help them set up at the gallery in Redfern, a suburb that has been colonised by young white couples who work in design or law. Mike and Jacob are expecting more than a hundred people. Old college friends. Folks from the National Art School who come for the free craft beer and spend their Centrelink payment on tattoos and Status Anxiety tote bags. Mike and Jacob both graduated from there several years ago and tell me each opening is an excuse to bitch about other artists and find new people to fuck.

Four large canvases hang in the front room of the gallery—black, with a white vertical brushstroke. The line is marked at different points on each canvas. The idea is for the four paintings to be acquired together as a set and displayed in a small room facing each other.

In the second room, Mike hands me gaffer tape and scissors. 'Make sure the corners are flat against the wall.'

I'm sticking cardboard cut-out signs onto the walls. I stop every now and then and tug at the sleeves of my denim jacket to cover my wrists. Nobody knows about the other night. How close I came to starring in a white man's midweek fantasy.

A young woman walks into the room holding a stapler. Her hair is bleached blonde, witch-like, her eyes the only giveaway to her ethnicity.

'You an artist here?' she asks.

I look at her nose ring. Single white stud. 'I'm Mike and Jacob's housemate.'

She nods coolly. 'I'm Val. You look like someone famous.'

Her Drew Barrymore mouth is painted blood orange. She smells expensive, a blend of musk and jasmine.

'I played the violin well once.'

She stares at me, tiny head stilled. I'm tempted to tell her I know who she is, regurgitate all the things Mike and Jacob have let slip about her in my presence. She's the latest artist to sign a six-month lease on the spare room at their studio. She graduated from the Victorian College of Arts last year and moved to Sydney to be with her boyfriend of seven years, only to be dumped a few weeks later. Her mega-wealthy parents live in Shanghai and got her an apartment in Bondi Beach.

'So, you're shit at the violin now?'

'My teacher might say that.'

She lets out a blunt laugh, lifts the stapler in her hand, presses it to my shoulder.

Mike shouts from the other room, 'Oi, Valerie Li! Watch it. That girl needs her shoulders!'

'My fingers weren't on the trigger, Mike, chill.'

She's wearing a white T-shirt with FUCK ME SAFE printed in the middle, in block caps.

'Nice T-shirt.'

She pulls her hair in a bun and asks me if I know who she is quoting.

'No.'

'David Wojnarowicz. A New York artist. He died of AIDS in the early nineties.'

She bends down to pick up staples off the floor and inserts them into her stapler.

Jacob calls out from the other room; he is struggling to adjust the ceiling lights. I go to help.

When I return to Val, the room is punctuated by the sound of her thunder-clap stapling. CLAP. CLAP. Pause. CLAP.

'Why's there no music playing?' I ask.

Val pinches her nose. 'Music takes me away from myself. I don't want that when I'm painting. It's such a distraction, no offence.'

'But you're not painting.'

'I'm working. It's the same thing. I got out of an abusive relationship with music years ago. It's too persuasive. My parents made me play the piano. Could you pass me more staples?'

I want to please this girl, though I've only just met her. Is it because we're the only Asians in the gallery?

I pass her the staples.

'So, if I play Debussy right now . . .'

'Please don't,' she says. 'I'll have traumatic flashbacks to art school. Our teacher used to put on Chopin and expect us to paint flowers and lakes.' She makes a retching sound. 'Mozart used to be interesting. Until he wasn't.'

'And if I play AC/DC?'

She twists her wrists in circular motions, looks up at the ceiling. 'Don't even.'

At 7 pm, a crowd amasses. A group of five enters. Then couples trickle in. I go to the bathroom to splash my face with cool water. When I return, the crowd has poured out onto the street, smoking, holding wineglasses, talking, laughing, some looking serious, like they are talking about the famine in Yemen. When I wedge myself into one of these serious-looking conversations, I find them instead discussing the merits of living in Paddington versus Woollahra. Noah and Olivia drop by. Olivia is wearing a black dress with white heels, making her a head taller than me. In ballet flats we are the same height.

'It's our anniversary,' she announces. 'We've got a booking at Tetsuya's at eight so we can't stay long.'

'Congratulations.'

Mike slaps Noah on the back. 'Such a good boyfriend. Maybe he'll propose tonight?'

'Don't be ridiculous,' Noah says.

Olivia smiles at the floor. 'We'd better not be late.' She pulls on Noah's jacket sleeve, waves us goodbye.

Later, Mike makes a speech. People raise their glasses as he begins a long list of acknowledgements. I'm standing to the side near the speakers, holding a bottle of beer by its neck, scanning the faces in the crowd. Mike has just cracked a joke when a savage noise outside punctures the space, redirecting our attention. There's a screech of tyres and a voice yells something obscene. *Cunt* or *fuck* or *dick*. I can't hear the word, but I register the tone.

Then the eggs start coming. The first one cracks against the front window, a second and third smash against the door. Then they start landing near the feet of those who had spilled out onto the footpath. There is screaming. Some of the men shout, take off after the car. Women scuttle inside. The car disappears down the dark street.

Later, inside, Mike and Jacob are hunched and small in the back corner of a room.

'Are you okay?' I put an arm around Mike and rub Jacob's arms, which are crossed in front of him. 'The important thing is that nobody was hurt,' I say.

Val inserts herself between me and Jacob. 'This is bullshit. We should call the police.'

'No,' Jacob says. 'I don't want this in the papers. My mother would kill me.'

'But think of the publicity,' Val says.

Mike shakes his head. 'We want it for the right reasons. Not because we got egged.' He extracts a Juul, and begins inhaling deeply.

'At least we weren't bombed.'

Jacob stirs. 'Mike, I'm Jewish.'

As we're cleaning up, Val takes her phone out and snaps pictures of the cracked eggshells swimming in pools of yolk.

'Hashtag real art. This'll be my ten thousandth post.'

She invites me back to her apartment in Bondi Beach. We take an Uber. She is currently subletting to a Chinese artist, an old friend, though she doesn't think he'll last long. The man is a sculptor. He hires models and sleeps with them after. After the art. Or maybe the art is the intercourse. She laughs as she tells me.

'The apartment smells constantly of wet clay, and in the evenings I can't eat my dinner without the sound of a woman being pleasured. Which is why I'm always eating out. I can't cook either. Which reminds me, I should probably start looking for a new place. Or rent out that room to someone else.'

She looks over at me, she can tell there's something on my face I'm not expressing.

'You're tired, huh?'

'Yeah.'

She takes my phone and texts herself. *Yo. Val here.*

'Driver, can we just do a detour and drop off my friend here?'

She turns back to me and clasps my shoulder. 'You can visit me some other time.'

The driver drops me off in Newtown. It's just past midnight, though I feel awake and alert. I close the front door behind me and go to my violin. Thirty-three days till the audition. I can fit in another hour of practice.

11

The following evening, I make miso bolognaise for the boys. Mike comments on the unusual mix of Japanese flavouring and I tell him my mother showed me how to make it when I returned from Wayne. She was a good cook, but never had time. And she liked cleaning too. Typical feminine activities. Part of me was disgusted that she'd be talented at such simple, ordinary things.

The boys are still traumatised about the egging at the opening. I suggest they take a few days off to relax. Binge on *Harry Potter*. Go for a two-hour massage. Double jack-off to Michael Fassbender in *Shame*. Instead, Mike returns to the studio that night, and Jacob stays in his room.

I spend all weekend in the lounge room practising. I eat dry cereal for breakfast because there's no milk left in the fridge.

On Sunday afternoon Jacob comes out of his room in his Peppa Pig PJs holding a bottle of beer and a bag of corn chips.

'You sure I can't do anything?' I ask.

He slumps onto the couch. 'No.'

'Want me to practise in my room?'

'No, but the scales are kind of annoying.'

I make a small noise. He returns to his room with a fresh pack of chips.

I turn to the tricky passages of Mahler's 4th. Slowly first, then at twice the speed. Slow, fast, slow, fast. Alternating between slurs and staccato, ricochet and dolce. The bow is the voice. It's all in the right hand. I play until the sun weakens. Birdcalls replaced by bat croaks. Sometimes, when I'm playing Mahler, I am tempted to butcher his music deliberately because of what he did to his wife, Alma. He is another man, a composer, who probably never dreamed a girl like me would replicate his melodies. But I shouldn't be so cruel. None of that matters. They'd written the notes that once saved me, and for that, I ought to be grateful.

The following Friday, I get home from a concert to find Jacob sobbing on the couch.

'What's wrong?'

He tells me he'd gone to visit his mother in Vaucluse for Shabbat and they had a fight. He'd wanted to take Mike, but his mother refused. 'She said she'd rather die than see me with a man.' His shoulders are trembling. 'Now she says she never wants to see me again. She's cutting me off. And I can't afford to live here without her help.'

'What do you mean?'

'Mum owns this place.'

He looks at me. Eyes glassy. 'I'm sorry,' he says. 'She's said she's selling it in a few months.'

'Oh.'

The skin around his eyes is swollen and pink. 'There's no rush, though. You've got at least two months, maybe three.'

'That's okay,' I say. 'Don't worry about me.'

•

They move out a week later.

For three days it rains without stop. The canvas chairs in the back yard collect ponds of rainwater in the seats. I take pictures of the sad ponds and Mike and Jacob's empty room and send them to the boys accompanied with sad-face emojis. The kitchen has been stripped of all their possessions. It's a kettle-less, toaster-less, espresso machine–less kitchen; a gallery with no art.

I make another round of miso spag bol, listening to the excerpts as I squeeze miso paste into the cold mince. Mozart. Beethoven. Singing along to the violin line.

I plate up, grate parmesan on top, light a candle.

'It's ready!'

My voice cuts through the empty house. Hollow.

I reach for my phone: 9.45 pm. I shove a few mouthfuls into my mouth, then realise I am not hungry at all. I thumb a text to the bass player, holding my finger over the blue arrow, but I don't press send. It's too early for a booty call. Too late for a satisfying fuck. But he was never satisfying.

Screen off. A sombre face stares back at me from the grey reflective surface. How does anyone survive alone?

I press on Val's name.

She picks up after the second ring. 'Are you dead?'

'No. What? How could I call if I was dead?'

'Are you in hospital?'

'No.'

'Why else would you be calling me?'

'You said the other night that you might be looking for a new place to live.'

'Yeah,' she says slowly. 'Are you thinking of moving out?'

•

A few seconds after we hang up, I text Geordie because he is reliable, and because it's the right amount of time since we last saw each other. As I'm clearing the dishwashing rack, I feel that old sense of euphoria return. Waiting for my lover to come. I check my face in the bathroom mirror and readjust my hair. When he texts that he is outside, I go to answer the door. Inside, I let him do what he wants to me because I don't want to spend another night alone. I need someone's breath to distract me from my anxieties. I need a shawl over my gaze to prevent me from looking too closely at my small, defective heart.

12

The hand physio calls to ask about my wrist. She is interested in the way mayors are interested in their constituents; at a distance. We are allocated four appointments each season and this will be my last. She has a spot at three in the afternoon. I arrive half an hour early to lift weights at the gym next to a rehearsal studio. I forget how quickly I sweat, even when I'm just lifting dumbbells, and end up embarrassed by my collar of sweat on my T-shirt when I arrive for my appointment.

She squeezes my wrists gently.

'Are you over-playing?'

'I've got an audition coming up.'

'Stop after an hour. You can't play more than an hour at a time. You'll damage the ligaments around your fingers.'

'I played six hours a day for more than a decade.'

She stills her face, a mother to a child.

'You're not young anymore.'

Olivia comes over for a practice session after dinner. She brings a bottle of red wine.

Two weeks out from the auditions, she's had to take a week-long break from playing after spraining a finger playing netball. We argue about the dangers of sport for the hundredth time. She insists netball is the safest sport for violinists.

'There are plenty of other sports that don't involve the potential of losing a finger,' I say.

She pushes the sleeves of her sweater up and follows me into the kitchen, red-cheeked and frowning.

'I've done it for so long.'

'That's no excuse.' I pull two wineglasses from the cupboard. 'Why do you play with only girls? Women's sport is so . . . catty.'

'You're such a sexist.'

She opens the bottle and pours herself a glass of wine.

'There's some strange competitive thing happening when there are only women on the court.'

'What about men?'

'Well, all-male spaces are inherently bad.'

'You don't really mean that.'

I take a moment to think about it.

'No, I really do mean that.'

We return to the lounge room and pick up our violins, play a few scales, go through the excerpts at half the speed. I sense her lagging half a beat behind. I pull her up on it. She asks for the metronome.

'Ninety,' she demands.

'That's too slow.'

I thumb the dial in my hand, the lever jumping from the low tens to three digits.

Olivia picks up her glass of wine and readjusts her music stand.

'Before I forget, Noah said he needs a second player for his show in September. You know, the one he's been roped into by his school friends?'

I nod my head to the click of the metronome. Place it on the stand quickly and begin playing along. Olivia follows and we continue playing, applying less pressure to our bows at the phrase before the big climax in bar 127.

Later, as she's clipping on her helmet and mounting her bike, she mentions Noah's concert again.

'Oh, yes. You said before. What is it, a charity concert?'

'Sort of. It's an alumni event at Newington. Can I put you down?'

'What about you?'

'I can't. My mother needs me on Monday nights.'

I fold my arms, feigning irritation.

'I hate Noah's friends.'

Olivia puts her arms around my neck. In that embrace, I know I have lost.

'You're a godsend,' she says.

'I know.'

'And don't forget it's Noah's birthday this weekend.'

As she rides away, I turn to shut the door behind me and glimpse my own reflection in the glass panel. For a moment, I think there is somebody inside the house, standing in the hallway waiting for me. My heart stops. And then I step inside, untie my hair. I walk to the bathroom and use the toilet.

Later I check my phone, hoping for a text from Val. I'd sent her three messages earlier in the day, asking whether she'd thought any more about moving in together. I even told her I'd started looking at places, which is a half-lie. On the toilet seat, I scrolled through real estate pages of apartments in the Eastern Suburbs.

My heart leaps at a text banner, but it's just Olivia reminding me to pick up a present for Noah.

What to get for your best friend's boyfriend? A book? A sex toy? A subscription to GQ? Nobody reads magazines anymore.

I stare at the phone, willing Val to text me. I'm sure she would never make me go to her boyfriend's birthday party. She would never make me do anything I didn't want to do.

13

Noah turns twenty-five and Olivia insists on throwing him a party at his parents' penthouse in Cremorne, a white wealthy suburb that hugs the shores of Sydney Harbour on the north side of the bridge. His parents are in Croatia for a month on sabbatical, so the place is free all of April. I invite Val as my plus one because she's relatively new to the city and wants to widen her circle of friends. We arrange to meet at her place to get ready. The sculptor has moved out, she tells me. She still eats out most nights.

Her apartment is on the top floor of a renovated art deco building on Campbell Parade. I knock twice on the metal flyscreen and she comes to the door almost immediately. I follow her into the lounge. There's a smell of wet cardboard and jasmine. Delta blues play from her laptop.

Her eyes are ringed with heavy black kohl. She's wearing denim overalls over a white T-shirt, camel-coloured socks with pink spots, black boots, kitten earrings.

'I thought you said you wanted to get—'

'I know, sorry. I got excited.'

A lady is singing about her lover who has run away to Chicago.

'Is this Bessie Smith?'

'Memphis Minnie.'

We sit on a three-seater, green retro couch in the open-plan living area. Against the far wall opposite, the kitchen is one long bench and a large two-door refrigerator. The furniture is sleek and grey, discreetly expensive. There are framed sketches on the walls; pencil drawings of a man's face, a typewriter, a willow tree.

'This place is nice.'

She shrugs, indifferent.

'The fridge is too big. I don't cook.'

She says 'cook' the way one might say 'masturbate' in public.

She walks over to the fridge and opens the two doors. 'See? Nothing.'

Empty except for a carton of long-life milk, a can of tuna and a bottle of Diet Coke.

'You weren't kidding.'

'I never cook. I don't know how. Anyway, you still haven't seen the view.'

I follow her onto the balcony.

The expansive line of blue ocean. Seagulls dot the blush-red sky, wheeling in an invisible wind.

'Must be nice to live here,' I say. 'Why don't I just take the sculptor's room?'

She wrinkles her nose. 'This place reminds me of Damien actually. He was here a lot.'

The gum-snapping scat of Memphis Minnie's voice jives in the background, a third party to our conversation.

'Come on, I need to finish my make-up.' She walks back into the apartment.

In Val's bedroom, there are jars of scented candles scattered on top of books. It's a tarot-reader's room. Lamps in each corner. A large frameless mirror by a bookshelf, a scarf rack.

I sit on her bed and watch her fix fake eyelashes on. She asks if I got Noah a present. I tell her I didn't have the mental capacity to think about it, so I got him a gift voucher for a music store in the city. She tells me she's bought him tickets to Boy and Bear. 'How do you know he likes them?' I ask.

'Everyone likes Boy and Bear. Especially nice, white, private school boys. They're so predictable.'

'What are these for?' I point to a bowl of condoms on her bedside table.

'They stop me from making babies.'

'Aren't you on the pill?'

'Damien is not the only person I'm sleeping with.'

'I thought you guys broke up.'

She pats her forehead with a cotton ball.

'Is it an open relationship?'

She doesn't say anything.

I slip off my shirt and jeans and grab the slip dress I'd brought from my bag.

'If it's not an open relationship, isn't that cheating?'

She walks across the room to tie the back of my dress. I feel her cold fingers brush my skin.

'I think being in a monogamous relationship is just another patriarchal trap set by men to keep us from taking over the world.'

Only Val can make such sweeping statements.

We take a selfie and she posts it. In the picture, I look uncomfortable, like a teenager off to her first party, anxious and trying to hide it unsuccessfully.

The penthouse is on a quiet street lined with European cars and large fig trees. Lights pulse from the third floor, announcing the location.

As we approach, the door to the apartment block opens. Two men walk out.

'Hey!'

Noah and I hug awkwardly. His cologne is thick; cinnamon and wood. The scent of affluence embedded deep into his flesh.

The man standing beside him is distracted by the phone in his hand. Face gaunt, cheeks tight below dark eyebrows. He's wearing dark blue jeans and a black long-sleeved shirt with small aeroplanes on it. Cufflinks. He looks like Christian Bale in *American Psycho*.

'This is Mark,' Noah says.

We shake hands. His cufflinks are 747s. He is older. Maybe ten or fifteen years. He returns his attention to his screen, as if his height and natural good looks demand respect, regardless.

'We're just heading out to get more beer,' Noah says. 'You guys want anything?'

'We've brought whisky,' Val says.

'But I'd like more.'

'More?' He looks at me strangely.

'No, I'm joking.'

Noah smiles, no teeth. He waves as he turns to leave, his friend trailing behind, eyes still fixed on his phone.

We take the elevator to the third floor. The sound of beats muffled by the tiled walls. We emerge to the flesh-throbbing thump of techno slapping us in the face. The door to the penthouse is open and we step inside tentatively. At once the music is killed. A collective chorus of boos thunders across the room. People are squeezed together like sardines in the narrow hallway, drinks in hand, mouths in speech. We push through to the lounge room. It smells of chlorine, citrus and sweat, like a freshly cleaned bathroom at an upscale gym where white towels are provided and Aesop products are freely distributed.

Val sees someone she knows and disappears, leaving me alone to navigate a sea of trimmed, vacuous hipsters. I find bottles of beer and wine in an ice bucket in the kitchen and pour myself a drink. I take a quick sip, surveying the living room from the relative obscurity of a corner by the fridge.

I look around at the groups of people laughing and talking, and I am suddenly aware of my own isolation. For a brief moment, I panic. No one is going to speak to me. It feels like failure, this involuntary solitude.

I spot Olivia sitting on the arm of a couch next to a boy. She waves to me. 'You made it.'

'What happened to the music?'

'Neighbour was complaining.'

She leans over, her expression serious. 'It's a Newington craze-fest. Everyone here either went there or dated someone there. Seems like a bit of a social decline, don't you think?'

'Hanging out with your high school friends?'

'Yeah.'

She excuses herself, pulled away by other voices. She returns a few minutes later, pulling on the arm of a girl; Val comes up behind me at the same moment.

'This is Dresden,' Olivia introduces. 'She went to Barker too.'

Val shakes her hand.

'What's your connection to Newington?' I ask.

'My boyfriend worked there as a sports coach for one term,' the girl says. 'He was also a mentor to a lot of these boys.'

'Wait, you're dating Mark?' Olivia's mouth is open and frozen.

The girl nods. 'He's the one that looks out of place, evidently.'

Olivia is still shocked. 'Noah never told me. But then again, he never tells me anything.'

'We met him outside,' I say. 'He went to get more drinks with Noah.'

'Is that where they went?'

Olivia nods with authority. 'Noah likes to be stolen away.'

The four of us are talking about the boys. If this were a scene in a film, we wouldn't pass the Bechdel test.

'I'm going to go and spread my wings,' Val says. I watch her steer through a stream of people, leaving me to pretend to care about the significant others of my best friend and a stranger.

'Where are you guys living?' Olivia asks.

'Mark's in Darlinghurst, but I'm studying in Melbourne.'

'Long distance is impossible,' I say.

The girl looks at me as though I've offended her. 'It's not impossible. We make it work.'

'Of course. What are you studying?'

'Business and finance. I'm the only child of Chinese immigrants. I suppose it was inevitable.' She flashes her perfect teeth, satin black hair sliding to part her face. 'I met Mark here in Sydney when I was interning at EY.'

'EY?'

'Ernst and Young.'

Olivia and I nod politely.

'We got a lot of bad press because Mark was going through a divorce. That's sort of why I left. Then I won a scholarship to Melbourne Uni. It worked out well in the end, though of course I'd rather be here in Sydney. Mark flies down almost every weekend, so I can't complain. Oh look, they're back!'

Noah and Mark walk in with bags in each hand. Their entrance is greeted by a soft cheer. I feel an urge to move towards them. I want to untether myself from the conversation with this perfect Chinese girl. Her perfectly delicate frame, perfect cheekbones and perfect hair. Even her name, despite its novelty, seems perfect. Who gives their Chinese daughter a name like Dresden and then makes her study finance? Who says, 'evidently'?

'Which one is your boyfriend?' she asks me, narrowing her eyes.

'I don't have one.'

'Oh, are you friends with someone here?'

'This girl,' I say, putting an arm around Olivia. 'We're best friends.'

'Oh! How sweet,' she says. 'I didn't even know that was still a thing.'

'What? Friends?'

'Best friends.'

I walk away. I don't know how to continue the conversation. I help the boys unpack beer, vodka, whisky onto the kitchen counter. They ask me what I want to drink.

'Something healthy,' I say. 'I have an audition in a few days.'

Mark hands me a glass of clear liquid. 'It's nutritious,' he says, smiling.

'What is it?' I bring it under my nose and smell nothing.

'H-two-oh,' he says, patting my shoulder and nodding like a football coach.

'Your girlfriend is nice.'

He looks at me more closely. 'You met Dresden?'

'She's very pretty.' I keep my shoulders square to his face.

'Smart too,' he adds.

'I know. She's Asian.'

He laughs, his whole face breaking into a crinkled map of rivers.

Noah calls out from the other end of the bench where he is slicing lemons into wedges. His white shirt clings to him with sweat.

'Don't get too close to that girl, Mark—she's dangerous.'

Mark raises a brow.

We watch Noah hand a drink to Olivia, who is still talking to Dresden, theirs heads dipped forward as though sharing some wild speculation.

'I've got to make sure these girls are not misbehaving,' Mark says. He walks away. I return to my state of aloneness in the corner of the kitchen.

•

The rest of the evening passes uneventfully, until someone spikes Val's drink and she throws up in the bathroom for more than half an hour. Mark and I end up taking her to hospital, because we are the only sober people. My car is parked too far away so Noah insists we take his parents' BMW.

Mark's girlfriend wants to come but he tells her to go back to his place. She has a seven o'clock flight to Melbourne the following morning.

'Don't come back too late,' she calls out to him as we leave.

Val staggers along the footpath, one arm slung over my shoulders.

'Do you want me to carry you?' Mark offers.

'I get motion sickness when I'm being piggy-backed,' she says.

'I'll carry you in front of me.'

'Like a lover?'

He bends down to lift her, her body falls back into his arms like a sack of cement.

'Get the door.'

I run ahead as instructed.

When he lays her down in the back seat, her hair gets tangled in his cufflinks.

'Who wears cufflinks to a party?'

'Dresden gave them to me.'

We get lost on the way to the hospital because neither of us know how to use the sat nav in the car and neither of us knows the area. I take out my phone only to find it dead.

'Where's your phone?' I ask. He pats his pants.

'I must've left it at Noah's.'

In the back seat, Val is half weeping, half moaning, head lolling against the seatbelt. We take turns looking back like concerned parents. We drive through McDonald's to ask for directions. We get fifty-cent cones and French fries to share because suddenly I am starving.

'Don't tell my girlfriend I'm doing this with you,' he says.

'I don't think I'll ever see your girlfriend again.'

By the time we reach Royal North Shore Hospital, Val is asleep. Mark carries her into emergency, where the triage nurse panics at the sight of them because it looks as though he is carrying a dead body.

'She's only sleeping,' Mark tells her.

The nurse leads us to a bed where Mark deposits Val, and then we're asked to stay in the waiting area.

I arch my back against the chair.

'This might be the nicest thing I've ever done for anyone.'

'Glad I could help.'

There are a few people in the waiting area. A television suspended from the ceiling in one corner. Jack Black being an idiot with school kids.

'You don't drink much, do you?'

He takes his time to answer my question.

'I'm a bit older than you. A hangover is a nasty thing at my age.'

'How old?'

'Forty.'

An hour later, the three of us leave the hospital. Val is given tablets and told to drink lots of water. We never find out what had been put in her drink. We are the typical youthful weekend crowd being reckless with our bodies.

Mark drops us off in Newtown.

'I better take my girlfriend to the airport,' he says as we get out. The sky is brightening into a faint, meandering blue. A glow on the edges of the trees.

'Nice to meet you,' I call out, not turning to meet his eyes.

'Nice to meet you too.'

'See you never.'

'See you never.'

14

Before New Jersey, before the breakdown, I wrote long passages of sex scenes. When I wasn't playing the violin, I filled pages of graphic details, getting thrashed, fucked, whipped, slurped, nipped, slapped, hit. I'd describe the way a man would take my body; pummel it. I imagined my body as the most desirable thing, a machine to please men. I knew that they had more power and I saw my body as the only way to get closer to them. In my stories, the sex was always rough and expedient. I'd write long sentences and then feel the meat between my legs loosen and pulse. I'd write my stories and then staple the pages closed. When I felt the urge to touch myself, the staples would come undone. Much later, I drew inspiration from the boys I was taking to bed, but they were never as rough as I hoped. I never knew how to make them do what I wanted.

There were days when the boys were not around. Days when I was convinced I was the ugliest girl in the world. I'd read the lines I'd written and make myself come. Afterwards, my repulsion would compel me to staple the pages together again. I'd promise myself that I'd never do it again. But I'd do it again. And again. And again. And again.

Once, I saw Rebecca at the computer looking at photos that appeared as though people had acted out my stories. Solid white flesh colliding.

Bodies entangled like weed to coral. I watched as she scrolled through pages and pages of images. Then she cleared the browser history. Later, I went to the computer and typed 'sex scenes' in the internet browser.

At first, I watched people kissing. Then I watched people do things to their bodies I'd never seen before. When I heard someone coming inside the house, I closed the browser and grabbed the metronome, which was always next to me. Nobody would suspect me of anything as long as it was ticking.

I spent weekends watching men fuck women in the mouth on the internet. Whole days whiling away the loneliness that felt like a fist inside my throat, always threatening to choke me to death.

I guess living with my father and being a normal teenager was a strange time for me. I had to go to school every day. I'd seen movies set in American high schools, but I had no idea how to act around teenagers. How did one conduct a conversation? And about what? The only thing I knew was how to play the violin and how to perform.

The boys saved me. They taught me I was good. Their hands and mouths taught me to overcome my self-doubt. And I was an open fruit, ready and willing to be consumed.

My father was hardly around. I suppose he was trying to build his dental practice—and start a new life with a woman who was not my mother. I didn't like her. I'd never spent so much time with a woman who was not my mother. But I thought about my mother so little during those two years in Wayne. Before then, I think our lives had become a single existence. Now I was building an identity of my own, and I wanted someone to tell me I belonged. I didn't know how to do it without my mother—but I did it. And I have the boys to thank for it.

The morning after Noah's party, I wake to find a note from Val next to my pillow.

Damien has come to pick me up. Thanks for saving me last night. PS. Don't fuck the old man.

I take a train and two buses to get to my car, which is still parked in Cremorne.

In the afternoon, I get back to the violin.

At certain moments during the day, I shift my position so my body doesn't shadow the music on the stand. After a run-through of the concerto, excerpts, sight-reading, scales, I put my violin back into its case and go into my room. I leave the door open because I live alone now and nobody will hear me scream.

I pull out a dildo from the top shelf of my wardrobe, click open the green lube, turn the bottle upside down and let it ooze over the tip of the glass phallus like maple syrup over ice cream. I lie in bed and watch some ordinary, gonzo porn on my phone. Man eats woman. Man straps woman. Man hurts woman. Woman screams in pleasure or pain, I don't know. I hold the dildo between my legs and slide it in and out. It doesn't feel deep enough. The position is wrong. I get on my knees and stand the dildo upright, riding it like a cowgirl, reach down and part the lips of my vagina with dry fingers. I rock back and forth, watching myself in the mirror. My body is perfect and museum-portioned.

After a while, orgasm-less, I collapse onto the bed.

I close the porn tab on my phone and scroll through my contacts list. I want someone to make me scream operatically. When was the last time I came like that? Two weeks ago? Who had I been with?

Bass player? Bassoon? Geordie? Maybe I was alone.

At the end of the week, I visit Mike and Jacob's studio in Marrickville. I decide I am confident about the audition, four days out. I need something to distract me.

From a distance the warehouse looks like an abandoned factory. A mechanic's shed. A textile mill. A place where basic parts come together, loud machinery churns for hours. Inside, golden lights flicker like small detonating bombs.

Mike and Jacob are preparing for another exhibition, this time in Shanghai. The collection is based on the theme 'White', and the curator is from Iceland. Ai Weiwei will be at the opening. I ask if they are excited about meeting him.

'He's just another sensationalist artist,' Jacob says. 'And he's Chinese, so everybody has to love him. You can't not love him. At least, not publicly.'

Val chips away at her hair, which is piled on top of her head in a loose bun. 'Can you stop China-bashing?'

I ask her how she's feeling after the other night. She shrugs, tells me she's fine, and that Damien has found himself an actress to date and hasn't called her since he drove her home.

She's wearing khaki overalls, a white undershirt, black canvas shoes. Her wrists are stained with black spots. She never looks entirely clean.

'Tea?'

She goes into the kitchen area.

I wander through the artists' individual spaces, partitioned off by white walls. Entering an artist's studio is like stepping into their mind. Loose sheets of paper strewn across tables. Coloured crayons, tubs of paint, bottles of poison. Turpentine. Rabbit-skin glue to prep canvases, illuminate the subject. Toxic paint remover. Tubes, heavy with reflective aluminium, exotic colours. Naphthol red, Windsor emerald, cobalt violet, burnt umber, blue hue, yellow orchid, magenta. Magenta. It even sounds spectacular.

An assortment of cigarette packets, some crushed, some unopened. Marlboro Blend No. 27 and American Spirits. 'These are American,' I say aloud.

Val emerges from behind me and hands me a warm mug.

'Peter's a new artist here from Chicago.'

'Cool.'

More snooping around. In another space, on a trestle table, a diary opened for any passer-by to read. In messy childish handwriting:

Grow up and start using oil paint.

Be fucking quirky or quirky as fuck.

Try to have sex outside.

Try to have sex in your parents' bed.

Try to sleep with the cheater.

Next to the diary, charcoal sticks lie scattered like bodies on a beach. Jugs of water, plastic cups, paper plates. Tissues. Heap upon heap of tissues. A spectrum of waste. All white. Dyed. Paper towels spotted with shadow-coloured smudges. Colours on white. Paper. Life, the world outside, inside tubes, eager, waiting to be squeezed out.

Tubes of toothpaste in silver. Foil. Yellow gloves. The sink. There is always a sink nearby. Staple gun. Pins. Rolls of canvas propped against walls. If only musicians were able to accumulate this detritus of cum, blood, sweat, tissues. Human excrement. Snot. Saliva. The preparation for the real thing. The white, the beginning with nothing and then the putting in love. The crumpled tissues. If only I could wipe away my mistakes. A note here. A bad bow there. Intonation miscalculated. Rhythms maligned.

If only I could wipe it all away.

Val is designing a logo for the upcoming Pro-Choice March. The feminist group WE CUNT WELL has commissioned her for the event. It needs to be red, loud and include the word CUNT.

We talk while she sketches on the fabric.

There's a knock at the door. 'Val!'

Mike sticks his head into the room. 'There's someone here to see you.'

'Tell them I'm working,' Val says, without looking up.

'It's Damien.'

Val's mouth collapses. She puts down her pen and stands up. She tells me she'll be back in a few minutes.

I wait for her; ten minutes, then twenty, then I go out to ask Mike where she is.

'She and Damien left.'

Back home, alone, I get a text from Val, apologising for skipping off. She and Damien are back together.

15

There is always a place for me to land; a place for me to deposit my urgency. I text Olivia and ask her what she's doing. She's at Bondi Beach with Noah and his friends. I remind her that it's only two days until the audition. She tells me to join them.

I take a train, and then a bus. It is well into the afternoon by the time I arrive. It is warm for late April. As if summer is reluctant to leave. The beach is a strip of white speckled with bodies. I find the group between the flags. They are playing Frank Ocean on their Sonos. Bottles of kombucha stand on top of a large esky. I recognise a few faces from Noah's party, including Mark, who is lying on his stomach reading a book.

I spread my towel next to him. He is reading Helen Garner's *This House of Grief.*

'That's pretty intense for the beach,' I say, slipping off my dress.

'No such thing as a beach read for me.' His expression both invites and resists interpretation.

I ask after his girlfriend and he laughs. He tells me she's too good for him.

I stand up. 'I'm going in.'

A heavy relief plummets through my stomach when he puts his book down. 'I'll join you.'

I approach the water like I approach everything else. No hestitation. Head first. Eyes wide. When I resurface, I turn around to see his body only halfway in. Shoulders lifted, fingers skimming the surface of the water.

'You're making it painful for yourself.'

In the bright light, I dive under again. The blue-green underwater, a blurry abstract art.

We swim for a while then head back onto the sand and lie on our towels. I lie close to him, positioning my body for his full viewing pleasure.

We have dinner at a Thai restaurant in Surry Hills. The crowd has thinned by now, only five of us left; me, Mark, Olivia, Noah and Noah's friend Tom. Mark sits next to me and orders wine for the two of us. At one point, as we're talking about Lars von Trier's *Nymphomaniac*, he puts his hand on my leg and squeezes it. I pretend it is the most normal thing.

Afterwards, Olivia, Noah and Tom head home, leaving Mark to sink his hands deep into his pants pocket, waiting for me to say something. I twist the straps of my calico bag, waiting for him to say something.

'I have an early morning,' he says.

'What do you do again?'

'I trade funds.'

I nod slowly.

'Want to go for a short walk?'

My legs follow his. We walk until the streets are empty, and then he stops.

'This is me.'

In the elevator, we hold our bodies erect as though principled, disciplined. We know what we are about to do. We are patient. We are still. My restraint is impeccable. I follow him like a prostitute in a French film. His apartment is at the end of a long corridor.

As he pulls his keys from his pocket, I hold out my hand. 'Is your girlfriend here?'

He stops abruptly. 'No, she's in Melbourne.'

We enter a large, open space. Black marble floors. A huge window. The city skyline flickering in spots of red, white and yellow. The bridge, a symmetrical ornament.

'Would you like a drink?'

'No.'

'I'll get you some water.'

I sit on the sofa, which is leather and blue.

He emerges from the kitchen with a glass in his hand.

He sits close. Hand on my knee.

I take a sip of water. Place the glass on the coffee table.

'We're good people,' I say.

'Yes, we are.'

'We don't cheat.'

'No.'

He looks at me with measured eagerness.

I lean forward to meet his mouth. How quickly these things escalate. Our bodies collide, rough and hurried. Our hunger is mutual. The violence of his mouth and hands. We kiss like we are trying to bruise each other's mouths.

That night, we have sex three or four times. I lose track. I want to go home and write about it in my diary.

In the morning, I lie in bed and watch him put on a shirt. The crinkled skin on the back of his neck—three rolls disappearing into his collar. He strolls across to his walk-in wardrobe and returns with a briefcase.

It is large. Something for an overseas trip. He places it at the end of the bed.

'What's that?'

He smiles and opens it.

A three-tiered jewellery box. Cufflinks, set in neat rows, silver and gold and diamond and copper. There are numbers and letters and hearts and dogs and crosses and bows-and-arrows and cars. Lots of cars. A Beetle. A Ferrari. A Jeep. A Cadillac. A teapot. Wheels and bikes, and smiley faces and sad faces and trees.

'A little obsessed?'

He shrugs. This is all I get. This is all he offers. He picks up a pair of dogs. Terriers. Locks them on his sleeves.

We part at the door, a brief swipe of his lips on mine leaving me with an anxious sort of pleasure. I smile as I walk towards the station in my weekend dress, hips slanted, mouth bruised, chin red, as though I'd rubbed a piece of sandpaper there for hours and hours.

When I get home, I peer into the mirror. The skin under my lips is chafed, forming a yellow layer of pus. It dries out, then cracks; and re-cracks every time I smile.

It gets worse over the next few hours.

16

On the day of the audition I wake early to take a long shower, scrubbing off the residual sweat of sleep, washing my hair, shaving my underarms and legs. In the bathroom mirror, I squint at my own reflection. I rub anti-rash cream into my hands, place dots of white cream strategically around my face. Cheeks and forehead, avoid the chin which is still red like a sunburn patch. Rub. Smooth. Rub. Repeat.

I curl my eyelashes, coating them in mascara, dab my cheeks with powder and blush, apply a thin coat of lipstick. I pull my hair back in a tight ponytail and slip on a black dress and ballet flats.

In the kitchen, I pour cereal into a bowl and eat it dry.

It's a ten-minute walk to the station. The air is damp, a hundred sponges pressed against my skin. The weekend's autumn warmth has been replaced by a sharp wind, a harbinger for winter. My headphones are strapped around my skull covering both ears, no music. I use it to silence the sound of cars and pedestrians on the street. I am still sore between my legs from the evening with Mark. Extinguish it. At this moment, all I should have in my mind is Mozart, Brahms, Beethoven. Sound. Tone. Smooth.

On the train to the Opera House, I spot another girl with a violin case strapped to her back. She's wearing black too, the standard uniform for an audition. Her eyes are closed, Beats on, probably listening to the excerpts. My stomach constricts into a ball. Heavy and hot. She is prettier than me. She is white. She is petite. I wonder if this will play against me.

At Circular Quay, the girl eases off her seat and turns. We exchange brief smiles.

The entrance to the backstage area is manned by a technician in a black T-shirt who waves at me with his walkie-talkie and smiles like it's his first day on the job. He tells me to sign in at the desk inside and warm up in a studio room.

'Don't we get a practice room each?' My voice is small.

'It's a quick in and out I'm afraid.'

The studio; carpeted walls, upright piano. I unpack my violin on the piano stool and play a few scales, moving my torso about, closing my eyes to focus on the sound. I spot the pretty girl making her way towards the concert hall. Her back is erect, face a measure of calm. Involuntarily, my mind turns to Mark's face. Thin lips. Wet lips. His scent imprinted on my senses.

I adopt the same attitude I've had since I started performing almost two decades ago. I'm just telling a story. Everything is inside me. Emotions belong on the fingerboard. Steady, breath, flight.

A woman with a black lanyard emerges beside me, hands clasped in front of her. 'They're ready for you.'

I follow her through a series of narrow corridors. Framed black-and-white photos on the walls. Nobody's face resembling mine. At the end of a long corridor the woman pushes open double doors. I follow her in. A black chair sits lonely in front of a music stand on the stage. White partitions, two metres high erected a few metres away. Presumably, the panellists are on the other side. The woman recites my number aloud—'This is candidate B-R-4-5'—and disappears through the door.

I take my seat, place my music on the stand, tune an A. Bach's Sonata for Solo Violin. The first. The stock standard. The basic. But the basics are hardest. The basics are stripped back. There is no orchestra. There's just you and your violin. No elaborations. No mask to hide behind.

I melt into a bodily stillness inherited from my grandpapa. My arms feel weightless yet heavy at the same time. Like I could caress the cheek of a newborn on one hand, while lifting a car with the other. My bow strokes are confident and wide. The sound flies across the stage, through the hall. My mind wanders into a clear blankness. I close my eyes during the final phrase, letting my corporeal memory take over. The last chord hangs, lightness, in the hollowed, open space. I relax, pushing my shoulders forward, collapsing them for a few moments.

'Thank you,' a voice on the other side. 'The excerpts, please. From the top.'

I take deep breaths. In and out. Close my eyes. I hear the tempo in my head, lock it in and begin.

I use a slower bow for the first excerpt, a slow movement. Sixteen notes to a bow. I tilt the bow on its side to catch the least amount of hair across the strings. The white powdered dust of the rosin clouds the space between the bridge and fingerboard. I pull back, ease on the pressure. The violin whispers. I breathe in small, shallow inhalations.

Twenty minutes later, I play the final note of an excerpt. I tuck my violin under my right arm and feel the damp cotton on the back of my dress, stuck like honey against my shoulder blades.

In the green room, I notice my hands are still shaking. Banks calls as I'm leaving the Opera House—wanting to debrief, no doubt. I let it ring out. We're encouraged to talk after an audition. What went well. What could have been better. Trauma counselling for musicians.

I am always good at these post-performance talks. I conjure another version of myself. One where I am able to relay most of the good parts of the playing. I never make a mistake, so there is really nothing to speak of in terms of failures, but maybe I moved too much this time and they could hear the sound of my torso adjusting to the weight of my bow. Maybe I rushed the allegro section. Did I exaggerate the dynamics? Why couldn't I just have played with more control? More restraint? They want a malleable, reliable musician. Why did I have to show off?

Instead of calling Banks I text Olivia, expecting her to respond immediately. Her audition was in the morning. I watch my phone for the three white spots jumping up and down at the bottom of my screen.

How easily these feelings of rejection and abandonment fold into my existence. How easily they form, coagulate and surface, contaminating everything good about my life. There is nothing. I board a train back home and begin listing the boys I can call tonight.

At the pharmacy, I buy cream for the sore beneath my lip. The man behind the counter looks at my chin and tells me it is a fungal infection, which makes me feel like I am something to be discarded. I thought fungal infections only happened between the toes or legs. I swear never to kiss a man with a stubble again.

But then I do, the following evening. This time, he draws blood. We find each other between the sheets. In the shower, he holds my face between his two large hands.

'Would you mind shaving?' Mark asks.

'What?'

'Shaving your pussy?'

Something hard clamps in my throat. He begins lathering soap on my breasts.

'I don't like furry pies.'

17

I'm sitting in the waiting room of a local salon, waiting to get the hair between my legs waxed. Olivia finally texts. We haven't seen each other since before the audition; nearly a week ago. She doesn't mention it, so I don't either. In the past, we've always debriefed post-performance, either in person or on the phone, but this time it's like the audition never happened. She speaks rapidly into the phone. An electro-pop duo from Sweden is in Sydney for a music festival and Noah has tickets to an exclusive party. I hate the rave scene. I hate the sound, the bodies, the noise. The darkness, the smell, the liquor. On the other hand, I need to let loose. I am trying not to think about what I'll do if I don't get the position with the orchestra.

I'm in the waiting room alone, cupping the phone to my ear. 'I hate dancing.'

'Please come,' she says. 'I don't want to be stuck alone with Noah.' She sighs into the phone. 'Last night he accused me of cheating. He counted the number of condoms in my drawer and said that two were missing. Can you believe that?'

'That's a bit neurotic.'

'And apparently he's been tracking me on his phone.'

'Is that legal?'

'I don't know. So where are you?'

I hesitate. 'At a cafe waiting for coffee.'

'You don't drink coffee.'

'I felt like one today.'

The wax job is painful, much the same way pap smears are painful. Awkward, showing your genitals to a complete stranger who tries to make conversation. The woman, a hundred piercings and sleeves of tattoo, tells me to lie back and not look. This is the third time I've been waxed down there and I'm not sure why I am doing it.

Afterwards, at home when I pee, the liquid runs down my thighs and then all over the toilet bowl, making a mess.

I practise the excerpts for a few hours without a break, ignoring the pain in my wrist. I make some toast and eat it standing up in the kitchen, phone in hand, mindlessly scrolling through Facebook. I get dressed and Uber into the city, settling on a black skirt and silk blouse. It's late by the time I reach the CBD. Olivia is waiting outside the club in a line twenty people deep. She's wearing a leather jacket with pressed-on roses, a red miniskirt and calf-high boots.

'Where's Noah?'

'He's on his way on a bus.'

'You guys didn't come together?'

'I was in the mountains with Mum.'

Inside the club, it's a tropic, smoke-filled dungeon of bodies throbbing to a radiant electronic track. The strobe lights needle through the dark space, slicing faces in half, then quarters, a wide beam from a shuttered lamp on the ceiling shadowing faces, then exposing them in micro-second pulses.

Olivia grabs my hand and takes me to the bar for a few shots. Between our fourth and fifth drinks, she tells me she's not happy.

She and Noah are becoming two different people. She is weary of his indifference to her mother. He doesn't seem to care for her the way he used to. I wince each time she says he doesn't care, because it always seemed to me as if he cared. He always seemed to behave with great sincerity and gentleness. Was Olivia mistaking his kindness for passivity?

At some point, we look at each other and it's clear that we are both waiting for the other to bring up the audition.

Finally, I do. 'You know, there's only one spot. One of us might get it.'

Her tone is bland, careful. 'Or neither of us will get it.'

'It will be one of us.'

Noah arrives, hair uncombed, shoulders slumped. He is wearing a white T-shirt and dark jeans. We down more shots then slide into the mass of bodies on the dance floor. I forget the rest of the world exists and move my body the way it yearns to move, grazing my flesh against a man with small eyes and gropey hands. My body becomes a porous thing, pushed and pulled by the convulsion of other people's desires. The whole room vibrates.

I pound my fist in the air when the bass twists into a rhythmic pulse. The low tenor of its intonation hits me across the chest, like I am coughing each time it thrums through the space, dense with flashed torsos weaving in and out of shadows and beams of light.

Noah and me. We are thrusting our bodies together, gazing at each other as though entranced. At one point, his lips sink into mine, and all the noise disappears. Something in me wants to be found out. It scares me to discover this; makes my heart scream at a decibel nobody can hear.

In the bathroom, I find Olivia standing by the sink. She leans towards the mirror to check her hair. 'Have you seen Noah?' she asks.

'You look fine,' I say. 'Go!'

I take her place at the mirror. A white bulb beams from above. Shadows fall on my face in all the wrong areas. It's just bad lighting. It's just bad lighting. I want Olivia's glassy skin. I want to go out and find her and carve her face off with a penknife and put her skin over my face.

I take my lipstick out of my clutch and reapply it. I wonder whether Olivia will notice the shade of Spring Pink! on Noah's lips.

In the mirror, I see the pale mounds of my breasts exposed. When I lean forward, a hint of nipple. I take a step back and pull my dress down.

Outside, blue lasers flick around the room like police sirens. The thrashing beat of music on my chest. Someone grabs my hand and pulls me close. Noah.

He looks at me with wild eyes. 'Don't tell Olivia,' he breathes into my face. Hot alcohol.

'Don't.'

'She's looking for you.'

He lowers his eyes until they reach my breasts. I feel his left hand grip my hip.

'What's going on here?' Olivia doesn't know how to wear confusion on her face.

'Noah's being a dick,' I say.

'She was just trying to hit on me,' Noah says.

Their hands find each other in the darkness. I call after them, squeezing through strobing bodies. Someone pinches my arse.

When we reach the entrance door, the bouncer tells us there's no re-entry.

Olivia turns and holds up a hand.

'Don't follow us.'

On the street, they hail a taxi.

I climb into the next one and arrive home just after five. I check my phone. No texts. When I call her, it rings out. I leave messages. Ten. Eleven. Twelve. I give up after the thirteenth.

I think about Noah's lips. Something inside me wanted to be found out. Ruin Olivia's life so I can feel better about my own deficiencies. Lying in bed, alone again.

18

A bruised grey sky hangs low over the harbour as I walk towards the Opera House for morning rehearsal.

The concert hall is empty. I arrive early hoping to practise without the stage crew knocking around chairs and equipment. I check my phone; an email from Bryce, the orchestra's manager.

Late afternoon, I am in his office. He enters dressed in a suit. A few moments later, Banks.

I sit up straight, trying to convey confidence and ease. An adult.

'Jena, I know you weren't expecting to see me here,' Banks clasps his hands behind his back, relaxed.

Bryce leans forward.

'We're offering you a permanent position with us.'

The news doesn't surprise me. They'd have been stupid to pass on someone like me. Though it occurred to me in the days following the audition that my history as a soloist might make me fundamentally unfit as the second desk of the firsts. An orchestra player is the most reliable and emotionally steady of all musicians. I'd only been doing a few concerts a week. How could they know I'd be suited to the rigid routines of playing four nights a week, four daytime rehearsals? Olivia might have seemed like the better choice on paper. She'd been playing with orchestras since she picked up the violin in year six. If her mother wasn't sick, maybe she would be the one being offered a permanent position. In many ways, she is more deserving.

I smile a painted-on smile. 'Thank you. I'm really happy.'

I text Mark the news. After a concert that evening, I wait for him outside his office. Twenty, twenty-five minutes. When he emerges from the revolving doors, he strolls slowly, arms swinging by his side, smiling with the ease of a fifteen-year-old boy who's just aced a chemistry exam. He stops a metre from me and waits for me to take the final steps towards him. We walk to an Italian restaurant between two office buildings. We have margaritas and share a pepperoni pizza. After the meal, I think about Ubering to the studio to surprise Val and the boys. I'd promised to go to their exhibition opening but then told them I had a concert. Which was true. But my concert is done and I could see them now. I could still make it. I think about how I am going to tell Val. Olivia. My thoughts foam, and then crust into something fragile and cracked.

When the waiter brings us the bill, Mark rolls onto one butt cheek to fish out his wallet. He takes out his card and throws it onto the small padded tray. 'Thanks,' I say quietly.

He nods, looking at his phone.

Later, we check into the Hilton on George Street. 'A treat, for you,' he says.

We have no bags, no luggage. The man at reception looks at me while I wait beside Mark who is filling out a form on an iPad. I smile weakly and turn my back to him.

The room is on the forty-second floor.

We fuck like we always do. Hard. Callous. Quick. Afterwards, we lay in bed, our bodies loose, resting against the headboard. We are characters in a French film yet to be made. I tell him we should be smoking. That's what you do after a tremendous fuck.

I look at his face, impassive and grey. It must be the shadows in the room. He is staring at the television screen, which is switched off.

A calmness settles over my body. I move closer to him and rest my head on his shoulder. He hadn't noticed my new youth, even when he went down on me.

He has many flaws.

And yet.

And yet.

And yet.

19

I am pleased that now I can tell people I have a full-time job. I am legitimate, finally. Normal. This is what I'd wanted, during the period before my breakdown. To stop touring. To stay put.

We have rehearsals four times a week, evening concerts from Wednesday to Saturday and matinees on Saturdays.

The weeks pass in a steady routine. Soon, I find the late evenings suit Mark too, and I stay over each night after a concert, except when he's in Melbourne. Occasionally, he takes me out to eat, though mostly we just fuck. On Mondays and Tuesdays, he doesn't call. I stay home and practise, read, and occasionally drop by the studio to see Val and the boys. I try not to think about Olivia, who does not call.

I don't know how Noah explained what she saw to her. Would she really think that I would seduce her boyfriend? I wonder what she'd think if I told her about Mark.

May threads into June. I feel myself grow weary of the new reality, the routine. When Mark is in Melbourne it is especially hard. I crave his body and nobody else's. On a cold Sunday afternoon, weeks after I've joined the orchestra permanently, I get a text from Olivia. It's brief, asking me if I'm going to the White Cocktail at the end of the month. No congratulations. No apology. I feel petty anger stirring. I wonder whether I'd treat her the same if she'd been offered the position instead of me. I send a brief text; yes, I'll be there. Then, nothing else.

Social functions are a test. I know how to charm the elites. I've been doing it since I was a child. The Russians threw the best parties. In St Petersburg, the conductor would hand me a shot of vodka and I'd down it when my mother's back was turned. In America, it depended on the city. In New York City, the parties were like Gatsby's. Over the top. Beautiful people. I was part of this world because they made me stand at its centre, but I also understood that I was completely outside of it. I did not return home to a mansion with a fridge stocked with French champagne.

I wear a backless, halter-neck gown to the dinner. Dark blue.

At Bennelong, I am greeted by a waiter who asks for my name. He leads me to a table at the front of the restaurant with the best view, close to the principal leaders. I am seated between a flautist, and Trumpet, who I knew from the college orchestra. Throughout the evening, we bond over our shared distaste for caviar, which is served alongside each dish in the à la carte menu. He tells me about his long-distance relationship with an opera singer in Germany.

'It's hard. The worst thing is she's based in Walldorf, which is a tiny village in the mountains with no internet.'

'How do you guys keep it together?'

'Love, I suppose, and trust.'

The conductor makes his way over and wedges himself between us. Tonight, he is not the Maestro. He is dressed down, a simple grey suit. He's pasted a slab of grey hair across his high forehead and left a small soul patch below his bottom lip.

'How's your night going?' His eyes are intense.

'We're good.' I turn my body to include Trumpet, who looks slightly alarmed by this.

'Can I get you and your friend a drink?' The conductor is trying.
I place a hand on Trumpet's forearm. 'He plays second desk.'
They shake hands like businessmen.

'Enjoying your season so far?' Trumpet asks.

'Yes, it's been good.'

We exchange social graces, and then Trumpet stands.

'Bathroom, excuse me.'

Part of me wants to follow him, but the conductor is now pressed forward, elbows resting on his knees.

'Now that you're a permanent member, you should apply for the Philharmonic exchange.'

I recall him mentioning something about it on his first day.

'I know some people on the panel. I can give you some advice.'

'I'm happy with where I am.'

'I know you're happy—but it's the Philharmonic. Don't you want to try?'

His eyes are shadowed by a huge flower piece at the centre of the table. In the subdued lighting his face looks forlorn. He could be any old white male. He shifts in his seat, readjusting his angle to me.

'Is he your boyfriend?'

He glances over at Trumpet, who is talking to a trombonist on another table.

'No.'

'Well, that's good. Nobody's worth staying in this city for.'

I laugh. A stupid, short laugh. 'I haven't thought about applying.'

'You ought to.'

His gaze is searing. I look away because I realise what he is doing and I've forgotten what to do in these situations.

'Why don't you take a taxi to my place later? I can give you some advice. I've been with the Philharmonic for decades.'

•

The conductor is staying in a serviced apartment on Macleay Street in Potts Point. The first thing he does is lead me to the balcony. The view is expansive across rooftops rolling towards the harbour, the blue horizon of the city.

He shows me around the rest of the apartment, finishing with the bedroom.

The sex is disappointing. Almost as soon as he takes a condom out, he goes flaccid and then tries for the next ten minutes to make his penis hard again using his hands. I lie beside him watching, gown hitched up to my waist.

He tells me to get his laptop from his desk. We watch a video of a man going down on a woman in a bus. He finally gets it up, but it's so quick we don't bother with the condom. He pulls out quickly, his face contorted in a half-agonised half-ecstatic grin. He grabs my chin in his hand and squeezes my cheeks. 'I'm sorry.'

'For what?'

'Coming inside you.'

'That's okay.'

He rises and goes to the kitchen; returning with a glass of water for himself.

'I'm sorry.'

'I know, don't worry.'

'You need to go now—it's orchestra policy.'

On the way to the train station, I pass a man lying in a foetal position by the side of the road. He is wearing a torn polo shirt, ripped shorts. His eyes are shut, hands clasped together in front of his mouth, like he's suppressing a cough.

'Are you okay?'

I can't tell whether he's dead or alive.

I ought to call someone. Nobody is around. I dial triple zero, then hang up. I speed walk like a maniac towards Kings Cross Station, glancing behind me every few steps.

At rehearsal the following morning, I sit in my usual seat behind the concertmaster, willing the conductor to look at me. I want an acknowledgement of last night, accede that he'd taken my body and used it for his pleasure, that I exist for him in a way others do not.

I play forcefully, even in pianissimo parts. The other players turn to look at me. But the conductor erases me. And that erasure makes me want to scream. I imagine myself exploding, the pink tissue of my brain strewn across the stand, spilling onto the laps of those unfortunate players nearby. The anxiety runs through my veins, reaching every part of my body. I can't locate the source of its itch, I only know that as he is thanking the orchestra at the end of the final piece, the blood pulses beneath my skin, and it takes all my willpower to stop myself from leaping off my chair and spearing my bow into his face.

20

After a concert one Thursday in June, my phone vibrates in my coat pocket.

'Hey.' Olivia's voice sounds muffled, like she has a piece of fabric over her mouth.

'Hi.'

'Where are you?'

'Walking home.'

'Want to grab a drink?'

It's been over a month, the longest we've ever been apart. She wouldn't call unless she had something to say. She hasn't been playing in concerts and leaves all my texts unreplied.

We meet at a bar near her apartment and sit on high stools by a fountain in the courtyard, heat lamps blazing above. It's a cool, windless evening. Blue night. Orange light. Her cheeks are rosy and full. We drink beer and skirt around things we don't want to talk about. I want her to apologise. Tell me she knows it was her boyfriend who was being an arsehole that night. Instead we talk about the string groups forming around the outer suburbs of Sydney. She asks if I've thought about the New York Philharmonic exchange; the conductor has been talking about it in rehearsals. 'How do you know? You haven't been coming.'

'I've just heard people talk about it. Anyway, are you going to audition?'

I shake my head. No way. She asks about the SSO. I smile, pleased that she's acknowledged it at last. I tell her it's going well.

'I'm stoked for you,' she says, though she doesn't sound it. 'But I have to say, I think it was unfair that they let you audition. I mean, you were the world's best violinist once. It was hardly a level playing field.'

I take a long swig of beer and stare at the screen inside the bar to distract me from the pain of her criticism. It's the first time she's ever voiced an opinion about my past.

'Look,' she says, 'I'm sorry I didn't tell you this before, but I got the can. They took me off the casuals list. I was missing too many calls.'

I wait for her to catch my eye, but she keeps her gaze on her fingers.

'Is it because of your mother?'

She nods. 'I wanted to tell you earlier, but I thought it would seem like such a small thing.'

'What do you mean? You never tell me anything about her.'

'But it's really nothing to you. I mean, someone like you, you were never going to be a casual forever.'

'That's not fair.' I fold my arms and then unfold them. Why do I feel like I need to defend myself?

'Anyway, it's fine,' she says. 'I'm a bit of a mess right now, but I've got a job, at least.'

'Teaching?'

Another soft nod.

'I'm not sure what to say.'

She looks up. 'Don't worry. You don't need to say anything.'

We finish our drinks and part at the junction where our two suburbs separate. I watch her turn the corner into another street. She doesn't look back.

When I get home, there is no text from her. No text from Mark.

•

I wake the next morning to a throbbing wrist and a ricochet of loud knocks.

Val is at the door with two drinks.

'So, I didn't know what to get you because you don't drink coffee.'

She pushes a takeaway cup forward. 'Chai okay?'

'Thanks.' I stand aside to let her in.

'I was just on my way to the studio. Mike said he left some brushes in a kitchen drawer.'

'You're not here to see me?'

She slips her shoes off with one hand.

'I love that you know that,' I say, shutting the door.

'I'm Chinese.'

She follows me into the lounge room, making small talk about the weather, the election, the greyhounds.

'Have you decided about moving?'

Her forehead creases as if she doesn't know what I'm talking about.

'The two of us—moving in together?'

'Of course, sorry. Didn't I already text you? Sure, I'm up for it.'

I leap off the couch and jump onto her.

'Hey, watch out. Coffee.'

She holds a hand up, distancing herself from my enthusiasm. 'Let's just see how it goes.'

'I'll be good, I promise.'

'I don't want you to be good.' She stands and makes towards the kitchen. 'Anyway, I'd better look for those brushes.'

I follow her, blinking hard, excitement mounting in my chest. My loneliness was just beginning to make me feel like I might commit violence against myself.

21

Mark calls after rehearsal. He's booked a table for dinner. He tells me to dress up. He tells me he has a conference call at nine, but it is short so I should be ready by nine-thirty.

We meet at Jade Temple. He is in a suit, tie, blue cufflinks the shape of soccer balls. He looks at the waitresses then at me and smirks. 'You should wear that.'

The women are wearing tight-fitting traditional *chi-pao*. Hair in a bun. No lipstick. I've never worn a *chi-pao*. It is strange to have a white man tell me to dress in a cultural uniform, put myself into a box, a box he's created for people who look like me, this face, this skin colour, and all that it means. We sit at a small table. Bamboo fans spin above our heads, leaf green panels hang from the walls.

He pushes a ceramic cup to the side and extends an open palm. My cue.

I'm still offended; I don't want to touch him. But I put my hand in his.

He carries on with the same racist, sexist rhetoric through the three entrees. He talks about women the way one might talk about nut milks. What's the latest trend? Which one is lowest in fat content now? Cashew? Almond? Macadamia? Hazelnut?

'I think white women are too plain,' he says. 'I don't learn anything by being with them. They're too vanilla. I went through an African-American phase, but I'm into South-East Asian now. They have such delicate features. They're more feminine. Especially TAGs.'

'TAGs?'

'Tiny Asian Girls.'

I want to let go of his hand but I don't, because I want someone to hold my hand and he is holding my hand.

'You know, we're human beings too,' I say.

He laughs, a sharp exhalation. Even his laugh sounds cruel.

'I think I might have UTI. It's really painful and itchy when I pee.'

He releases my hand. Leans back in his chair.

'Jesus, we're eating.'

The waitress in *chi-pao*, who is not Asian, places a bowl of hand towels in front of us.

'Can we still have sex?'

'I'm taking antibiotics. We'll have to use condoms.'

'Whatever.'

The mains arrive. He's ordered half a lobster, which comes on a large silver platter.

'I didn't realise it would be so big,' he says.

I am no longer hungry, and we leave most of it untouched.

'How much was it?' I ask, gesturing to the platter.

'I don't know. Two hundred.'

'That's a lot of money.'

I sip green tea from a tiny porcelain cup and tell him there's a Taiwanese joint my mother and I used to go to when I lived at home. It's on the North Shore—out of the way, but worth the trip.

'You should take me. I've never had Taiwanese food.'

He flicks a few pieces of lobster shell off the table and looks around the restaurant.

Then he tells me about a blind pussy taste-testing competition he recently discovered on Reddit.

'I'd do well at that,' he boasts. 'If you were to blindfold me and get me to go down on multiple women, I could tell which is which.'

'What do you mean, *which is which?*'

'Which pussy belongs to which woman. You all taste slightly different.'

'Should I be offended right now?'

'Why?'

'Because it's . . . weird.'

'What is?'

'Your blind pussy taste-testing competition.'

'I'm just saying something objectively.'

'And I'm saying we're not objects.'

Back at his place, he undresses himself methodically, placing his cuff-links back in the box, his shoes onto the shoe stand, hanging his shirt on a hanger. He walks over to me and bends down to slip off my shoes.

I reach for my handbag on the edge of his bed.

'Come on, we don't need it.'

'I don't want to take risks.'

'It'll be fine,' he says. 'I'll pull out. I promise.'

In the morning, when we are doing it in doggy, I feel a finger slide into my arsehole. I cramp up. He puts his hand over my mouth. 'Let's try it.'

He pulls my butt cheeks apart and jams his penis inside. Something comes out of my mouth. Sounds I don't recognise. But he keeps going.

I try to relax thinking this might ease the pain, if only slightly.

Later, I feel as if I have progressed in some way. Adultified.

When Mark goes to shower, I reach for my phone on the bedside table and call Val. I tell her of my new achievement. I wait for her response. I wait for her to tell me how bad I am for sleeping with a man who is in a relationship with someone else. I wait for her to tell me how I'm doing it all wrong. Instead she asks me a question.

'Did you make him give you the dirty sanchez?'

'What?'

'The dirty sanchez.'

'What's that?'

'After he pulls out, tell him to wipe it across your lips. You'll make a Mexican moustache.'

'You're disgusting.'

'So are you. You just had a cock up your arse. Congratulations.'

His shower has a metre-long window with a view of the city. I trace a line across the products perched on the sill. Facial cleanser, facial scrub, body scrub, gel cleanser, blackhead remover, anti-ageing lotion, anti-fatigue exfoliating powder, intense hydration beard conditioner, anti-fatigue eye gel, charcoal cleanser, exfoliating tonic, aloe shave gel, post-shave soother, dark spot corrector, cellular three-minute peel, anti-gravity wash-off serum. They are all in dark colours. Grey. Black. Khaki. I snap open the facial scrub and apply some to my forehead, cheeks and chin, rubbing it gently in a circular motion. I wonder if I'll start growing a beard. I flick the side of a bottle onto its back and read the label. *Life-changing skin care.*

Afterwards, I stand on the bathroom mat, drying my hair with a hand towel. Mark comes in and kisses the back of my neck. I turn around and wrap my arms around his back.

'I'm seeing my girlfriend this weekend.' The shower tap is still dripping. 'You can't make any new marks on me.'

We have sex again. The whole time, my hands are clutched in tight fists.

22

Val and I are in the studio negotiating how we're going to live together.

'Perhaps we just need to stop thinking and start doing.'

I tell her that is the best thing she has said since 'I CUNT WELL'.

On the weekend, we meet on Francis Street in Bondi Beach to view some apartments. As I'm parking my car, I spot Val walking on the footpath, dressed in black leather pants, blue sweater, denim jacket tied around her small waist. Everything wants to be close to her body.

The first apartment is on the ground floor of an old block. The front gate is unlocked, the windows frosted. Val manages to hide her distaste until after we leave.

The second apartment has two bedrooms and a balcony that over-looks a quiet street. I see a man in a wetsuit, upper half undone, racing across the street with a surfboard under one arm. I walk back into the master bedroom, where Val is testing the sliding closet doors.

'It's a bit old and smelly,' she says.

'I love the view.'

'We can do better.'

The agent wanders in. We shrug noncommittally. She tells us its winter. There is less on the market. She suggests we see a property that has just come up this morning; hasn't yet been listed. She makes a call then gives us the address.

The apartment is on the top floor of a modern building. There are two bedrooms. One is significantly larger than the other and has a balcony that overlooks rooftops and a tiny slice of the ocean. The kitchen is small but the lounge room is huge. We walk past each other in the corridor. We exchange grins.

Val takes the larger room and agrees to pay an extra hundred dollars a week.

We move in the following Friday evening—15 July—the weekend I turn twenty-three.

I call my mother to tell her the news. She invites me to dinner. It's been months since I've seen my father, and even longer since I've seen Rebecca, though she usually doesn't visit my parents during the week.

At the table, my mother executes a warning. 'You've only known this girl for a short while. How do you know you can trust her?'

'She's a woman.'

My father emerges from the study, sullen and hunched. Since we returned from Wayne four years ago, he has resumed the role of my mother's husband as though nothing had happened. When I allow myself to think about their marriage, a spark of terror lights in my mind; how easy, the performance of spouse-hood. He asks me again where I am moving.

I tell him and say I want to be close to the beach; he says I might as well be living in another country.

'It's only half an hour's drive away.'

'If it's near the beach it's probably very expensive,' he says.

'It's alright,' I say.

'Do you have enough money?'

'Yes.'

After dinner he helps me load bags into the back of my car. Chinese containers of leftovers.

I get into the driver's seat then wind down the window to say goodbye.

'Call your mother,' he says.

'I do.'

'Call her more often. She's got things to say.'

I drive away. An old grudge rising in my throat.

23

The combined housewarming and birthday celebration is Val's idea. Her vision: Andy Warhol's The Factory meets the Met Gala, though we're not sure about the dress up.

We theme it, the Coconut Party.

The man in the fruit store on Campbell Parade asks me why I am buying so many coconuts as he helps me load the five trays into my car. I tell him about the Coconut Party and he gives me a lingering look. I feel pressured into inviting him. He says he's not free on Saturday night; that's when he goes to his second job.

'What's your second job?'

'Being a husband and a father to a three-year-old and a six-month-old.'

'That's nice,' I say, even though I don't think that's nice at all. 'You're a good man.'

'I'd rather be going to a party hosted by a pretty girl.' He winks.

I get into my car and drive off, feeling violated. Intuitively, I reach for my phone to text Olivia, but stop when I find her name in my inbox. I'll see her in a few hours. I'll tell her then.

Back home, coconuts are cracked open and placed strategically around the apartment—on tabletops, the ledge of the balcony, on our heads, spread across the bookshelves. We fill them with a variety of booze. Vodka, whisky, bourbon, champagne, red wine, white wine, port, gin, sake. We slice up cheese and put it in coconuts.

People arrive and crowd onto the balcony, where two tables of coconuts and drinks are laid out. They laugh at the sight, then take selfies posing next to rows of coconuts neatly arranged like bowling pins. I check my phone for messages, but none of the names appearing on my screen is the one I am waiting for. I wonder when Olivia will arrive. Even if she doesn't stay long, I want her to be here when the party is at its full capacity. I want her to know I can be without her.

'Hey!'

Noah appears at the door. He's wearing a white T-shirt and chinos. A Bondi Lifesavers cap hides his thatch of blond hair. His smile shifts something inside me.

'Where's Olivia?' I ask. 'She said she'd be coming.'

'She's at her mum's.'

For a few seconds, all I want is for everyone around me to disappear; she is the only person I want to see tonight.

'She said she'll call you,' Noah adds. 'Sorry.'

The crowd continues to swell. The Sonos is at max volume, hammering ordinary, trippy house beats.

I busy myself filling coconuts, cutting more cheese. In the kitchen, a few people are doing shots; someone has broken up some coconuts, using the shards as bowls to drink from. I join them for a couple of shots, then retreat to the balcony to breathe. I look around. There are music producers, writers, filmmakers, artists, teachers, chefs, editors, lawyers, policemen, Uber drivers, personal trainers, graphic designers, social workers, sculptors and a few journalists. One public defender who looks out of place.

I decide I need to drink more and start squeezing through the crush to get back to the kitchen.

'Where are you going?' Noah shouts into my ear.

'What?'

He doesn't need to repeat himself, but I want him to lean closer to my face.

'WHERE ARE YOU GOING?'

I stab the air in the direction of the kitchen. He indicates for me to lead; puts a hand on my hip and leaves it there as if he owns me, and I wonder why this small gesture feels so validating. I push through the crowd.

In the kitchen, all the cupboard doors are opened. There are coconuts on each shelf, between bags of muesli, bottles of wine, boxes of Lavosh.

There are people clustered in the kitchen. They're orchestra members from university, mostly brass players. Potheads. Anarchists. They have names like Pippa, James, Marcus and Charlie. They're doing lines of coke on the kitchen counter.

'Join us!' Charlie reaches for my arm.

'I'm just doing coconuts tonight,' I say.

'How boring.'

The four of them collapse into a laughing fit.

'At least they're having fun,' Noah says. He takes my hand and leads me out of the apartment through the back door.

We walk to the end of the street, far enough to lose the sounds of the party.

'I wanted to ask . . .' he begins. Pauses. 'I was just wondering if you and Olivia are okay.' He raises an eyebrow.

'Yeah, of course. Why wouldn't we be?'

'I think she's still annoyed you got in.'

I shrug, not sure what he wants me to say. And then I realise I don't have to say anything. 'Well, there's nothing I can do about that.'

We look back at the party. The balcony is glowing with pink and orange fairy lights. The heads of people outlined in a quivering black landscape.

All I wanted was for her to see how successful I could be without her.

All I wanted was—

'Thanks for agreeing to lead the event at Newington,' Noah says.

I turn to face him. I'd expected him to bring up the kiss from that night two months ago. But it seems he's forgotten about it.

'Lead? I thought I was just playing in the ensemble.'

'Olivia said you'd be happy to lead it.'

There's nothing to do but walk, so I walk.

Noah follows. At the next corner, I stand and look up at the street sign, pretending to read it.

'You want to go someplace else?' he whispers.

'No, let's head back to the party.'

My phone pings and I pull it out of my pocket. A text from Mark. For the first time, I feel irritated.

'Friend?' Noah asks.

'Nobody'.

24

A few nights later, Val and I watch *Frances Ha* in bed on my laptop. The air is still thick with the smell of honey and garlic from dinner— baked kingfish with pomegranate sauce. The sauce takes half an hour to make and leaves my fingers stained crimson.

Greta Gerwig leaps through the streets of New York's Chinatown. I relax into a joy-by-osmosis as the camera follows her twists and turns and pirouettes. Next to me, Val is sucking on her fingers, rubbing the red off her knuckles. I yearn for a friendship like the one between Frances and her best friend, Sophie.

Olivia and I saw the film together when it came out a few years ago. It had become a sort of emblem of our friendship. I always saw myself as Frances and her as my Sophie. But Olivia said she was Frances and I was Sophie because I was the more successful one.

In the film, Frances and Sophie are madly in love. Friend love. That's what we're made to believe. In the beginning, they're best friends who also live together—'like a lesbian couple that doesn't have sex anymore,' Frances said. I want that closeness, that intimacy, that acceptance.

I glance at Val. She looks bored. I try to hide my devastation.

•

In the second-last week of July, it rains without respite. I carry an umbrella around like a spare limb. An annoying, spare limb. The final concerts with the American conductor draw closer. Relief settles in.

The return of our chief conductor marks the month of his seventieth birthday. Bryce announces a special birthday concert. They bring me on for a small ensemble because they want a high-profile musician to lead and Banks, who is a friend of the conductor, has nominated me. The program has been selected by the conductor himself—works by Brahms, Mozart and Haydn. At the first rehearsal, I propose we add Schubert's 'The Trout', the conductor had always said it was his favourite piece of chamber music. Bryce is reluctant but I stand my ground. To my surprise, the rest of the ensemble support my suggestion.

After our first rehearsal, I bump into Banks in the green room at the Opera House.

'You should think about the exchange,' he says.

'I'm not sure.'

I remember the American conductor had mentioned it on the night of the White Cocktail, and then Olivia had raised it, but that was weeks ago and I hadn't thought about it since. 'When is it?'

'It would run from November through to the beginning of March next year. All your travel and accommodation would be covered. There are only four spots being offered across the world. Four in total. It's a big deal, Jena. You'll need to audition, but your chances are good.'

'I just started with the SSO. Wouldn't that look bad?'

'It's New York City. It's the Philharmonic. Who knows? You might even be considered for a permanent position there.'

I press a palm to my cheek.

He leans forward and places a hand to his hip. 'There is one thing I need you to know though . . .'

I look at him, steady gaze, waiting.

'Christopher Jennings will be on the audition panel.'

Christopher Jennings. That name. My arrogance. My humiliation.

When I was fifteen, I debuted at Carnegie Hall with the New York Philharmonic. The concertmaster was a steely man from England, a visiting artist who Banks had known when they were both students at the Royal College of Music. During a break one rehearsal, he walked back onto stage where I was still practising. He stopped me with a friendly wave and told me casually that he could not play without an occasional rest.

'That's why you're not a soloist.'

I remember the look he gave me; a blend of astonishment threaded with admiration and offence.

Banks heard all about it, of course. Jennings seemed like the least surprised person that evening when I didn't finish the performance. It was like he'd known what I was about to do.

'There's no chance I'll get in,' I say.

'That was eight years ago.'

'You haven't forgotten. Why would he?'

He shakes his head. 'I'm only telling you so you aren't caught by surprise. The audition is the first of September. I will help you.'

25

My mother is my motor. She *was* my motor. When I call to tell her about the exchange, she suggests I set a practice recital in preparation for the audition. It's always good to perform your audition program to get a feel for the order of things. Like putting up a series of paintings in a new gallery and going for a walk around the space.

'How about we raise money too?' my mother suggests over the phone. 'It's Alzheimer's Awareness Week next month—perfect timing.' She assures me she'll arrange everything. Venue, accompanist, promotion, catering. We'd need at least two rehearsals.

'I don't know,' I say. 'I'll need to run it past Banks. We'd have to invite him.' It's been years since my mother and Banks have seen each other. Neither asks about the other. And yet, the sensation I felt when I saw them backstage that night is still fresh. I think about the possibilities of reopening old wounds. 'Would you be okay with that?' I ask.

She tsks, as if I've offended her. 'Don't worry about me.'

In the lounge room, I set out two stools next to the stand: one for the rosin, tissue box, wrist band; the other for a water bottle, pencil, rubber. Metronome. I click it on and listen to its repetitive knock. I close my eyes and bring my violin to my neck. Without the shoulder rest, without the weight of clothes, I am free. I bring the bow to the G string and begin playing scales, ascending, descending. Weight and gravity. I think about the way my left wrist feels solid and tight like a compressed piece of aluminium, the single vein running from the start of my thumb to the bony part of the hand. It throbs as I move it from side to side, a braised pink groove circling my flesh like a friendship bracelet.

The other night, my wrists had been bound by a thin leather rope. Mark had run his nose down my body, slow breaths like the sea lapping on the shore. I feigned ecstasy, moaning and lifting my body off the bed.

I spend longer on the E string because the higher registers are harder to get in tune. I do it over and over, until my finger pads feel like they're being sliced by a thin blade.

As my fingertips navigate the floss-thin string, my mind disappears into a cave and all I see is darkness and light, existing in one frame. When I hear the intonation crystallise underneath my fingers, I wonder how it came to be that I can no longer tell the difference between pain and pleasure. That I might never truly know the difference.

When I arrive at the church for our first rehearsal, Sandra, the accompanist, is already waiting near the entrance, a folder of sheet music clutched to her chest.

'Sorry to make you wait.' She shakes off my apology.

She's a small woman with wiry black hair and rimless glasses, serious, mid-thirties with a competent, feminine face. She was a student of Dr Resling, and I have played with her a handful of times. She is quiet, reliable and astute, which is exactly what I need in an audition accompanist.

I open the front door to the church with the keys left under the doormat, instructions sent to me by the minister, an old friend of my mother's.

I find the light switch behind the curtains. White light pours over the interior of the church. The industrial haze of organised religion.

Sandra shields her eyes with a hand.

I unpack my violin at the front pew, while Sandra takes her position at the piano, readjusting the height of the piano stool, bouncing a few times to test its stability. She wipes the low keys with her sleeves, taps across the black and white. It's cold. Wine cellar cold. The chill of unventilated timber floors and high walls. It takes a while for my fingers to warm up.

We run through the program, a standard spread of Franck, Mozart and Brahms sonatas. Crowd-pleasers. I breathe in the spaces between phrases and melodic twists, and watch for Sandra's changing expressions.

We lock eyes at simultaneous entrances. Her motion is fluid. Her eyes possess the steady focus of an aerial skier gauging the jump she is about to make. Soloist–accompanist relationships take years to build. A good combination is hard to manufacture. You have to trust each other completely. It's not just the soloist who is performing; the pianist is also a musician, also onstage.

My mother walks into the church during the slow movement of the Mozart. She creeps forward slowly, taking a seat in the front pew next to my case. At one point, I see her reach for Monkey and pat him on the head, adjusting his body upright.

Banks enters a few minutes later and sits in the back row. There was a time when I wouldn't think twice about how to perform around him. Long ago. He was my teacher. My confidant. My everything. All those years. We toured the world together. Now, after years of absence, he has re-entered my life. I have to remind myself how to be around him.

At the end of the second movement, my mother comes over to greet Sandra. 'You're playing well.'

Sandra smiles politely.

Banks remains seated at the back. 'Well? Keep going,' he says.

My mother sits back down, this time directly in front of me. Sandra and I continue onto the third and fourth movements without interruption. Neither has acknowledged the other.

Banks calls out from the back, 'Go from the start!'

Sandra and I blink at each other and start from the beginning.

After the first phrase, Banks gets to his feet. 'The tempo is wrong.'

I see my mother's face change. She plays with the straps of her handbag.

Banks makes his way to the front of the church and stands next to the piano. He leans over to read the score on the stand. 'Allegretto moderato. You're taking it too slow.'

'Oh?' Sandra looks offended. 'I've always played it this way.'

'Try again, this time a bit faster.'

Sandra and I lock eyes. I swing the tip of my bow from side to side, indicating the new tempo. We burst through the opening phrases. Out of the corner of my eye, I see Banks nodding enthusiastically.

My mother walks to the back row, sits where Banks had been sitting before. By the time we reach the end of the movement, she's made her way to the front again. Her face is sour, her fingers now clamped firmly around the handles of her handbag. 'It's much too fast,' she says.

Sandra and I share a fleeting look of frustration. We turn back to Banks.

He is looking at my mother with a confused grin. 'How so? I think it's the perfect tempo.'

'Well, if you sit at the back, you'll hear a jumbled mess of noise.'

Banks crosses his arms in front of his chest. 'The acoustics in this hall will not be like those in the Opera House where Jena will have her audition.' His tone is condescending.

My mother looks at him coldly. 'I know that. But this is a performance.'

Sandra is the only neutral individual I can rest my gaze on. I look at her, pretend there's only us.

I hear raised voices outside—a group of kids walking past, boys arguing about ball possession.

Banks rubs his temples with his thumbs, concealing his eyes behind his large hands.

When I was touring, they'd never once had a disagreement in front of me. Back then it was just me, my mother and Banks. The newspapers and anyone else who cared about child prodigies called us 'the Three-headed Beast'.

We toured three weeks on, one week off. I had a tutor who accompanied us. Banks didn't like her. He thought she got in the way of my musical development. He would often interrupt our lessons. I didn't mind. To me, he knew best. I trusted him completely. It was only later that my mother told me that she and Banks had different views about my playing; that Banks would always win because he was the teacher.

'Perhaps, if we just make sure nobody sits near the back?' Sandra offers.

Banks and I look at each other.

'The acoustics aren't great in here,' she continues. 'The sound will reverberate more than usual anywhere you sit, really.'

I look down at my ballet flats; the bow on the left pair has disappeared.

'Could we try it again in the speed we started with?' I ask.

Sandra nods and plays a few bars at that speed. I look across to Banks, who is assuming a seat. We play the first few lines, and then I nod, stop playing. This time I don't look at Banks.

•

Two days later, my mother sends me a picture of the recital ad. My face is serious, my hair clipped behind one ear, my forehead dominating. It's a picture taken from my final year of touring. I look deceptively calm. Fifteen. My mother posts the event on Facebook, Twitter, Instagram, all the platforms she is active on through her work on the boards of numerous charities. She does not call. I don't call either.

26

My grandpapa was a famous child prodigy. He began playing the piano when he was five years old. He burned out before his twelfth birthday and then became like any other child in China at that time. Once he grew up and moved away from home, he tried his best to resume his music, but he didn't have enough money to travel and perform.

My grandpapa had perfect pitch and knew how to play the violin, so he became my first violin teacher. Before he arrived in Australia, my mother asked him to bring a 1/32-size violin. It was too big for me but my grandpapa insisted that violins didn't come any smaller.

From the beginning, I played without a shoulder rest. With my arm stretched out, my fingertips only just scraped the bottom of the scroll. For the first three months, I played open strings. Grandpapa said the foundations took the longest to get right. I know all this because over the years my mother would tell me stories about those early days. The stories lodged in my mind and became indistinguishable from my own memories.

Before the start of each lesson my grandpapa would say, 'When I'm teaching you, I am not your grandpapa, understood?'

At the time, my mother was working at an accounting firm in the city. Sometimes, she'd come home and see red marks on my face. She asked me what happened.

'Grandpapa wasn't happy with the way I played the scales.'

I heard them whispering in the kitchen later, but all I remember is the way the low tone of my grandpapa dominated the sounds of the house. He lived with us after my grandmama died.

As I played, he would push me into position. If my body didn't move the way he wanted, he had ways to change that. To fix my sometimes-wavering bow arm, he tied a thin wire to my wrist and attached the other end to a doorknob. Then he opened and closed the door slowly, so I'd get used to the motion of the moving bow arm, steady and still and always at precisely the right angle. Sometimes, he'd move the door so fast that by the time we finished my wrist was encircled with a bright red ring. When that happened, my mother would ask me to cover my wrists, so she didn't have to see what my grandpapa was doing to me.

By the time I turned six I was playing Beethoven, Mozart, Shostakovich, Brahms. Grandpapa told my mother I needed a new teacher. He had heard of a Russian woman who was reputed to be the best violin teacher in the world. At the time, she'd just moved to Shanghai for a two-year teaching residency at the Conservatory.

My mother got in touch. The woman's reply was frank—'I don't take children.'

But Grandpapa told my mother to buy the plane tickets anyway. 'Just go and have Jena play for her. See what she says then.'

My mother and I flew to Shanghai. I played for the Russian woman. I played the first page of the Brahms Concerto.

'Your daughter needs to come and study with me,' she said.

So, I was taken on by Nadia. Nadia, who had long silvery hair tied in a ponytail; a tail that reached her lower back. Nadia, who said tears were the hallmark of progress, so I cried every lesson. Nadia, who never laid a hand on me but used the tip of her bow when I played a wrong note. She'd place the pointed end against the small of my back and when my intonation slipped—which it did only rarely—she'd jab me and yell, 'Wrong! Wrong! Wrong!' and then, 'Again!'

Sometimes even when I thought I'd played flawlessly she would whip her bow across my back. For two years, my mother and I flew to Shanghai every fortnight, leaving on Friday night and returning on Sunday evening. We could afford it because my father fixed a lot of people's teeth. All his money went into those tickets and lessons. I never saw much of my sister, Rebecca, during that time. I rarely saw my father either. He was a shadow at the edge of my life. And perhaps my mother's as well.

Two days before my eighth birthday, Nadia died of a brain aneurysm in her apartment. The cleaning lady had found her. She'd died alone.

We did not go to her funeral and it would be another year before we returned to Shanghai. That time I debuted with the Shanghai Symphony Orchestra playing Mendelssohn's Violin Concerto. My mother became my agent and started booking concerts during my school holidays when managers began hearing about me. And then we heard that Professor Niall Banks, an old friend of Nadia's from Moscow, would be teaching in Sydney. He was an emeritus professor from the UK, married to an Australian flautist half his age. When she fell pregnant, they moved back to her home in Sydney. He was offered a teaching position at the Conservatorium and took on local and international students. They lost the baby, I later found out, and soon after that, the marriage broke down. But Banks stayed in Sydney. It was another case of stars aligning. My mother said, 'It was meant to be. He could manage Jena's touring too.'

Grandpapa died a month later, and soon after Banks told my mother I needed to compete overseas. 'There's nothing here in Australia worthy of your daughter,' he said to her.

Within a year, I'd won seven international violin competitions and played with several orchestras across four continents.

During the year of my breakdown, I asked my mother why she gave up so much for me.

'Your urge was uncontainable,' she said. 'I couldn't stop you.'

'But you used to say you didn't want me to be a circus performer.'

'No. That was your father.'

What frightens me now is what had frightened me as a child. Nadia, dying alone in her apartment. How long had she been lying there? How long had she waited for someone to come to save her? How long before she realised that no one was going to save her? But then I realise if she hadn't died, I'd never have met Banks. I might never have become famous.

The recital is held on a Saturday night. When I asked Bryce for the evening off, he'd agreed, but seemed displeased. Why couldn't I have scheduled it for Monday or Tuesday? I told him my mother had organised the event and he gave me a look. I was embarrassed. I decided I hated him for making me feel like that.

The church is in a suburb heavily populated by immigrant families. Korean. Chinese. Vietnamese. Taiwanese. Malaysian. Filipino. Indian. Sri Lankan. I tell Mark about it; casually mention he is welcome. He laughs. He thinks I am joking.

Parents bring their young daughters and sons. The girls are dressed in pink frocks that reach their small calves. Frilled sleeves. Hair in pigtails, centre parts. Perfect little Asian kids. Me, fifteen years ago.

Val, Mike and Jacob are wedged side by side in the back row. My father is sitting in the corner on a single chair, alone, slumped with his eyes closed and arms folded. Banks is seated at the front next to my mother. He is looking at his phone. She is twisting the handles of her handbag.

In a small room behind the church hall, I roll my shoulders and take slow, deep breaths. I close my eyes, focusing on the inhalation. Exhalation. I pace around. I go to my case and reach for Monkey.

'You ready?' Sandra asks.

'Yeah.'

I pull my sleeves up. Roll my shoulders again. Inside my head, I'm running visuals of passages, chromatic leaps. The audience are murmuring quietly. A low purr.

Sandra and I walk onto the stage. I smile into the sea of faces. The lights are dimmed. For a moment, I think I catch a glimpse of Olivia in the back row.

Sandra is waiting for me. I blink. Raise my violin and tuck it under my chin.

We begin.

When I'm playing, everything is suspended. It's as though I've entered some other dimension. Somewhere nobody else knows. It feels good to play onstage, without the expectation of sixty other musicians behind me. I am the centre of everyone's attention, and that old thrill sluices me. Like glory. Heat. Entirely mine.

27

At fourteen, I won the Yehudi Menuhin Violin Competition. The prize was a solo with the New York Philharmonic.

I would play the Beethoven, a mature piece, one not many teenagers perform because of its emotional austerity. But I was going to do it. I would play the Beethoven Violin Concerto with the New York Philharmonic at Carnegie Hall. An impressive feat. Sarah Chang had debuted with the Philharmonic when she was eight, but she'd played the Mendelssohn; no one under twenty really touches the Beethoven. At least, not in public. It's serious repertoire.

I am waiting in the wings, breathing, counting each slow inhalation and exhalation. I sip water from the bottle my mother carries in her handbag, which makes me want to pee. Three minutes. I have time—just. I hurry through a corridor. As I open the door to my room, I see the back of my mother's head, and then a man's arms enfolding her. They lean their foreheads together. It's brief, but I see it. They are standing in a corner of the players' lounge. Banks and my mother. There is an intimacy between them I don't understand. An intimacy they have been hiding from me.

I become, in that moment, a child left out of a game. I feel hot with betrayal.

I want to tear at my skin. Rip my hair from my skull. That I could be related to the woman who is now having a private moment with the most important man in my life. Five minutes ago, I could not have fathomed a world where I was not at the centre of their lives. Something monumental must be happening. Or must be done.

Did I know what I was about to do?

A narrative enters my consciousness: it's effortless; I don't try to fight it. I am tired of this life; the touring and the late nights. I am tired of Banks's voice. Tired of the pressure, the restraints; tired of not being allowed to do anything that might damage my hands, which is just about everything. I'd thought we were a three-headed monster, but we are not; there is them and there is me. I want a way out—and they have given it to me. All at once I feel powerful, exhilarated. A roaring strength rises inside me.

The stage crew are rushing around. I hear the sound of applause. A woman with a clipboard and a headset gives me a nod. I stride onto the stage. Confident.

Onstage, I bow.

I make it through the first movement. The second.

And then. And then.

I slip the bow across the bridge. The audience stop breathing. I execute the wrong notes. I do not look at the conductor; he will try to help me recover. Instead, I look to the wings. My mother is standing beside Banks, her hands over her mouth. I'll never forget the look on her face.

I have never felt so powerful in my life.

It was a very public meltdown. That's what the newspapers called it. Performances were cancelled. Banks refused to speak to the press.

I'm not sure if either of them has ever forgiven me for what I did that night. I lied, of course. Blamed it on nerves. They knew me better than that. It was inevitable I would destroy everything. I'd been touring without substantial breaks since I was eight, and the older I grew the more aware I was that offstage I was nothing. I'd stare at myself in the mirror in the bathroom and wonder if one day I'd look and there would be no one staring back at me.

I don't remember much of the immediate aftermath. When I told my mother and Banks I could never play in public again, neither of them resisted. I'd thought they would counter, convince me to stay, to finish the tour. Play one more concert. I had engagements booked for the next two years. But they didn't. I wanted them to beg, to show me how important I was. But they didn't. Maybe they knew that on some level I'd been right to do what I did. So it was decided we would return home. That I'd put the violin aside and go to school, pretend to be a normal person. On our flight home, I took Monkey out of my case and held him in my lap the entire trip back.

Back home, my parents' marriage fell apart. My father had a cousin in New Jersey whom he'd once been close to. They reconnected and my father decided he was going to move to another country. Within a few weeks, it was settled. We'd go together, my father and me. I applied for an Extraordinary Alien Visa and my father accompanied me as my guardian. I was eager to detach myself from my mother and to put as much distance as possible between me and Banks.

For two years I hid out in Wayne. I'd taken my violin with me but didn't pick it up. My mother did not visit. I threw myself at boys. And they were my salvation.

28

I am lying in Mark's bed, which is Mark-less. He'd left early for work. Last night, I'd gone home around midnight after a two-hour rehearsal with the 'Trout' ensemble, tired and needing sleep, but then I caught a taxi to Mark's because he texted me during rehearsal.

Banks calls. It's been two weeks since the recital. We talk about non-specifics. The weather. Books. The news. We skate along a thin surface, until it cracks.

'I'd like to hear you one more time before your audition,' he says finally.

He wants to know how I am getting on. If my phrasing in the Brahms has improved since the recital. If my bow arm is strong. If my sensibilities are attuned to what I am playing.

I agree. He'd been my surrogate parent for nearly half of my life. When I picked up the violin again at the start of university, I had wanted to forge a musical career without him, but there was part of me that still craved his approval.

I arrive shortly after lunchtime, clutching a half-eaten bacon sandwich. The sky is a cool shade of pink and the air is wet with the prospect of thunderstorms. In his studio, Banks is wearing a cardigan the colour of bird shit.

He motions for me to enter. 'Okay, let's hear the Brahms.'

I play the entire first movement. He does not move. He keeps his eye on Monkey, whose body is leaning against the bows inside my case.

I play the second movement.

Then, two bars into the third movement, he rises off his chair.

'I didn't say to stop,' he scolds. 'Keep going.'

I place my bow back on the string and begin again. After a while, I realise I'm the only one in the room. He returns minutes later.

'Why'd you leave?'

He walks to his desk and shuffles a few books around. 'Tell me, Jena,' he says without looking up, 'what are the three components of musical prodigiousness?'

A dull weight falls over my shoulders. I have heard this too many times, but to him I can never repeat it enough.

I wonder what would happen if I refused to answer? If I pretend not to know the answer. Would he step out from behind the desk and hit me?

I can't pretend, though, because he knows I know.

I draw out each word slowly. 'The athletic. The mimetic. And the interpretive.'

'Good.'

'I have the first two, not the last,' I say wearily.

'Correct.'

'Why am I here if you're just going to be cruel?'

'*Cruel?* Is that what you think? Jena, why are you even doing this? Do you really want to be a violinist?'

'What kind of question is that? You're the one who put my name forward for this exchange!'

He crosses his arms and rocks on his feet.

'Do you know what happened to you at fifteen? You had nothing left. You failed because you had nothing new to say. But it's not your fault. Those things, they can't be forced. You had nothing left to say because you had no life experiences to draw on—and I contributed to that, I can see that now. You didn't . . . what you had was no life.'

He speaks with the air of a hospital chaplain, reflective and calm.

'Look,' he says, 'I never wanted to see you fail at such a young age. I wanted to give you a full and long career. But you were a child. You are still a child. You have no idea how much you still have to learn.'

The sound of a piano threads into the room, answering for me. I stay silent.

'Deciding not to develop a life in music after a prodigious beginning takes will.'

I turn my violin around, cradling its belly.

'What are you saying? That I will never reach my potential?'

'You were world famous. Wasn't that enough?'

I stare at him, unsure where the strength to do so comes from.

I want to tell him about the darkness that opened up inside me that night in Carnegie Hall. How it had always been there, lurking—a lack I never knew how to repel. There was a hole in me that was ultimately unfillable. An insatiable hunger I was born with. Like my talent.

'Of course it wasn't enough.'

That night, I lie awake, my head on the edge of the pillow, looking out at the neon skyline of Sydney from Mark's bed. He is on his laptop, fingers tapping the keys with metronomic discipline.

I think about Banks. Do I need to run away from this city to get away from that old self? Why can't people move on? I was fifteen. Most fifteen-year-olds do far worse than what I did. What do I need to do to get away so I can determine the kind of life I want, set my own terms?

I am stirred out of bed in the morning by a call.

'Jena, it's Bryce. You've missed two rehearsals. Is everything alright?'

I make a quick excuse. 'My mother was in hospital. I couldn't get signal there.'

It's a weak excuse, but he buys it and lets me off with a warning. I am afraid how easily lies come out of my mouth these days. I feel bad that I've stolen the legitimate excuse that Olivia had when she told them she needed to cut back on concerts. Maybe they knew they could no longer rely on her. And there is always someone else ready and willing to take our place. Our mothers. Our mothers.

29

When my father announced he was leaving after my return from New York—from that evening I cracked my world apart—my mother asked me what I wanted to do. We were sitting in the kitchen eating KFC from a huge bucket. She'd never asked me what I wanted. It was the first time I'd had fast food. I remember feeling pressured to give an answer immediately. And because I didn't want to upset them both, I picked the person I was least angry with that day.

That memory functions like a chokehold on me. The guilt is suffocating. I was so callous with my newfound freedom.

I call my mother after rehearsals and ask her to lunch. I text her my address. It's been three weeks since the recital. A thin chasm has widened into something invisible. She texts a single word. OK.

An hour later, she's at the door. At first, I'm unaware. I think it's my metronome, but then I stop playing and switch it off, hear the sharp rap at the door.

'How long were you knocking?'

'You're still using a metronome?'

Her handbag is slung across her shoulder and she's carrying a second bag with a cardigan and drink bottle inside.

I lean forward and awkwardly fold my body over hers. When we were touring, the photographers would say to my mother, 'Squeeze in closer to your daughter.' As though she had to be reminded that she was my mother. Today she feels smaller, like my body has expanded and hers has shrunk.

She follows me through the apartment as I shut each window.

'This girl you live with—'

'Val.'

'She's an artist?'

'Yep.'

She blinks and looks out the window. 'This view is not distracting?'

'No.'

We walk to a local cafe. On the way, I tell her how pleased I am that she's come to see me in Bondi. She is flicking her attention left to right as we walk, eyes alert.

'It's daytime. You won't get mugged,' I say.

She tells me she is always having dreams her handbag is stolen. The thief is always faceless. He is always a man. We talk about the recital, which parts I need to improve. We stick to the mechanics of performance and technique. She does not mention Banks.

She is concerned about my stiff bow arm and tells me I should visit the gym more often to build muscles in my right shoulder. I know all this. She knows I know all this. And yet, I listen with the sustained attention of an Olympic athlete. She talks and talks, recommending further exercises, and I look ahead.

'Are you listening?' she asks.

I blink once, deliberately, stopping on the footpath.

'I know how to do this.'

At the cafe, we choose a table by the window, looking out onto the street.

'Actually, can we move?' My mother rises and moves to another table. 'All that traffic whizzing by will give me a headache.'

The waiter comes over with menus.

'Do you have noodles?' my mother asks.

'This is a cafe,' I say. 'It's mostly sandwiches and salads.'

'Oh.'

The waiter smiles awkwardly, then leaves.

'We can go somewhere else if you like.'

My mother shakes her head.

Waiting for my mother to order is a monumental exercise in patience. I have learned to manage it by practising finger drills in my head. While she takes her time to order, I stare at the back of her menu and go through passages from the excerpts for my audition.

This is how I won competitions from a young age. On a plane, in the shower, on the toilet, at meal-times—any time I could not practise my violin. I'd focus on visualising my fingers. It worked. I won a lot of money. More than most eleven-year-olds. I went to London, Milan, Zurich, Prague. I was in Barcelona for my thirteenth birthday. On the plane ride there, I spent fifteen hours memorising an entire concerto. Glazunov, a Russian, mid-century. Something I wanted to do just for fun.

'I'll have the Caesar salad,' my mother says.

I nod, raising a hand to the waiter.

We order and my mother asks for dressing on the side. I ask for extra mayo in my burger.

'Are you sure you want extra mayo?' she asks. 'I saw those chocolate bars in your kitchen.'

'They're not mine.'

She sighs, shoulders droop.

We sip our waters and she asks whether I'm seeing anyone. 'You need to get out.'

'I don't have time for that. I want this exchange in New York.'

I wait for her to say something. But she doesn't. Instead, she picks up her glass of water and takes another sip. I take a sip of my water too. 'You know why I have to go back.'

A thick lump clogs the base of my throat, drumming at the centre of my chest. I want so much for her to love me, but this love is impossible. With my friends, there is no anxiety to be heard. I can relax into being. With my mother, I am always anticipating her next move. I keep morphing into different women with various faces and shapes. I can't stop shifting.

I can't stop burying parts of myself on call. I switch roles and amend behaviours to suit the people around me. Isn't that what being an adult is all about? I adapt and I adapt well. People should pay tribute to my abilities.

When our food arrives, we wait for the other to begin eating.

'Are the men in New York more handsome?' she asks, stabbing a piece of bacon with her fork.

I pick up the burger in my hands. 'Does that matter?'

She feigns casualness, bringing another forkful of greens into her mouth. Changes the subject.

Later, as we walk back to my apartment, I put my hand on her shoulder.

'I'm going to be fine. You have to trust me. I know how to take care of myself.'

30

Olivia calls mid-week. She's sobbing. Hiccups. Her cries are sharp and elongated. I don't know the words to make her stop, to calm her down. For a moment, I feel the rush of power surge into my heart. She's reached out to me. I have won.

After a few minutes she settles down. It's Noah, she says. He's broken her heart. Again. He does it incrementally, she says.

I presume he has slept with someone else, but no, she assures me, it's not that. He'd refused to spend the weekend with her in the mountains with her mother, choosing instead to stay in Sydney to see the latest Avengers film with his Newington friends.

'Can you meet me in a few hours? I need to pick up a few things from the doctors in Sydney.'

I tell her yes, but only after the concert, which will be after ten, I have plans with Mark though I don't tell her. I will decide later who I want to see more. She hangs up and the panic sets in; like a disease, it spreads across my collarbone, rises up my neck.

During the interval, I check my phone and see two texts from Mark. I text Olivia and tell her I can't meet her after all, I have an emergency. She calls immediately. I am backstage, preparing for the second half of the concert.

'What's your emergency?' she demands.

'I can't tell you. I'm just—I'm seeing someone.'

'But you said you'd meet me.'

I feel compelled to tell her about Mark. I want to be found out. The thrill of having won him no longer has a charge if no one knows about it, if no one knows that he wants me. I need to tell someone. Part of me simply wants to see how she will react.

She is pressing me against a wall. And then it comes out. I tell her about Mark because it feels like the right thing to do, despite all that I've done to her, or not done for her.

'What?'

There's a strange silence. And then soft sounds. I can't tell if she's curious or sad or disappointed or angry. I can't tell which side of anger she is on.

'How long has it been?'

Someone taps me on the shoulder. It's Trumpet, holding his instrument. He motions with his head for me to follow him onstage. 'We're late,' he mouths.

'Is that him? Are you with Mark right now?' Olivia's voice turns to indignation.

'No.'

I press the phone harder against my ear, wanting to catch her every breath.

'I don't know what to say to you right now.'

The line goes dead. I fling my phone into my case and walk back onstage.

During the second half of the performance, I try to concentrate on the music in front of me. My body has disappeared, replaced by a carcass. I carry on, play every note perfectly. Even execute a difficult winding chromatic passage. But that's another girl. One who was trained from a young age to follow instructions. I realise as I sit down to a few cheers from the audience and *whoop whoop* blows of the mouthpiece from the woodwinds that I am finally becoming a whole human being. Fracturing and splitting into multiple parts. Forgetting which Jena is performing when.

Over the next three days, I send Olivia multiple texts which go unanswered. It cuts through me. It's always a game, and we're always willing to play. She's pining for power and I hate her for it. My hatred scares me. I have never wanted to harm her, but suddenly, I imagine a world where she is injured, maimed, broken.

It rains continuously near the end of August. On the weekend, I peer outside Mark's window in the morning and see that a slice of cool yellow light has come through the low grey sky. Mark finds me composing an email on the toilet and snatches my phone from my hand. 'If you look at that thing again today, I'll kick you out of this apartment.'

I'd told him about Olivia; he wasn't impressed. In fact, he looked as though he was about to hit me, but then he moved into the kitchen and began to smash things.

Between rehearsals one afternoon, I check my phone.

Olivia's name shows up in my email. I click on it without thinking, hurriedly.

It is an essay. She calls me names. *Slut. Snatcher. Sly, conniving bitch.* She says I don't deserve her friendship.

You've always wanted to fuck other people's boyfriends. You've done it now. Are you proud?

Get your own guy. But you can't, can you? You just fuck people because you can't make them like you any other way. I say this because I care about you. You need to re-evaluate your morals.

It seems, suddenly, that all my feelings were never complicated, that my inclination to trust my instincts, which had always served me well in my performances onstage, were completely wrong. The violence of her words. A throbbing pain in the back of my head.

When I get home, I light candles by my bedside table and slip into my pyjamas. I want a quiet place to rest my head. Forget about the power others have over me. At eleven thirty my phone rings. It's Mark.

'I thought you were in Melbourne?'

'I came back early.'

If I wanted to play the game, I'd tell him to sleep in his own bed. If I followed the rules my father taught me, I would not have picked up the phone.

But being with Mark stops the sadness that creeps up on me when I am alone, when my heart pounds so loud I think my arteries might burst. Mark helps me forget all my inadequacies. I might be another TAG but out of all the beautiful TAGs he has chosen me. With him, I feel seen. I will take what he sees. That is more comforting than any award, any contract, any performance. To be fucked the way he fucks me feels more special than anything my violin gives me. I am not crazy. I am, in fact, normal.

He arrives twenty minutes later, smiling and sweating.

'I was at a house gig,' he says. 'My friend and I were dancing in the mosh pit.'

'Aren't you a bit old for that?'

He points to the metronome on my bedside table, still flicking side to side.

'Why's that on?'

I put my hands around his neck and sink my lips into his. I feel a haunting, confused lust.

'Can you turn that off?' he asks, pushing me away.

'I'm so glad you came over.'

'I'm glad too.'

I run to the bathroom to relieve myself before we begin.

When I come out, he is naked.

'I wanted to undress you,' I say.

'But I'm hungry for your body.'

'Have we reached that stage already?'

'What stage?'

'Undressing before sex? It feels so clinical—like what married couples do.'

'Shut up.'

He pulls off my top and shorts, briefly pressing his face between my legs before peeling my panties off. His eyes narrow. This must be what love feels like. A mouth pressed against the groin. Hands that slide to the places I was once told not to touch myself. He stands up and I kneel before him. He guides my skull down his body with one hand, and I let him control me. Domination and submission. A dizziness whorls down the back of my neck. My mouth becomes an instrument for his pleasure.

I feel the fleeting euphoria of achievement when he comes inside my mouth, hearing him weep with a pleasure only I can provide.

I fall asleep in his arms and wake the next morning with the stickiness of sex and exhaustion. The salty residue of his semen dried at the corners of my mouth.

I'm in the bathroom putting on make-up, listening to him talk about wanting to live till he's over a hundred.

'You're insecure,' I say, walking into the bedroom and stepping into a black skirt.

He reaches over and puts a hand over my head. 'About what?'

'Ageing. That's why you're sleeping with a twenty-three-year-old.'

'That's your opinion.'

'Men chase women because they're afraid of death. Having sex affirms you're alive, that you can be God, create life. What you're doing is so predictable.'

He grips the base of my neck and pushes me onto the bed. I stumble forward, hands steadying my balance. I stand to face him, wanting to resist. There are words to stop these things from happening. There are movements my body can perform to avoid this domination. But I don't know them. I let him take over.

'Let me give you a facial.'

I reach for my bag. I'll be late to the matinee if I don't leave now.

He shoves me back with a hand on my shoulder. 'Stay, please.'

'I need to go.'

'No you don't.'

When it happens, it feels like a quiet surrender. A great fall from a tall building. He comes on my face, two small spurts across my forehead. I blink hard.

I stand under the shower for a long time. I can hear him whistling in the kitchen. When I come out, my body is throbbing, glowing purple. The pain feels good.

I begin composing a text to Olivia, imagining a world where I performed human-beingness better and didn't tell her about Mark. Then I remember we're not speaking to each other. Perhaps today I will be asked to leave the orchestra. Why can't I carry the weight of my obligations by myself? Why can't I care more? Bryce picks up after the first ring. 'Your mother again?' he asks.

'Yes, I'm afraid so.'

'It's okay, Jena. These things happen. We've got subs in place. You can have the evening off too.'

'No, I'll be there tonight.'

'Are you sure?'

'Yes.'

•

That night, my phone rings during intermission. It's Banks. He talks quickly. A violinist from the San Francisco Symphony is visiting Sydney for one night only. He is holding a masterclass at the Conservatorium.

'You should come,' he says. 'He knows many people from the Philharmonic. You can talk to him about your audition.'

I make sounds, vague; like some stunted language. I wait for him to say something, to respond with the necessary incriminations. I imagine him standing in front of me, his mouth opening, then widening rapidly as though waiting for my reaction; his breath thickening the air around him.

'I can't. I've got plans.'

'This is important, Jena.'

He has never needed to convince me to put my music first.

'Why don't you come over? We can discuss this in person.'

I want to tell him about the part of my body that hurts. The invisible hand that grinds at some small, tender part of my chest and stops me from breathing normally. There are traumas written inside my body, cellular, larger than my own existence. The hunger for some affirmation which only Mark can provide. I am ashamed, and I can't tell him because he does not know me as someone who carries shame.

He sighs into the phone. 'Something is always rumbling inside you.'

I want to tell him it's his fault. Other things press into me like a foot on wet soil. The confident, abrasive mouth of a man. His eyes, his breath. His appetite for me. Banks would not understand. But then I remember his arms around my mother.

'If you change your mind, it starts at seven.'

I nod, though he can't see me. I make a soft sound to let him know I've understood him. Maybe he knows, too, that the things I hunger for are things he cannot give me. But he once gave them to another woman.

31

After an evening concert, I come home and look inside my fridge. There's half a pack of shaved parmesan, a dozen eggs, an open can of chickpeas and a bottle of beer. For a moment, I laugh; it's a laugh directed entirely at myself. How did it come to be that the contents of my fridge resemble those of a poor college student? At midnight, nothing is open except McDonald's. I order UberEats and fall asleep with a smear of sweet and sour sauce on my cheeks, a box of half-eaten chicken nuggets on the bedside table.

The next morning, I spend an hour in bed with my phone propped up against a pillow watching cheerleader porn. Post orgasm, I watch two hours of Janine Jansen playing the Beethoven and Shostakovich violin concertos. She is twenty-seven years old in the video, looking more like a Hollywood movie star than a classical musician.

I want to be her, much in the same way I wanted to be Ginette Neveu when she played the Beethoven Violin Concerto. How easy to go through life imitating person after person; it would be especially easy as a classical violinist. There are decades of role models to choose from. With the violin, you just have to look at what all the greats have done, play like them, flawlessly, and you're on your way to being known.

Ginette Neveu died in a plane accident on her way to perform in America. She had just turned thirty. I imagine my life ending at thirty. Seven more years. What would I do if I had only seven more years?

I want to talk to Olivia but can't bring myself to call her. Mark does not ring. I text him a few times and all of them go unanswered. I haven't seen Val in days. I am lying in bed watching a white man anally penetrate a Japanese schoolgirl. The screen changes to an image of my mother's face. I dry my fingers on the bedsheets before sliding the answer button. My mother asks about the orchestra and my audition. Five days away. I want the week to stretch out like a rubber band and then snap. Our conversation is brief. She needs an early night because she is working a charity stall tomorrow. When I ask her how my father is doing, she clears her throat but doesn't answer, says she has to go. I think about calling him, but I don't. I lie in bed watching a gang-bang scene instead. A girl with dark brown hair. Two small white round breasts. Nipples like olive pits. Erect and inviting. I return to roughing the edges of my clitoris until I come.

I hear the door open. Val has come back to me. Finally.

'Val? Is that you?'

The door shuts loudly. I step into the hallway to look. But there's nobody there.

The following evening, Val is home after spending the entire week at Damien's. She tells me he's asked her to consider being in an ethical non-monogamous relationship with another couple; and she's still deciding if it's something she wants. 'I've no idea what my own desires are anymore,' she says. 'Or if I ever even knew what they were.'

I'm in the kitchen when the apartment buzzer goes off.

I am making a salad, dicing almonds, crushing garlic. I call out to Val, who I hear opening the door. She lets the person in.

'Hey.'

Mark is standing at the entrance of the kitchen. He takes a step forward to plant a dry mouth on the side of my lips.

'Where've you been lately?'

Like a concerned principal checking up on an ill-behaved student.

'Just around, you know. Orchestra.'

Val walks in. 'I'm going out for some beer. You guys want anything?'

We shake our heads.

'I'll be back soon for some delicious food.'

She leaves through the back door.

Mark walks over to me. He unbuckles his belt and assumes a position. In a few moments, I am on my knees, that strange compulsion to let him do whatever he wants; outside, I can hear the wind combing through the branches, the dry leaves rustling against each other like a hundred maracas.

'I was cooking.'

'I haven't seen you in so long.'

'I have garlic fingers.'

'I don't mind.'

I collect him inside my mouth. Giving in is easier than resisting.

I stand up and go to the sink to wash my hands.

'I haven't eaten. Go get changed,' he orders. 'I'm taking you out.'

The water in the pot starts to gurgle. The eggs inside are panicking.

'I'm already making dinner.'

'Leave it. Take me to that Taiwanese restaurant of yours.'

'It's in Chatswood.'

'We can take a taxi.'

I open the fridge to fetch the tomatoes I'd been planning to roast. The oven is already pre-heated.

He walks over and pushes the fridge door shut.

'Come on now.'

On the street, we wait for a taxi. I text Val a one-word apology.

Mark is looking me up and down, assessing me. I've put on a slip dress and kitten heels. 'Your hair is a bit messed up. Do you want to fix it in the taxi?'

I look around for a surface to see my reflection.

He raises his hand and a white taxi pulls up. We slide in.

To the driver, he says, 'We want to go to . . .' He pokes my thigh with one finger. 'Can you tell him?'

I give the driver the address and he nods, eyes on the road.

It's after nine. On the main road, the restaurants are emptying. On the footpath, people saunter in twos and fours.

We reach Chatswood twenty minutes later. The restaurant is off the main road, down a one-way street. Mark walks slightly behind me. There is something disquieting about the way he walks, with his torso jutted out, hinting at some anxiety.

He reaches forward to grab my hand. 'I'm the only white person around here.'

Inside the restaurant, the kitchen staff and waiters greet us with a call of welcome. We're given a table by the front window. Maximum exposure. The waiter and I banter about the specials in Mandarin.

Mark leans across the table after we are handed the menus. 'She's not Chinese, is she? Because if she is, I'm walking out of here.'

'No, she's Taiwanese.'

'Good.'

He tells me that he and his friends avoid Chinese restaurants that have white customers. The same if there are white waiters at a Chinese restaurant. He's only interested in genuine cultural experiences.

'What about that time at Jade Temple?'

He thinks about this. 'Well, they were hot.'

He doesn't comment on my language skills as I translate between him and the waitress. I order pork belly rolls, pickled cabbage, pork dumplings and, at his request, two sorts of rice, and chicken popcorn.

'So, you don't like Korean people serving you at a Japanese restaurant?'

He shakes his head. 'I want my sushi served by Japanese people. I hate fake Japanese people.'

'What's fake Japanese?'

'Chinese,' he says. 'And Korean.'

After our mains we cross the road to a dessert parlour. A Korean joint filled with Korean people.

It is excessively lit for a Sunday night. Amber bulbs dangle above our heads. We order waffles to share and iced matcha lattes.

We sit down near the window and talk about pornography. Mark doesn't like the hardcore, violent sort, but he'd like to try choking someday.

When I ask him how he is so sure choking is pleasurable for the girl, he says that from a physiological perspective, it makes sense, the restriction of oxygen to the lungs, the pressure on a specific part of the throat, the blood vessels and the brain and the neurons and all that.

I keep prodding. 'Do you have first-hand experience?'

'No,' he says, but then he tells me how it's a well-known phenomenon and his friends' girlfriends get a lot of pleasure out of it. I wonder who these friends are because he never mentions them by name or profession. They're just 'friends'.

'When people hang themselves they end up ejaculating,' he says.

'They also end up dead,' I say.

He ignores me and looks at a girl across the table from us.

I persevere. 'Might their post-conscious ejaculation merely be the body's way of doing something final before their brain runs out of oxygen? How can you assume that such a thing guarantees sensory pleasure?'

He shrugs, eyes averted. My gaze roams around, and after finding nothing interesting to focus my attention on, I say, 'Let's try it then.'

I'm dismayed when he hardly reacts.

I ask him whether part of the reason he thinks he'll get off on choking is the power he will have while doing it.

'Yes, I think that's definitely part of it,' he says.

I wonder if he might accidentally kill me one day.

The waffles arrive. We eat them silently and finish our drinks, then take a taxi back to his place. I worry about not getting enough sleep before my audition, but I let him guide my evening anyway. I get a text from Val about the food I was supposed to make for her. I think about the salad, sitting alone, half dressed on the kitchen bench. The eggs placid and cooling inside the pot.

'Who is it?' Mark puts a hand over mine.

'Nobody.'

We sit on his couch for a few moments before undressing each other and getting into bed.

I reach for his body as he lifts his arm to tuck me in. I bury my face inside his warm armpit; inhale his maleness. I could hide in that dark crevasse forever. His phone thrums. Arms release me. I am a sack dropped on the floor. He gets up to check it.

'Who is it?'

'My girlfriend.'

He walks into the bathroom, phone to his ear.

I drift in and out of sleep.

I wonder if there is any way out of this loneliness. If there is a wall I can scale. I wonder if my mother has ever felt this, the lingering, vicious emptiness. I want instructions; I need someone to tell me not to feel this way. And then, maybe, I will stop feeling this way.

32

Three days before the audition. I practise for five hours without a single toilet break. It is the worst thing to do, but I do it anyway. Unthinking, I let my body fall into its natural state. My body carries the knowledge of a life before I was even conceived. Another life. This is what I believe.

My wrist distends, an aching tumour. I put ice on it, take four painkillers, rest for a few minutes, then resume until midnight. Val does not come home. I play with no clothes on in the lounge room.

The next day, I have a rehearsal at the Opera House with the 'Trout' ensemble. During a break, the cellist leans over while he's retracting his spike.

'Everything okay? You seem distracted.'

My mouth widens into a rigid smile, a cursory mask to deflect my irritation.

'I've got my audition on Thursday for the exchange.'

He nods. 'Good luck. This will help—Schubert always helps!'

'The Trout' is a good piece. I tell myself it is best played with a light bow, not overbearing, but I can't repress the need to hear my own tune rise above the others. Schubert wrote the quintet when he was twenty-two years old. When I first heard it, I was nine. It was 2002.

I'd gone to New York for the first time and watched a documentary at one of Banks's friend's home. It featured five musicians, all of whom I'd known intimately through years of listening to their recordings. They had beautiful names. Jewish. French. Indian. Poetic. When I saw their faces on the screen, I saw my heroes. They looked so happy. They were playing and laughing. There was never any laughter when I played as a child. Nobody told jokes around me. Itzhak Perlman was twenty-three. Jacqueline du Pré was twenty-four. Her husband Daniel Barenboim was twenty-six. Zubin Mehta was thirty-three. Pinchas Zukerman was twenty-one. *Twenty-one.*

I think about that film now as I rip into the opening chord. I think about the Faust story it is based on. The endless seeking of something that the hand cannot grasp. I wonder whether the other musicians in my 'Trout' ensemble can sense the emptiness behind my eyes.

Later, the pianist suggests dinner at the Argyle. Less than forty-eight hours now.

'Jena, you need a break.'

I think about what I told Christopher Jennings when I was fifteen. This is why I was the best. I never rested.

'You guys go ahead. I'll see you next week.'

'Good luck on Thursday,' the cellist calls out.

'Don't kill yourself,' says the pianist.

When I get home, I go to my bookshelf and find an old copy of Goethe's *Faust*. I open it to the second book and scroll down to the highlighted passages. I am looking for a quote. One that I used to recite to myself when I first came across it in Germanic Lit 101, four years ago. I flip through the pages. Then I find it; spoken by Helen.

Please think,
Whom you belong to!

How it would grieve us,
How you'd destroy too,
That sweet achievement,
Yours, his and mine.

Yours, his and mine. Yours. His. Mine. He is mine.

The afternoon before the audition, Banks calls. He clears his throat before making his request.

His voice is clipped, low. The rain smashes against the window of my room; trees pummelled by the rising storm, branches flinging against powerlines.

'It's too wet outside,' I say, surprised by how quickly I make up excuses.

'One last time. Come.'

When I arrive outside his studio, he is sitting on his chair playing a slow melody. Through the window, I watch his wrist move around the scroll of his violin. I pause for a few moments, keeping my distance as I gather my composure; study the limp frame of his shoulders.

He has worn away the cartilage between his joints, the bone rubbing the flesh of his fingers. He looks over his rimless glasses. This man made me who I was. He wants to help me. He wants to help me still. I push away the trailing doubts and walk through the door. I don't think about the things I did to make him hate me.

'Glad you could make it.' I close the door behind me.

He takes a cloth from his pocket and presses it to his forehead, patting away a thin layer of sweat.

'I heard your mother has been unwell?' He looks down at his desk. *Christina.* Say her name.

'No, why?'

'I heard from Bryce.'

I find some other lie to fill in the silence. He nods and puts his violin down.

Inside the studio, the air smells of sandalwood. He flips through a pile of music on his desk and waits for my response. I make a face, noncommittal.

'I have something to show you.'

He walks out from behind the desk and hands me a sheet of paper. It is blank.

'What is this?'

He returns to his chair and leans back.

'I'd like you to write down the worst-case scenario at your audition.'

I hold the sheet in my hand, unmoving.

'I break my arm and can't play.'

'How likely is that, though? Give me a real worst-case scenario.'

I shrug with irritation. 'Can I do this later? I'd like to go home early tonight.'

I slip the sheet of paper into the sheet music slot in my case and take out my violin.

I tune it slowly, twisting the wooden pegs with my left hand up and down, up and down. Stretching the strings. Warming up the bow hair. I begin playing from the first bar. Straight in.

He stops me after the first line.

'What are you trying to convey?'

'The first line?'

He nods, reaching into his case to extract his rosin. He picks up his bow and begins applying the amber brick.

'I guess . . . I want to be commanding.'

'Yes, but what are you trying to say? At the moment, this character you have has no personality at all.'

I swing my violin underneath my arm and readjust the weight of my body from one foot to the other. A coil of exhaustion rises inside me.

I pluck the rosin out of his hand and feign effort. I want him to play. To show me how to do it, the way he used to.

'I'm trying my best here.'

I stroke the rosin against the tip of my bow where the grip has loosened.

'Really? The Jena I remember had her own emotional gravity. She pulled me in.'

'I'm trying my best,' I repeat.

'You're not trying hard enough.'

He sighs and draws in a sharp breath. 'When I first met you, you played with your eyes closed.'

'That's because I memorised the music. I can't memorise every orchestral part that's ever been written.'

He puts a hand on my shoulder and I panic; he rarely makes physical contact. I draw back and walk to my violin case, bending down for the metronome.

'You don't need that now, do you?' He lifts his bow up and taps the air in front of him.

'I want you to know this,' he begins in a steady, slow tone, 'and I want to say it with absolute honesty, which is difficult for me. But trust me, I do this for your own good. I want to help you become a better musician, the way I did all those years ago. I know you can return to that glory. I know you can. But I'm not sure I like the musician you've become. What you did in Carnegie Hall all those years ago, that still haunts me. I don't know if I can ever forgive you. But I am also someone who is a slave to music, and you play good music. I still want to help you become a more capable musician. So let me. But that's all. I don't want to do anything more than that.'

The steady heart, the low thrum. Beating against my chest.

He looks at me, his bow still sweeping the air.

'You know more than you think you know.'

When I was thirteen, Banks said to me, 'Do you want to be happy? Or do you want to be famous? Because you can't be both.'

I'd been touring and competing in competitions for five years by then and I was beginning to grow into something I did not recognise. I suppose my intentions began to blur, to take on some strange, unrecognisable form.

It was during a lesson inside an airport lounge on our way to a competition in Finland. He stopped me, mid-etude; 'Do you know the story *The Little Mermaid*?'

'Yes.'

'Tell me.'

'She fell in love with a prince, and her wish was granted.'

'She became human, didn't she, with legs? But she had to give up her voice. That is sacrifice. If you want legs, Jena, you can't also have a voice. You can only choose one.'

'I want to have a voice.'

'Well, then, play. You don't need legs when you have a wonderful voice.'

By then, my ears had begun to lose their power of interpretation.

Later, I asked Banks why the prince did not wish for fins so that he could join the princess in the sea. He didn't answer. I imagined myself as this huge ball, empty, dark and hollow. I wanted to say, 'Fill me. I have boundless capacity. Teach me.'

But then I found that sex with men was easier.

33

At the Opera House, I spot Sandra sitting on a bench near the taxi rank, flipping through her music. She's dressed all in black. Her hair is parted in the middle and tucked neatly behind her ears.

'Hi!' she calls out.

I wave. 'You ready?'

'I grabbed a coffee on my way in and spotted some of the people on your panel at the cafe,' she says. 'Niall Banks was showing them around.'

'Banks is here?'

'I think he knows them from way back. Anyway, shall we?'

We walk through the main entrance to the foyer, where ribbons of light fall across the table at the centre.

Something shifts in my body. My fingers tighten, the muscles in my feet cramp.

'Are you okay?' Sandra places a hand on my shoulder.

I can't be frightened. It's too soon. But the fear accelerates quickly and I don't know why. I stare at the sign next to the backstage door.

NEW YORK PHILHARMONIC AUDITIONS.

SIGN IN AT REAR GREEN ROOM. STAGE DOOR.

I take deep breaths, straighten my back. Sandra looks on, a concerned bystander who has no idea how to help.

A security guard approaches us and asks if I'm alright.

I decide to do what I've always done. Let go of the body. Let it do what it wants to do.

We walk through double doors, accompanied by the security guard.

'She's fine,' Sandra assures him. 'Thank you for your concern.' She gestures for him to go.

I sign in at a table manned by a middle-aged woman in a lace top. She smiles, then says to Sandra, 'You'll have to wait here. I'll take you in when we're ready for you.'

The woman stands and leads me to a practice studio. Inside, alone, I unzip my case. I reach out and run my finger over Monkey's nose; the black beads of his plastic eyes, his stitched-on mouth; wide and permanently smiling. Like he is always deflecting the unanswerable things I ask him in my private moments. Am I going to fuck this up? Monkey smiles. He does not judge.

I start with scales, bow exercises, stretch my arms and legs. I focus on my fingers, the sound stored in audio memory. Implanted in my skin. My muscles know what to do. For a moment, all I can see is Mark's face. The triangular lights on his chest when he lies in bed. The intensity of the image distracts me. I push through it by playing louder, pressing it away.

After a while, the woman comes to get me. I follow her to the main hall.

The huge swinging doors open automatically, activated by a sensor, and I walk in, feet soft on the shiny floorboards, my eyes squinting against the glare of the stage lights.

The panel is seated behind a long table at the end of the stage. A man in a blue collared shirt introduces his colleagues then himself. Jennings. He looks exactly the same.

A spotlight illuminates the black stand. I walk towards it steadily, eyes forward.

For a few moments, the visuals in my head shimmer into something like a fantasy. I imagine the people on the panel taking off their glasses, turning to each other, unzipping their pants and giving each other head, inserting a finger, an erection, staring at each other's arseholes for signs of anal bleaching or waxing. I imagine them fucking like horses. Slurping, slapping. Flesh on flesh and chairs squeaking. Three, four bodies colliding.

They greet me with smiles, the ordinary mannerisms of audition etiquette.

Lips clenched; my arms heavy by my side.

'When you're ready.'

I concentrate on the sound of my metronome. Drummed into my bones. Eyes blink, draw breath. Exhale slowly. Inhale.

'I'll start with the excerpts.' My voice sounds constrained, like there's something under my tongue.

They ask for four of the twelve excerpts.

I operate as I always do, hands stilled by the calm resolve I've learned to perform. Fingers braced in a tight grip around the fingerboard. Then, relax.

It happens like magic. My body becomes, momentarily, a thing that does not belong to me at all. When I'm in motion, channelling the melodies of men who have died long ago, I'm suspended in time, like an aerial surfer gliding through space, undiminished by gravity. I am at once beheld to the notes of each frequency written on the page, and utterly free, consumed by a gracious state of being.

When I finish, they ask me to choose a fifth and final excerpt to play.

I press my lips together, then open them quickly. 'I don't know; I can do any of them.'

'We'd like to hear your choice,' Jennings says, then adds, 'Please.'

I decide on the Mozart. His music shows the best of me. Mechanical, clean, flawless. It is my job; I have done it so well for so long. As I play, the memory of that day, the rehearsal, the moment I had with Jennings, all of that surfaces to my consciousness like bits of dead coral floating up to the surface of the sea. As I'm playing Mozart, my life becomes ahistorical; for a few minutes, I am a descendant of his geniuses.

I end on the double stop, bow pointing towards the stage floor, then look up at the lights above.

They bring in Sandra. She smiles as she takes her seat. I realign myself so that I'm facing her side on. I keep the f-holes of my violin pointing to the panel.

'I'll do the Brahms Sonata,' I announce.

Sandra rolls her shoulders and waits for my cue. I tilt the scroll of my violin towards the ceiling, place my jaw onto the chin rest.

The first movement is momentous, rough. Sandra's piano intro rips through the hall. She is confident. She is unapologetic. I come in a few bars later. We fly through the first movement flawlessly, then the second. I forget the ease with which all of this comes. And then there are moments I remember. My mind flicks on and off.

At the end of the third movement, something extraordinary happens. On a busy descending passage, my fingers feel as though they're about to slip off the fingerboard. I think I'm about to lose my place and I want to stop, I'm compelled to stop and start over, but I can't. I close my eyes and let my fingers take over. My palms are slick, high with adrenaline. I can feel that rapid wildness gathering at my navel, then rising to my chest.

I am fifteen again. A fear that grips my shoulders, paralyses me into a state of hellish panic. It returns like a simmering heartburn, then dissipates just as fast when I realise I've always known what to do. There is no fear. Only the shock of finally knowing how inevitable all this is.

A hushed silence falls over the hall.

'Is everything okay?' someone calls.

I stop and look at my fingers. The calluses, normally hard, have burst, leaving damp layers of skin peeling off, half attached. It feels like I've plunged my fingertips into a bowl of razor blades.

'Yes, I'm fine.'

I have finished, somehow, and everything is still again. I see Sandra nodding at the piano. She is beaming.

I feign confidence. The sharp pain is replaced by a numbness I thought had left me years ago. Today, it saves me.

The panel dismiss Sandra and indicate a chair for me. I sit, legs crossed at the ankles, posture straight, violin on my lap.

'Why are you the ideal candidate for this exchange?' one of the panel members asks. He's tapping his pen on his temple.

I take my time in answering. I always take my time.

'I'm a good player.'

They chuckle.

The man who'd asked the question says, 'Yes, but everyone who auditions is a good player. What makes a Philharmonic player stand out?'

I smile.

'Well, I remember rehearsing with them when I was fifteen—'

'That's right, you had a big concert with us in 2008?'

'I did. But I had a nervous breakdown. I've since recovered from that.'

I scan their faces. One of them looks down at a sheet in front of him, writes something.

'What is your favourite performance by the Philharmonic?' a woman asks; she's the only woman on the panel.

I had not expected this question, but immediately, I know how to answer. A year before the end of my career, I'd been touring the East Coast of the US, giving small salon recitals. Banks had talked to a few people and had managed to arrange for me to spend a day in New York accessing the archives of the Philharmonic's past performances.

'Sarah Caldwell's 1975 take on Lili Boulanger's "Faust et Helene".'

The woman turns to the man on her left, her eyebrows raised. I can see I have impressed them. Jennings folds his arms.

She turns back to me. 'And why is that?'

'It's not widely performed. I like smaller, quieter pieces. Pieces history has forgotten. It's for three voices. I'm not usually someone who seeks out vocal repertoire but a teacher of mine played it for me once. She loved French romantics. And Lili wrote this for her sister, Nadia. Of course, you all know this.'

'I don't actually. Tell me more.'

I inhale and scan the panel, reading for boredom. Jennings leans forward and places his chin on a hand.

'It's based on a poem by this poet, Eugène Adenis. He based it on the second part of Goethe's *Faust*.'

'You're a reader?'

'I studied literature.'

'Why did you do that?'

She's firing questions without pause. I think it might be a trick.

'I guess I needed the stories to help me be a better person and then, maybe, a better musician.'

The woman nods, expressionless.

'Do you have any other interests, besides music?'

Another panellist speaks. 'You've played with Americans?' he asks.

'Of course.'

'What do you think?'

I chew the tip of my tongue. 'I think Americans are great. They're flamboyant. I could learn a lot from them.'

'We're flamboyant? What makes you say that?'

Porn. I want to say: Americans do it best. I want them to know what I'm really thinking, because then they can answer their own questions. I glance around for somewhere to deposit my gaze.

'It's something invisible. The energy, maybe.'

'Energy?'

My breath fractures. I wait for someone to say something, to help me articulate what I mean, but they are silent. I fumble with words, I am incoherent. The lights burn my cheeks and the top of my skull.

A man clears his throat. 'No matter, thank you very much.'

I replicate the motions of a defeated athlete. Hang my head. Move slowly. I make it all the way to the exit without tripping; a small light inside me, clicking off.

34

Two nights later, I lead the 'Trout' ensemble for the conductor's seventieth birthday.

In the green room, the pianist asks me about the audition.

'Not good,' I laugh.

He gives me a sympathetic smile, which makes me want to jab my bow into my mouth. But I tell him thanks as I'm walking towards the stage door. Patrons and board members are seated between rows E and J towards the centre. In the wing, the five of us take turns peeking out to the audience.

'Looks like they're all here,' the cellist says.

The viola player and I exchange quick grins. We are dressed in matching emerald gowns and black heels. There's a split in our skirt, strategically designed for maximum thigh exposure when we're seated. The men wear grey suits.

'Okay, Jena.' The bass player looks at me. 'Any words of wisdom from our leader?'

I nod, look at the floor in front of me. 'Right, let's give them a good show.'

They smile encouragingly, wait for more, but I'm already walking onto the stage.

The applause thrums in my ears.

We stand in a single line, collecting the loud eruption from the audience. I step forward in front of the empty chairs. We bow, gesture to the chief conductor who is sitting in the middle of row E, dressed in a black suit, red bow tie. He's smiling ecstatically, nodding his head.

We take our seats and the applause diminishes. The stage lights are exceedingly bright. Already, I can make out the particles in the air; small traces of dust.

We make small adjustments. Chairs screech, weight on feet, check bow hairs. All eyes on me, a small lift of the scroll. We launch into the first movement.

My fingers feel spright and responsive. I love this momentum, catching my breath on the higher registers. We play the five movements without rest. There is no interval. Between movements, I watch as the cellist extracts a handkerchief from his pants pocket and wipes his fingerboard. The fabric is flung across the black ivory, I see more particles fly, suspended in air. The last piece finishes with a counter-melody conflict between all the instruments. We flick our gaze from one instrument to another. I see drops of sweat collect across the cellist's forehead as he sways violently beside me, like raindrops shifting sideways along a gutter.

My melody soars above the accompanying lines and triumphs. Our bows fly into the air. We stop, statue-still. I relish those few seconds of transcendence, right after the end of a piece, before the boom of the audience's applause.

We rise and stand at the edge of the stage. Bow. I feel that old, whistling exhilaration return. The audience leaps out of their seats. After the fifth bow the viola player leans over and whispers, 'Invite him up onstage.'

My face burns in wild panic. Bryce had reminded me before the concert, but in the relief of finishing I'd forgotten. I place my violin on my chair and gingerly make my way down the stairs to the side of the stage, lifting my gown just enough to expose my ankles. I tread slowly to the chief conductor's row. He is crab-walking past seated patrons. When he reaches me, he bends forward to press his lips to my cheek. I link my arm through his, and we walk up onto the stage. At the top of the steps, a stage crew hands him a microphone as he aims a soft, faint smile to the audience.

His speech is long. Well-rehearsed praises and gratitude. When we finally step offstage, my hips feel misaligned. I'd been hyper-aware of maintaining good posture, feeling the gaze of more than two thousand eyes on me, constantly redistributing my weight from foot to foot. At the afterparty, former players and current players from the orchestra take turns talking to the conductor. I hang around the exit so I can make a quick departure. I have one beer, and then find an excuse to leave.

When I arrive home after midnight, my phone buzzes. It's Mark with a single request.

I ignore his text and walk towards Val's room to find the door open, lights off. I walk in and switch on the light. The room is neat, bed made, nothing loose scattered across the dressing table. As though the room is preparing for a new guest.

A few seconds later, there's a knock on the apartment door.

'Why didn't you reply?'

Mark walks in and pushes me against the wall.

'I'm sorry. I was about to.'

We move into my room, shuffling our feet slowly. He unbuckles his belt and I assume my position on the floor in front of him. He fucks my mouth, then lifts me up onto the bedside counter and clamps his chest against mine as I push against his legs, his eyes flicking between my genitals and neck, something convulsive and wild in the way he looks at me. He flips me over and takes me from behind, shaking my torso, legs hard against my hips. He stops suddenly, pulls out. I bend down to see red cascading down my legs. I have made a small pond of blood at my feet.

'Christ, there's a lot of blood,' he says.

'It's the last day of my period,' I say calmly.

I want him to stop talking, to keep pounding, because it doesn't hurt-hurt; it just hurts. He puts his hand on my lower back.

'I've got blood all over my hands too.' He walks into the bathroom. Runs the tap and washes his hands.

I shuffle to the mirror, leaving a trail of red spots behind me. I turn to see red paws left on my lower back. I've never seen so much blood on my body. My own blood.

35

I wake from a violent dream. A car accident. My body dismembered. Bones exposed among a wrecked pile of metal and glass. Ligaments and blood. Open veins and crusted hair. I reach for Mark's arm. He opens his eyes immediately, as though he'd been waiting for me to wake him. I tell him about the dream. Loose flesh and flowing blood. Limbless torso. Open wounds. He wraps my head inside a tight grip.

'Stop talking.'

I reach for my metronome on the bedside table. He pushes my hand away.

'I'm here.'

In the morning, I ask him why he won't leave his girlfriend. He turns around and opens his mouth. I give him my full attention; I want to hear his reason. But then he closes his mouth and doesn't say anything. In the shower, I suck on his cock for longer than I want and end up choking, coughing hard from the rush of water, cum blasting into my mouth. He bends down and slaps the side of my face. I look up at him. His eyes are black shadows. I am suddenly terrified by what I might do for him. Part of me reaches into that old self, the girl who only knew how to play the violin. The girl who had not yet discovered sex. Part of me wants to resuscitate her. Otherwise I might kill myself. He cups the back of my skull and pushes his full length into my mouth. I relax into the motion, and let my bladder go. I pee on his feet. He lifts me up, bends me over. His cock is so large that at one point it feels as though I am being split open by a blunt carving knife, but I let him continue because he begins to make sounds like he's about to come and I am relieved. It'll soon be over. When he loses his grip, my head slams against the glass door and I feign unconsciousness. He gathers me up and lays me on the bed, still wet.

Each time he returns from Melbourne, there's a newness about him, a dark yearning I want to cling to.

'Can you skip tonight?' he asks as we are towelling ourselves dry. I shake my head.

When he pushes me onto the floor, I tell him no. 'I'll be late again.'

He adjusts my body so I am on all fours. A sharp pain slices my wrist. I wince, collapsing onto my side.

We are both exhausted, but it seems nothing will satiate our hunger for each other's flesh. I roll onto my back, wrap my arms around him and make red marks on his scapula. He presses down on me. I dig my nails deeper.

In the bathroom, I switch on the light as he turns his back to me. I have accidentally created a masterpiece, red lines made with a thin brush. Lines that wobble. An artist with Parkinson's. Cat marks and scratches, red whorls when he pushed deepest inside me. There are faint bruises, the shape of a single thumbprint for the times I lift my lips above his skin and bite into his flesh. He tells me he likes it when it hurts. I enjoy hurting him.

'Take a picture,' he says, raising his arms over his head—a young boy waiting for his mother to undress him. Afterwards, we study the picture together like it is anthropological evidence of an ancient tribe, a ritualistic painting, the symbol of an inexplicable deity. I make drawings of pleasure and pain on my lover's body. Soon, the pigments will fade just like our love for each other. But the picture on my phone remains. A photographic document of a woman's artistic abilities and a man's ineluctable appetite.

36

He goes away for an entire week. I want him more when he is not around. A song spins in my head. I sing it over and over and over. Something about being talented at missing someone. About loving from afar.

I take the train to Stanmore, walk the five minutes to Newington where Noah and his high school friends are waiting for me. There are gold plaques and sandstone sculptures every ten metres or so, commemorating old boys. The grounds are immaculate and broad; each building carved out in reflective glass panels and laced with trimmed rose gardens. Inside the hall, men in suits and polished shoes mingle in groups, holding beer and glasses of wine. The small chamber group are gathered at the front of the stage.

I call out to Noah when I see him. He's holding cables in one hand, his phone in the other.

'Can you text Olivia and tell her I'll be here till late?' he asks.

'Why can't you do it?'

'I don't want her to think I'm overbearing.'

'Olivia and I aren't talking. Hasn't she told you?'

He blinks. 'I didn't know it was that bad.'

'It's bad. I didn't even think she'd let us see each other.'

He winces.

'She doesn't own me.'

The concert lasts a little under an hour. Most of the ceremony is taken up by speeches listing the names of men who've given large sums of money to the school. Lots of applause, and then we're packing up again. Noah is different tonight. His eyes drop to the floor when he's talking to me and his hair is gel-flattened and he is clean-shaven. We head to the local pub on the main road and I walk behind him, staring at the back of his head. He's talking to a young man I've never met. They laugh, slap each other across the back. At the pub, we talk about our jobs, shows we've seen. Some people talk about real estate. Rent. Noah returns from the bar with his third beer of the night.

'Great show tonight,' he says, smiling. 'Did you want a beer?'

A young teacher joins us at the table. She flirts with Noah, laughing at his jokes, brushing the back of her hand across his shoulders. When he excuses himself to go to the men's, I say to the teacher, 'You know he has a girlfriend?'

She opens her mouth in an exaggerated O, puts a hand over it, an expression of mock alarm. 'It's not you, is it?'

After eleven, the bartender asks us to leave. The three of us walk out together.

'I'm going to walk home,' I announce.

Noah takes a step closer. 'I'll give you a lift.'

'But you're not going in the same direction.'

'I need to pick up that thing.'

'What?'

'You know, that thing.'

It takes me a second. 'Oh, yes. The music for that concert.'

The teacher walks over to Noah and stands on tiptoes to kiss him on the cheek. 'See you around,' she says.

We watch her cross the road.

'Not very subtle, is she?'

He scoffs, pulling out his car keys.

'Hey,' he says, 'you want to go for a swim?'

At Rushcutters Bay, everything is dark. We scale a fence near the boatshed, his hands hovering close as I weave one leg over the other. We strip down to our underwear and slip into the water, which is icy and dark. I glance down to see if my nipples are showing underneath my white bra. In the water, the chill of a new sensation. We swim around the yachts, trying to find one to board. All the ladders are retracted.

'There's one over there,' Noah calls. He points to a medium-sized yacht about fifty metres away.

'It's a fair bit out,' I say. 'Can you swim that far?'

I wade through the black liquid. He follows close behind. Soon he passes me, reaching the yacht's ladder first. When I get there, he turns his back to the ladder, grabbing the bars above his head.

'Password?'

In the black water, it seems easy to bridge the physical gap. I hold his hip and curve one arm around his neck. He pulls me towards him, eyes fixed on my breasts.

'Thank you.' My face is wet with saltwater.

He pushes his face close to mine, our noses colliding as the water ripples.

'What are you doing?'

Then his tongue is inside my mouth, knocking against my teeth. There is no rhythm to his kissing. I tangle myself in his oral mess. The confusion is pushed to the edge of my mind, present only when I open my eyes and see he has kept his eyes open while kissing me, like he wants to be awake to what he is doing.

We climb onto the yacht and push open the door to the galley. The urgency between our bodies is palpable. We have sex standing up against the kitchen bench. He is tall and has to bend his knees to slip in at the right angle. I grip the bulkhead for support. At one stage, as he wedges me into a small space between a cupboard and doorframe, something pierces my tailbone.

I let him continue. I don't ask him to adjust my body, don't ask him to loosen his grip on me, even though after a while I think my back is bleeding. I let him drive himself inside me.

Later, I find his face in a crack of light. He is still shaking, tired, slack, a mix of elation and shame in his eyes. We swim back to the shore; the wound in my back stings in the saltwater. We pull our clothes on and drive through the empty streets back to my place. We get out of the car and he follows me to my apartment building. At the front door, I stop him. 'Maybe don't come in.'

He nods.

'I don't want anything from you,' I say.

He shuffles his feet, taking a step back towards the street. 'I know.'

37

I listen to Coldplay for five days. I eat entire blocks of chocolate in one sitting, mindlessly jamming pieces into my mouth. I order Thai takeaway each night and I stop brushing my teeth before bed. I am paralysed. Noah ignores my texts. I grab Monkey from my case and push his furry head between my legs. Nothing works. I have yet to hear any results from my audition, and it's been two weeks. I fill my life, all its gaps, with anxieties; I push in things to worry about until there are no cracks at all. I take thirty-minute showers and emerge with my skin bruised all over. I stare at the foggy mirror in the bathroom, towel wrapped tightly around my body, wiping steam from the glass with the soft melancholy of an introspective heroine in an American indie film, looking deep into my own reflection. Feminine affliction has never looked so good. I sigh at my own face.

Val knocks on my door and tells me I'm starting to look creepy and sad and not in a cool French way.

She doesn't know about Noah. To the rest of the world, I am just another girl screwed over by a boy who has vanished after a one-night stand. Nothing has shaken me up like this since the breakdown, and I don't know why I feel so bad. Each passing hour, the horror of the reality I've conjured up feels frightening, a freight train careening towards me, forever a few metres away but never colliding. I'm waiting for it to kill me. I am short of breath the moment I wake from sleep. I'd gone and thrown a bomb on any chance of reconciliation between me and Olivia, the person who'd saved me from my old self. It has nothing to do with Noah at all. I realise, too late, there are lines that should never be crossed.

'You're being totally ridiculous,' Val tells me. 'Is it Mark? Did he do something?'

'It's not Mark. I need Ben and Jerry's to make me feel better. Could you go and buy me some?'

'I'm not your slave. You know, women like you were locked up in mental asylums a hundred years ago.'

'Women like me?'

'Angry and promiscuous.'

'I'm mourning.'

She rolls her eyes. 'Stop being so dramatic.'

'I can't help it.'

'Men never feel this bad. Women are always feeling bad about something. It's called the patriarchy and you're perpetuating it right now.'

In the evening, she takes me to a bar on Crown Street. I pull on a wrinkled T-shirt and dark jeans.

'I've taken the liberty of asking a few of my friends for some available dick for you. You need to stop moping around. We're meeting my friend Sam's new housemate. He's just moved into their place in Darlinghurst and apparently he's very tall.'

'What does he do?'

'I don't know. Does it matter?'

'I don't want to fuck a plumber.'

'Jesus Christ, you're worse than a racist.'

'My prejudices don't need a label.'

'I have to Skype my parents. I'll be in my room with my headphones on so you can be as loud as you want.'

'What makes you think I'll bring him home?'

She orders another drink but leaves it unfinished on the bar and walks off to catch the bus when Sam's new housemate arrives.

Sam's new housemate is not tall. He's not tall enough. He does not smile much. After two beers, he gets up. 'Coming?'

I follow him back to his place and I let him take off my clothes in the dark of his bedroom and I let him go down on me and I let him fuck me in that ordinary way men fuck women they barely know.

38

A week later, I'm washing my hair in the shower when I hear my phone ringing in the bedroom. I race to get it. Between the bathroom and bedroom, I slam my right shoulder against the doorframe of my bedroom and tumble to the floor, landing on my right hip. I lie there for a few breaths, wailing quietly. Then I get up and limp to my phone on the bed. One missed call. Unknown number.

At rehearsals, someone asks me about Olivia. I tell them she's fine and leave it at that.

In the afternoon, my phone rings again while I'm walking to the train station. I fumble for it in my handbag. When I answer the call, the person on the other end asks if I am Jena Lin. He has an American accent. My heart hammers against my ribs.

'Jena, this is Nelson Williams from the New York Philharmonic. We met at your audition.'

It's been three weeks since the audition. I'd tried to forget what had happened, but the voice reminds me. Nelson. Williams. Perhaps he was the one dressed in a suit. The only member of the panel who'd smiled at me.

'Yes, I remember you.'

He clears his throat. 'Congratulations. I have good news.'

I stop at the entrance of the station. My chest erupts, a steel plate breaking against the surface of my ribs. I feel the hollow force of each hit, hit, hit; thump, thump, thump. A low baritone. Rolling timpani boom. I calm myself by looking up then closing my eyes. Breathe in. Breathe out. Breathe in. Breathe out. The sky is Play-Doh blue. Everything looks artificial.

'Hello?'

'Yes, I'm still here. I'm just surprised.'

He laughs. It's a warm, generous laugh. 'It was one of the most impressive and powerful auditions I've ever heard,' he says.

'What?'

'Truly. We're excited to have you join us in a few weeks' time.'

Back home, I put on the kettle and refill my water bottle. While I'm waiting for the kettle to boil, I call my mother and tell her the news. I move to the balcony and linger in the sun.

'I thought you said you slipped up?' She is perplexed.

'I know. I thought I did. Maybe my brain is no longer working properly. I might need help.'

'How strange. Could it be some sort of hoax?'

'Maybe they were desperate to get me.'

'Don't think so highly of yourself.'

'I don't think highly of myself.'

She fires questions at me. Logistics. Money. Schedules. Plans. I am thirteen again, only this time I have to take responsibility for these things on my own. 'And who's going to stay in your room in Bondi while you're away?'

I hadn't thought that far ahead.

After we hang up, I walk into my bedroom and stand in front of the mirror, pressing my cheek to the glass, trying to see my own reflection in my pupils.

I take a step back and measure my body, my face, my ears, my unbrushed brows. How will I manage without my mother? How will I play without Banks?

In the evening, Mark walks out of his office building a few minutes after nine. I wait by the traffic lights outside for him to catch sight of me. He's looking at his phone. I step in front of him. He presses a dry mouth to my lips, pockets his phone. We walk in silence, neither of us looking at the other. In a bar on Kent Street, he pats me on the shoulders, a brother to a sister.

'I'm proud of you.'

I'd texted him the news right after I spoke to my mother. 'I leave first week of November.'

'That's good. I still have a while with you.'

'You have your girlfriend.'

'That's not the same.'

He leans forward.

'Don't let anyone tell you they're a better fuck than me.'

I see Mark each night, between the long days preparing for my trip. I let him take me as though nothing has changed between us and nothing will change. I arrange to pay my bills by automatic debit, get new passport photos, do an inventory of my underwear. One evening, Val asks if I want to sublet my room, tells me she won't cover the rent by herself while I'm gone. But I don't like the idea of someone sleeping in my bed without me. I'll be getting a stipend from the exchange and all my travel and accommodation is paid for. I think I can cover the rent. I want my room to be waiting for me when I return, to smell only of my body.

•

On the weekend, I visit Mike and Jacob at their studio after they return from Shanghai. Mike asks after my mother.

'I left you a message and you never got back to me,' he says.

I don't remember a message. 'My mother?'

'Val said she was unwell, that's why you couldn't make it to our show last month.'

The show. The night at the Hilton.

'Oh, yeah. Sorry about that.'

He's readjusting a frame on the wall, eyes darting between me and the silver wall clips. He tells me we'll need to celebrate, gather with a few artists and drink to New York. They seem more excited than I am. Every time I get what I want, the thing that I want loses its power.

Nelson Williams sends me a schedule for my first week in New York City. I buy two jackets and a new pair of boots, some sweaters and a beanie. Val makes me promise to visit her favourite Warhol works and museums.

'Why don't you just fly over and join me?' I say. 'It's not like you don't have the money.'

She flips me off.

I've made this sort of mistake before. I assume that as the daughter of billionaire parents she can do whatever she wants.

'Not true,' she tells me. Her parents keep her on a tight leash, giving her money for rent and nothing else. She is lucky to be allowed to paint.

In the next few weeks, I see Mark frequently. We don't leave his apartment, staying in the bedroom, writhing with some bottomless need. My head dips into a mild, persistent haze, a dream-like state, half conscious, half asleep. Drunk on sex. Drunk on misdemeanour. He takes my body and I collapse into a vortex of orgasm and spit and semen. Time is indistinct, like the period when I was a child between concerts and practice, when time seemed to halt, when the hours passed like days. When the air around me felt like it was melting, slow, dripping like a Dali painting.

Banks calls, leaving messages, short words of congratulations. Somebody must have relayed the news to him. His calls go unanswered. I can't escape the feeling of panic and inadequacy from the last conversation we had. The disapproval on his face. I wonder if he'd planned the speech long ago. If he knows the wound I'm still nursing.

Silence is my most powerful weapon. He will know what I want from him, even if I can't say it myself.

The night before I leave, Mike and Jacob come over for dinner. We roast a chicken and make a watercress salad. They ask me specifics about the exchange and then list the artists whose work I have to see, the museums—the Hoppers at the Whitney—the arthouse cinemas and jazz clubs.

I remind them I've been to New York several times.

'But not as an adult,' Mike says, skinning a piece of chicken breast on his plate. 'It'll be so different. Now you can drink and make love.'

Jacob drizzles balsamic vinegar over the salad and tells me his favourite neighbourhoods. 'Borough Park, South Williamsburg and Midwood. Midwood is crazy. The Jews call it Flatbush, but it's not really Flatbush—the real Flatbush is somewhere you should hang out. There are a lot of Caribbeans there and the culture is way cooler. Also, don't go to Seagate. Or Rego Park or Floral Park or Forest Hills. Though since you're Asian, you'll probably just get death stares.'

'I'm not going to Syria.'

He pinches my forearm. 'It's only going to get more dangerous if Trump gets elected.'

We laugh, open mouthed.

'I'll drink paint if he does,' Mike says.

Jacob is not smiling. 'I hope I never see you drink paint,' he says soberly, taking a sip of beer.

I am smug and proud and my certitude is strong. The US is about to elect its first female president, and I'll be at the centre of it all. We're giddy, optimistic, electrified by a new confidence. There is so much newness ahead of me. There is so much to look forward to.

After dinner, the boys hand me a parting gift; a small framed canvas the size of a paperback. The canvas is painted black with a single white brushstroke down the centre.

I study it for a few moments, trying to think of something clever to say.

'What does it mean?' I ask finally.

'You're the white line,' Mike says.

'But I'm not white.'

'That's not the point.'

'I'm a white stroke?'

'Look at it carefully.'

'Yeah?'

'Look at the space around the line.'

I am quiet for a moment, studying the image, then I think I see. 'I'm alone?'

'Or you could put it another way,' Mike says.

'More like, you're this incredible aberration of a human,' Jacob says.

'A girl.'

'A lonely girl.'

'But you make it look cool.'

'Not sad.'

'Dangerous.'

'Like I said, cool.'

39

Val comes into my room while I'm still in bed. My last few moments of comfortable sleep for the next thirty hours.

She smiles her big smile and leans forward, pressing her body over mine. She's being interviewed for a possible commission early next year at the Museum of Contemporary Art and cannot stay. She rushes out, stopping at my door to wave.

'Don't be good,' she says.

I get up and put on David Bowie's 'Modern Love' on repeat while I make a snack to take on the plane: Medjool dates stuffed with roasted almond butter. I split the dates down the centre, spoon a heap of almond butter into the opening, seal it like a clam. Each date is cling-wrapped and slipped inside a zip-lock bag which I stuff into the backpack I'll take as carry-on luggage, along with my violin. I have one suitcase to check in.

My flight is in the afternoon. I take the train to the airport alone; I don't want a big send-off.

During the second leg of my journey, the flight from LA to New York, the woman seated next to me asks why I am going to New York.

I reach over to the seat on my other side and pat my case, which is clipped tight in a seatbelt.

I ask her what she is doing and she tells me she is following a man.

'It's only been six months but I have a good feeling about it.'

I nod and start rummaging in my backpack for my headphones.

'Have you ever been in love?' she asks.

'Sure,' I say. 'Yeah.' I slip on the headphones.

Across the aisle, I see a couple, mid-forties, white. The man looks like a fuller, rounder Michael Fassbender. The woman is lean with pronounced cheekbones and dark eyes. She is wearing block-coloured athleisure. They look utterly in love. Fingers interlaced on the armrest. Eyes beaming.

They must be having an affair, I think. They have either recently left their spouses or left them in their respective cities. The man has the *New York Times* spread open across their two seats and is reading with glasses. The woman is looking at a photo on her phone, flicking through the filter options of a picture of herself in a black cocktail dress; she cannot decide whether she looks better in sepia or black and white.

Later I look at them again. The man is devouring the woman's face like he is eating chocolate mousse. When the flight attendant comes past with the trolley, they pause, and I watch the man order. ('A glass of red wine for me, please,' he says, like he is in a fancy restaurant on the Upper East Side.) The flight attendant hands him a small bottle and a plastic cup.

The couple flick through a magazine together, their heads close. They are definitely having an affair. Their giddiness is unnatural for a married couple of that age.

Then the man goes back to the newspaper and the woman picks up the magazine. She is reading an article titled 'Trust Your Instincts and Don't Play Games'. It is accompanied by a picture of a black catwalk model in a purple robe. The woman glances over at me, she senses my stare. It's as though we can each read what the other is thinking.

I know your secret.

I know you're jealous.

Later, when the man extends an arm between the woman's legs, she pulls the blanket over his hands, turning her head with a smirk of accomplishment. I know that look well. I have worn it myself. On the streets of Sydney, on the rare occasion when he claims my body in public, I enjoy having Mark's face buried in my neck. I know that particular pride. *I've got something you don't.*

It's the crafted look of a woman who tells the world: *I have the love of a man, and that trumps everything else.*

I wonder what I am afraid of. Without Mark, am I missing some essential fact of womanhood? Alone, am I an anomaly? A thing to be laughed at? A thing to be pitied?

I want so much to touch myself between the legs. Make it all stop. Drive down that road I know so well. But there is nowhere I can go to make myself come. Nowhere to shed my shame, unburden myself from the dark cave of my own construction.

I reach for music to calm my panic. I thumb through my phone and stop at Mahler. Fifth Symphony. It blasts through my headphones, fiery and full of dissonance and rage. Mahler, the truculent master of twentieth-century music. The brute. The controlling man. One of his lovers said that being with him was like being on a boat that never stopped rocking. Thinking about Mahler always makes me sad, because when I listen to his music, all I can feel is the sadness of his wife Alma, who was also a composer but whose creativity he discouraged. She has been forgotten. What happened to the wives, the caretakers, the invisible humans who worked tirelessly for the men we now revere? Musing on this distracts me for an hour.

In the dark of the cabin, I see the woman's small head disappear beneath a heap of blankets on the man's lap. The man's eyes are shut, head tossed back, mouth gaping. Small gasps. I think my heart might explode and cause the plane to fall out of the sky.

It's night-time when we land. I collect my bags and walk into the arrivals hall to find a man in a grey Philharmonic T-shirt holding a sign with my name on it. I wave. He rushes over.

'Glad to meet you, Jena. I was just watching your performance this afternoon.'

'My performance?' I follow him through the crowds towards the exit.

'When you played with us. I was going through our archives because I wanted to watch you before I met you.'

I'm not sure whether to be flattered or on guard. 'That's nice, thank you.'

He tells me we can't leave yet; we're waiting on another person—a girl from the UK who'll be arriving soon. The man has a strange accent. Not quite from New York. I think about asking him where he's from, but he keeps talking and talking and I can't get a word in.

The girl arrives and the man leads us to the cark park. It's cold. It hasn't begun snowing, but the air and wind are the same thing, tossing our hair in front of our faces, burning the tips of my nose and ears. I pull a beanie out of my backpack and put it on.

'You're not used to cold weather, are you?' the girl says.

The best way to enter a city is late at night. Like sneaking into a party through the back door.

We check into a hotel near the Lincoln Center. We're staying here for two nights before we move to our own apartments in Greenwich Village, which are owned by an orchestra patron. In the hotel, I peel back the curtains and peer out onto Sixty-third Street. Against the black sky, a thousand coins of light shimmer and pulsate. In the en suite, the shower taps are reversed. H is cold water and C is hot.

I take out my violin. Lean into the familiar. After a few minutes, I grow listless, unfocused. I look out the window at the landscape, an arcade game.

I need to get out. Reorientate my body to the freezing air of the city. I pull on a woollen sweater, thermal pants, a scarf, beanie, gloves, boots, woollen coat. I take the elevator down and step into the cold night. My phone tells me it's eight degrees Celsius. It feels like minus twenty.

The last time I was here, the three-headed beast was doing a full tour of the East Coast and my mother and I had a fight. I had wanted to stay in New York longer to see Ground Zero, but she refused. My violin was the most important thing. Banks didn't say anything, but I knew on such matters, he would tell me to listen to my mother. We did twenty-three cities in three months. They didn't even remember my birthday.

It's after ten and the pavements are still jostling with crowds. I walk along Seventh Avenue towards Times Square. I walk steadily, eyes drawn to the footpath in front of me. I listen to the sound of dirt crunching beneath my boots, walking past bars heaving with people, past restaurants and dark rooms. I turn my head for a moment, long enough to catch glimpses of laughing faces and animated hand gestures. Stories being told, laughter being shared. I am outside of it all.

The immensity of the city presses against me. It feels both liberating and suffocating. The city wants to make an impression on me, and I want to make an impression on it. It feels like a duel. I'm too tired to fight. I stop at a crossing just past Times Square, shivering at the chilling breeze on my face.

A woman next to me talks loudly into her phone. 'I feel like when you write it down, it makes it more real,' she is saying. 'You of all people should know this. Write down how it makes you feel. You don't have to share it with anyone.'

A group of three strolls briskly towards me. As they pass I hear one of them say, 'I only go to parties where everyone is married now. I don't go to parties where there are single people.'

I wonder if he is single. I want to turn around and tap him on the shoulder and ask him to invite me to one of these parties.

At Twenty-eighth Street, I turn and walk back to the hotel. It's 3 am when I return to the room, face cold, hairline damp with sweat under my beanie. In bed, I stare at the ceiling, making shapes out of the cracks and stains of its surface. I imagine all the people who've ever looked up at the ceiling and wonder what shapes they saw. I wonder how many women stared at the lines while being fucked in this bed.

I reach for my phone and download a dating app. Upload the photo of me and Val taken before Noah's party. The men on the site have pictures of their torsos, bulging biceps. They are brawny and they are white and they are black and everything in between. I swipe right. Right, right, right, right, right. Four messages slide on my screen.

Do you want to have sex tonight?

This, from an Eric Bana–Hulk doppelgänger. In the picture, he is sitting at the end of a bed, taking a picture of the mirror which reflects his hunched shoulders and sleeve of tattoos.

Delete.

Another: *hey*

Delete.

Another: *hi sexy, what's up?*

Delete.

Another: *why are u on this app?*

I scroll through this one's profile. A few pictures of him working out at the gym, holding a massive wheel above his head, pumping his fist like Rambo. His mantra: *Be honest, and you'll get no bullshit from me.*

I zoom in on his face. He is black, attractive. A young Denzel Washington.

I type: *Because I am cripplingly lonely.*

My thumb hovers over the send button.

I backspace and retype: *I want to make out with someone.*

He writes back: *meet@3pm tomorrow@starbucks on 42nd.*

The cold is paralysing. It restricts airflow; lungs, chest, breath. I put on two layers of thermals, a sweater, a large jacket. I'm still wrapping my arms tight around myself for warmth. Pedestrians scurry along the pavements like ants in a colony. Women in longline puffer jackets. Conehead beanies.

App-man is taller than I expected, though I'm not sure what I expected. His skin is the colour of charcoal. He's wearing a scarf that covers his mouth and jaw. He pulls it down to say hi, then pushes it back up when we step outside. As we walk downtown, the traffic of pedestrians moves in one direction. At a set of lights, yellow cabs crawl by. I glare at the ads for gentlemen's clubs affixed on the vehicles' roofs. I wonder if App-man is looking at them too. It's the same blonde woman in each ad. She's wearing black lingerie, breasts about to tip out of her bra, lips thick with sex. I look away for a moment, ashamed at how far I am from resembling her. My breasts are the size of limes. My hair the colour of tar. My lips are small. The exact opposite of sex.

He doesn't seem to notice. We walk and he asks me questions. We can't decide where to go. In the end we slip into TGIF. Inside, a bored-looking waiter shows us to a table upstairs. The second floor is near empty. Mid-afternoon.

A middle-aged couple nearby. App-man orders a bowl of glazed chicken. I have an iced tea. It tastes like watered-down Fanta. I ask him how many brothers and sisters he has. I stare at his lips, which are full, thick, swollen. Pink. I wonder what we look like. Two lovers – no, we are too polite. Too formal with each other. Our bodies give it away. High school friends. Work colleagues. Neighbours who decided to hang out. Church buddies. Classmates. We're a strange combination of people. In New York, though, there is no such thing as strange. I tell myself he must do this with a new woman every day.

Outside, I place my body in front of him.

'Do you want to come to my hotel?'

We walk side by side, arms wrapped around ourselves to seal out the cold. I decide we must look like amiable old friends. Ex-lovers. Newly divorced. We've subtracted to the formal because we can't stand to be with each other any other way.

In the foyer of the hotel and then inside the elevator, he keeps a respectable distance.

In my room, he asks to use the bathroom. I hear the toilet flush. He comes out and sits on the edge of the bed next to me. I watch him unlace his Nike sneakers slowly and place his shoes by the foot of the bed. He tucks his socks inside the shoes. I glance at him nervously, a schoolgirl waiting to be kissed.

'I don't know how to do this.'

He leans over and presses his mouth over mine. It starts, just like that. We push our bodies against each other, hungry, filling a need. In between his body and the mattress, eyes closed, I feel seen.

While he takes me from behind, my face is buried into a pillow. A sadness moves inside me, something heavy, burning. Wet. I sob into the pillow, the feeling something entirely new yet entirely familiar. He bends over and cups a hand over my breast. 'Are you okay?'

'Yeah, keep going.'

His cock is thick, warm and full. But all I feel is the trembling grief of something in my body. All I can think about is Mark and how easy it is to betray another person.

Everything else functions on auto. My hands reach for those familiar places. This is all rote work. Nothing is as simple, as effortless as making love to a man, especially a stranger.

He does not make me come.

After he finishes, quietly, like he is trying not to be heard, we lie side by side, staring at the ceiling. I listen to the soft inhale and exhale of his breath. He doesn't say much. Eventually, we pull on our clothes. I walk him to the door.

'See you soon?' he asks.

'Yeah, sure.'

I reach for my metronome and climb into bed. Accidentally, I fall asleep.

40

When I wake the next morning, I take a shower. The water blasts directly onto my nipples. I lower myself into the bathtub and make myself come. If I can't orgasm with a man, why do I keep taking them to bed?

I've learned to go through the motions. I make loud grunts. I know they love hearing it. I perform for them. With App-man, I no longer see the point of that performance.

I get a message from him and read it quickly as I'm pulling on boots. Without thinking, I type a quick response.

I gather my bags and violin and take the subway down towards Greenwich Village. My new apartment is on the sixth floor of an old building on the corner of Fifth Avenue and Twelfth Street. The Philharmonic's administrator is waiting for me outside. I follow him up to my apartment and he hands me the keys. It's a one-bedroom place with a walk-in kitchen and a spacious lounge. The ceilings are low, windows large; looking out onto Fifth Avenue, the view extending onto the First Presbyterian Church and The New Shul.

When the administrator leaves, I take out my violin, play scales, warm up my fingers, adjust them to the northern hemisphere. A few hours pass. Schubert, Mozart, Ravel.

It is late when I finish. I have a shower, eat some corn chips, lie in bed waiting for sleep. The rumbling of the cars below keeps me awake; sirens.

I wake at five in the morning, having dozed for only an hour or so, and get up immediately, splashing my face with water in the bathroom. I get to David Geffen Hall early, walk around the space, remind myself of that other life. Geffen Hall. Geffen Hall. A new name. When I played here last time, it was called Avery Fisher Hall.

The hall through the main entrance is deserted. A security guard stands at the door to the backstage. I tell him my name and show him ID. Inside, the exit lights illuminate the backs of chairs, the music stands, timpani at the back of the stage. I sink into a chair and toss my head back, counting the silver and gold lines that trace the ceiling. The embroidery of a woman's hooped gown from the nineteenth century. Something worn by an aristocrat's wife. I shut my eyes for a moment.

'Jena?' Someone taps my shoulder.

I had not intended to fall asleep. The seats are uncomfortable and yet I have been out for almost an hour. I know this because Maestro is shaking me awake and asking what on earth I am doing here at 7 am. I tell him I couldn't sleep, wanted to see the place before it got crowded with musicians and tourists.

'It's a Saturday,' he says kindly. 'We don't have rehearsals.' He invites me to a concert in the evening. Zubin Mehta is conducting; the bass player whom I'd so loved, growing up watching 'The Trout' documentary, is leading, with a sitar world premiere, and some Haydn and Schubert. I go alone, later that night, even though Maestro has told me to call up some of his friends. 'You must still have some connections here,' he says. I nod. In the hall, I file in through a side door and find a seat by the aisle. Mehta walks onstage with the soloist; his face is dark, and appears to frown, even when he is smiling. She is beautiful.

The soloist, dressed in traditional Indian sari, hair perfect and full. She sits on the floor on a colourful rug and plays with her eyes averted.

On Monday, the rehearsals for the next concert begin. Onstage, Maestro is sharing a dream he had the previous night with members of the orchestra, only half of whom have arrived on time. 'My cleaning lady rang me and told me I needed to give up my condo on Fire Island.'

He sees me and waves me onto the stage. 'I trust you slept well?'

'Yes, thanks.'

'You all set?'

'Where's everyone else?'

He touches his baton. 'The election! Some of our players are stuck in a queue registering to vote. Anyway, we are extremely pleased to have you here.'

I look around and see half the chairs empty. I meet the concertmaster, Frank; who emigrated from China with his parents when he was two. There are three other musicians on exchange: a tuba, a flute and a cello. We're asked to stand and wave to everyone. We're the new kids in school. I glance at them throughout the rehearsal, trying to gauge how they're feeling. They look confident. Still. Their shoulders are square, faces stern, spines erect. I want them to catch my eye, to acknowledge me. None of them do. They're focused on Maestro and the music in front of them.

I'm seated next to a woman who has been playing with the Philharmonic for eighteen years. Her skin is powdered white, her expression ageless. She wears a gold bracelet on her bow arm that slides up and down as she plays.

At lunch, I follow the other players into the dining hall. I learn that the flautist is from the UK and the cellist is from Germany. They have names that are easy to pronounce. Katie and Anne.

Katie stands to shake my hand.

'Great accent,' she says.

I'm not sure whether she means I have a good Australian accent, or that I have good English for someone with my face.

During rehearsals the next morning, one of them suggests going down to the Javits Center to see Hillary make her victory speech. Everyone agrees it will be a momentous occasion to be in the city. We make plans to meet after rehearsal. Everyone is glad it's a Tuesday and there are no concerts. We can all be present to see the first female president make her mark in the city where dreams come true.

Later that night, the city transforms. Everything changes. The optimism has been replaced by something else. The televisions scattered; in bars and bodegas and cafes and libraries and restaurants; people are watching the nation light up in red patches. Each time I look at a screen, the country has turned increasingly red, like an infestation, a disease, chicken pox, a child's body turning infectious. It's terrifying, and I see it on the faces of the people around me.

On the subway, people are sobbing. A young couple are sitting side by side, the man holds a phone between them. The woman clutches a clump of tissues in her hand. It's just quiet. It's so quiet. Tuba looks at me on the street, wide-eyed. 'This is incredible,' he says. 'I've never seen anything like this. It's like the whole city is in mourning.'

We sit on a bench in the players' room with Maestro and watch silently. A glass panel dividing the dining room and lounge room is behind the screen. At one point, I glance over at four, dead-faced figures, eyes unblinking, mouths slack, jaws dulled by a hollow reality. Then I recognise my own face among the reflected expressions. The width of my lips, expressionless, catches me by surprise. I look at myself, then back at the screen, then back at myself again. Then I glimpse another pair of eyes following my flickering attention. The beardless face of a young man, pale, full-lipped, small nose. Tuba smiles. I turn to see his face in colour.

'What are you thinking about?' he asks.

'That maybe, if we go to bed now, we can wake up sooner and discover this was all a bad dream.'

41

That night, the sirens blare along Fifth Avenue.

I reach for my phone on the bedside table: 3.45 am.

App-man is asleep beside me, body curled in a foetal position, his body hidden under white sheets. I didn't want him to stay, but the news of the election had frightened him and he asked if he could spend the night. I write a quick note on a post-it and stick it on my pillow.

GONE TO GYM. SEE YOURSELF OUT. TONIGHT, SAME TIME.

The city that never sleeps also never stops working out. I find an all-night gym and do a few laps in the pool.

The night-time is still opaque, magical. The city throbs, always in some unplaceable anxiety of want. There are other parts of the city that are livelier. Here, the locals keep to regular hours. The pool is empty when I arrive and empty when I leave. The cardio room is busier, people running or rowing off their anxiety. When I return to the apartment just before six, my bed is empty. On the note underneath my writing, a scribbled handwritten word. OK. So much affirmation and consolation contained in those two simple letters.

•

Over the next few days, I manage to make some friends among the musicians. I latch on to a couple from Denmark, both violinists who live nearby on a street with NYU housing.

On the Friday, three days after the election, I visit them at their place on Fourteenth Street. Outside, the skin of the city feels porous. At the entrance to their building, I press a button beside the front gate. A man opens the door. It's the oboe player from the orchestra, and behind him is Tuba. He is taller than I remember, though the ends of his shoulders droop forward, as though pushed down by some invisible force. The Danish couple emerge from the hallway, take turns to shake my hand. They remind me of the flawless models on the pages of *KINFOLK*. Translucent white skin, salmon pink hair, ice blue eyes.

I follow them into their apartment and Tuba shuts the door behind us. The floor is littered with bread crusts and dead roaches.

'Come in. Sorry, we haven't cleaned up at all since we moved in,' the woman says.

The city lights slice through the windows like faint holograms, cutting my vision into strips of film.

Tuba pulls out a stool for me at the kitchen bench.

'Wine?'

'Sure, thanks.'

I ask them how long they've played in the orchestra.

Oboe talks over Tuba. 'It's not nepotism, I swear,' he says. 'I mean, we're not even from the same family.' He means family of instruments in the orchestra.

Nobody laughs.

'Yeah, I suppose there's no fun in those kinds of jokes anymore.'

'Maestro is the product of two musicians in the orchestra.'

'Yeah, have you talked to his mother?'

I nod. 'Just a few words. She seems nice.'

The Danish couple met at Juilliard fifteen years ago.

'Juilliard was a better place back then,' the man says. 'It wasn't as much about money as it is today. Sad how it's changed, very sad.'

The five of us sit around a tiled bench, leaning over glasses of wine. I scratch the tip of my phone case to occupy my hands.

'Can we go someplace to forget about the state of the world?' Tuba says. 'I don't want to talk about politics.'

'We weren't talking about politics,' Oboe says. 'Plus, what we do is inherently political.'

Oboe smooths out his hair looking in a mirror hanging on the wall.

'Play music?' Tuba replies.

'Yeah.'

'You said it. I didn't.'

'Where are we going tonight?' I ask.

'I don't know. Oboe suggested the Met,' Tuba says.

'No way. I'd feel like a kid on a school excursion.'

We spend half an hour debating what to do. A bar, a venue, a cinema. Anything that does not involve music. In the end, we decide on the Whitney because it is within walking distance—and because it is free tonight and because it is cold, and we don't want to catch the subway, where everyone is still crying.

On the street, I walk alongside Oboe, who is Jewish. He has an impish-looking mouth. It pairs strangely with his long locks which he ties into a low ponytail. He asks if I am a minority back in Australia and I tell him I'm not sure, it depends on how I'm feeling.

'How do you feel now?' he asks.

'I feel Australian.'

'Is that good?'

'I don't know.'

Tuba is from Austin, Texas. He was born in Yonkers but spent most of his youth travelling between Texas and New York, where his parents still teach at Sarah Lawrence College. For the past three years, he's been living in Cleveland where he graduated from the Institute of Music. He has a fantastically sharp accent. 'This is the only city in the world that will give you everything you want,' he says while we're waiting at a crossing, our bodies wedged against a group of European exchange students with matching backpacks and Beats slung around their necks. Tuba asks me if it's my first time in the city.

'No.'

He smiles knowingly. 'You're a hunter, I can tell.'

He looms over me like a bent tower. He is a bit older, mid-twenties, military-cut hair, inoffensive mouth, grey eyes.

'A hunter?' I say.

He nods. 'Absolutely. This city feeds the unsatisfied soul. The constant wanderer. The rumbling heart.'

'Are you a poet?'

He chuckles. A full-throated exhalation of excitable air.

'There are two types of people in the world,' he says, looking down at me. 'There are those who are birds and those who are trees. You're a bird. New York's full of birds. Every one of us migrated here. This place gives you somewhere safe to explode.'

Banks had said that, too.

'Who are you?' I ask.

'What do you mean?'

'Are you even a musician? Have you got a chapbook so I can read your poems?'

'Not yet. But watch this space.'

My temples throb with something red, anticipatory.

Inside the museum, we leave our jackets at the coat check counter. In the gallery lobby, a wall phone is stuck onto exposed pipes; red words engraved onto white panels. Tuba walks to one and picks up the phone. I watch as he communicates with his eyes what he is hearing. I focus on the smooth coil of copper of the telephone, hanging like a severed arm. A white American artist who calls herself MPA is preparing for a performance inside an enclosed space. There are photographic collages in various shades of red. We visit the enclosed space on the third floor where in February, the artist, with two other female artists, will cage themselves in a narrow space between windowpanes overlooking the Hudson. The light is red. Everything is red.

On the streets, there are people standing and smoking outside bars and restaurants. Everyone is talking in groups, animal clans.

We find a Turkish takeout and order falafel rolls, sitting at a table inside, eating them while talking about Edward Hopper and his famous painting, *Nighthawks*. There were too many people at the museum. The crowds swelled towards the end and we had a few seconds to glance at it. Oboe says Hopper was a genius. Tuba says he was a cunt who abused his wife. 'All geniuses are abusive towards women,' he says. 'It's a prerequisite.'

'That's a terrible thing to say,' Oboe says. 'You don't really believe that?'

Tuba looks at me.

'Well, maybe there's some truth to that,' I say slowly. 'I mean, if I were a powerful man, I'd probably abuse my wife too. And other women.'

For two mornings, I sit a metre away from Itzhak Perlman as he rehearses the program for a one-night-only concert. He runs through the Beethoven Romances for Violin at a faster tempo than usual and speaks slowly to the orchestra. When he smiles, one end of his mouth dips in a sly grin and the gap between his front teeth gives him a boyish charm, though he is now in his seventies, with a clump of ocean-foam white hair. I'd not played the Romances myself for years, but hearing him play them reminds me of the colour blue; how I reached for its cradling tenor, all those years ago. For the Brahms 4th, he is gentle with the tempo, gentle with his interpretation. He relaxes into the beat; he trusts us. I feel like we are giant kelp, waving under his direction. That evening, at the end of the concert, as he twists his wheelchair around to a standing ovation, Frank, the concertmaster, bends to shake his hand, and Perlman reaches back and clasps my hand too. For a moment, I feel part of history.

A week later, another violinist flies into the city to perform the Beethoven Violin Concerto. A Danish man with terrifyingly large hands engrosses everyone with the ease with which he plays the opening double stops, and the flair he threads through the rest of the concerto. I know the orchestra part by heart, so I spend the entire piece staring at the violinist's face; his slack jaw clamped firmly on his chin rest, cheeks jostling about; later in the players' lounge, he tells me he'd always thought that was the hardest piece. I stare at his mouth; his bottom lip protruding out slightly, like a little boy with an uncontrollable lisp.

During interval, I pace around the players' lounge, stretching my arms, massaging my wrists. Tuba is slouched beside me checking his phone. He asks me what it's like not to be in the spotlight. We're chugging water from plastic bottles. He looks vacantly at his phone. I tell him it's not as exciting, but I'm on the edge of the stage so I've still got the spotlight on the side of my face. It feels like being on the edge of a cliff and wanting to jump off. The lights cast shadows on my face. I miss the attention, the guarantee that all eyes will be on me. I want to be reminded of who I can be.

A bell chimes to signal the second half of the concert.

He bends down to clutch his gold instrument. 'You want to hang out some time?'

I smile, too eager.

42

We walk to rehearsals the following morning, the sound of a crowd chanting in unison rising across Columbus Circle. Something about Syria. The war. Invasion. The US army.

Tuba lifts his head taller and whispers the chant.

'Are there protests here every day?' I ask.

'Yeah, pretty much.'

'What a city.'

'What a nuisance.'

On Mondays, Tuesdays, Wednesdays and Thursdays, we have rehearsals for most of the day. Concerts are usually Thursdays till Saturdays, sometimes Wednesday night. At the end of the year, big drawcards bring in the crowds; Mozart, Beethoven and Dvorak. Stock-standard repertoire.

Each weeknight is filled with a concert or social gathering. The tempo of the city catches in my chest. Every face I pass looks affable. The hunched bodies race by in black puffer jackets, eyes permanently narrowed against the icy air. Soon, the snow will start falling. I track the motions of the city with my pulse, counting the number of times my heart leaps at the sight of something so gloriously New York. The yellow cabs, pretzel stands, water towers dotting the skyline. The familiar streets and avenues. Fourth. Fifth. Sixth.

Before long, the idea of returning to Sydney feels regressive. A quiet form of self-entrapment. I say as much to Tuba as we're walking to a local bar after a concert two weeks out from Christmas. New York City is constantly changing, but it's also always the same.

'This fucking city,' he says, glaring at a passing yellow cab.

'What, you don't like it?'

He keeps walking, slightly ahead now. I trail half a metre behind.

At the Carnegie Club, we find two empty stools and sit side on to a framed picture of Winston Churchill, who has a cigar trapped between his lips. The amber light from the lamps gives the space a romantic, nineteenth-century air. Everyone looks beautiful under these lights.

Tuba raises a hand and a waiter walks towards us. 'Would you like to hear our whisky specials for tonight?' she asks.

I nod eagerly. 'Please.'

'We've just received a new batch from Japan. Single malt. Very, very dry.'

Tuba rubs his palms together. 'Yes, yes.'

'Two of those?'

The woman whips around and disappears into a crowd of old men in suits.

Everything is leather, red, velvet, dark.

'Cigar?' Tuba taps the glass ashtray in front of us.

'No thanks, I think I'll consume it by osmosis just sitting here.'

'People come here to pretend it's 1955 again.'

'Pre-Bloomberg and all that?'

'Pre-feminism.'

'That's fucked up.'

'Precisely.'

'Is that why you brought me here? To molest me and get away with it?'

He laughs, open mouth. I can see his tonsils. 'Don't flatter yourself.'

While I'm in the bathroom, warm pee gushing, my phone vibrates in my bag. I scuttle off the seat, tear a piece of toilet paper off, clench it between my legs. The name on the screen startles me.

I swipe quickly.

'Hi.'

'Jena.'

It's the first time he's said my name aloud. Mark is calling from work; his voice is so clear I tell him it's like he is right in front of me.

'I miss you,' he says. I wonder if he is high or drunk. He makes other small talk. His new team. The weather. Always the weather. After a while, I realise that I'm still crouching in an awkward position, toilet paper between my legs.

'I need to go.'

'Wait, just tell me when you're back.'

'March.'

'You will come back, right?'

In the mirror afterwards, I stare at my reflection. He must love me. Why else would he call? Was this what I'd wanted all along? I run my hands under warm water, dry them on a paper towel. At the bar, Tuba is waiting for me with a glass of whisky, grinning.

43

The smell of pot snakes into my apartment on Fifth and Twelfth. It's everywhere I go, in the subway, on the streets, entering a building, coming out of a building. The city is in a constant state of re-wilding. On Sunday morning, Tuba and I go to Chelsea Markets for breakfast. He's never been because he tells me he'd rather die than be mistaken for a tourist. The previous evening, I met Nigel Westlake for the first time, and we reminisced about Australia. He conducts the score to *Babe* while the movie plays behind us on the big screen. It's a welcome relief after a week-long marathon of Handel's Messiah.

Tuba and I meet at Clement Clarke Moore Park and walk the High Line towards the markets. The morning is slow, air still adjusting to the day's fresh chill, a sharp brush on my cheeks. I put on sunglasses because the glare is blinding. The buildings look as though they're illuminated by fluorescent lights from the inside.

We find a table outside a matcha cafe. Last time I drank matcha was with Mark at the Korean cafe, so many nights ago. In another life. In that life, I was learning how to be a better victim of choking, and playing the role well.

I adopt an American accent when the man taking my order asks me to repeat myself. I order a green tea latte and Tuba gets a scoop of green tea ice cream.

'Ice cream for breakfast?'

We buy fish tacos and share a bowl of pesto hummus and fried eggplant. I ask for extra coriander and the man at the counter looks at me like I'm from Mars.

'Coriander?' I repeat.

'Cilantro,' Tuba says.

Even in the cosmopolitan centre of the universe, I am an outsider.

We sit at our table outside, eating. A stout, bearded man approaches us and taps Tuba on the shoulder. Tuba stands and hugs him then introduces me: Alejandro, an old friend from high school. They talk, trying to avoid the subject of the newly elected president. They fail. Tuba offers Alejandro a ticket to this afternoon's Brass concert.

'You're a musician too?' he asks me.

'I'm just here for the season.'

Alejandro says in a voice that is half irritated, half astonished, 'I've been in this city for six years and have never once ventured inside that place. It's full of rich white folks, isn't it?'

Tuba looks injured. 'You don't have to come.'

'No, I'll come.'

'I don't want to force you.'

'No, I'd love to see the inside of Carnegie Hall.'

'It's Geffen Hall, at the Lincoln Center.'

'Oh okay.'

'And there's no classical stuff, if that's what you're expecting.'

Tuba plays in the Brass concert at three in the afternoon, and Alejandro and I sit in the audience.

After the concert, we wait in the foyer for Tuba and decide to get drinks.

Tuba suggests a communist bar where local poets and writers with 'liberal values' give readings.

We walk, following Tuba, Alejandro smoking a cigarette with an ungloved hand. I glance over to admire his shoulder-length curls, his thick lashes. His mouth is so expressive. He'd have made a wonderful trumpet player. I tell him this. He smiles, a little hesitant, sucking on his cigarette, shaking his head and combing his hair back with his other hand.

'You think I have a good mouth?'

After a few blocks, we stop in front of a building that resembles a rundown industrial warehouse.

'This is the place?'

We walk up a set of metal stairs. At the top, we enter a crimson-lit space. Old propaganda posters of Mao's army, a row of faces looking out into the distance holding red books in the air. They are forceful and determined, unwilling to let anyone penetrate their line of fire. They look fierce. They look like me.

The boys push through the crush of people to the bar. I stand in front of a tall man in a grey parka and black beanie, peeking behind me every few seconds to make sure the position of my body doesn't suggest anything untoward. He ignores me, staring over my head at the poet onstage.

The boys return with beers as the MC introduces the second set. 'Eastern Europe is not Western Europe, but its impoverished, uncool cousin,' she begins. 'Eastern Europe lost the Cold War and everybody else won it, without even trying. Statistics show that Eastern Europeans are among the most pessimistic people on earth. But in light of recent events, let's claim that for ourselves.'

The crowd murmurs, some people click their fingers.

A woman walks onto the stage and reads a poem about the death of Paul Walker and how he'd reminded her of her ex-husband, an abusive Bulgarian. She's holding her phone out at waist height, glancing at the audience every few lines. 'Who will do Fast and Furious now?' she cries. 'Who will drive the cars and fuck the girls?'

The crowd chuckle, a choir of soft laughs. Alejandro leans over and whispers, 'I haven't seen a single film in that series. Can't stand cars.'

The next poet is an older woman. She reads a poem about the shifting politics of the country, and mentions the person about to take office. Instead of a collective chorus of boos, the crowd is quiet, solemn. Then the poet breaks into a Guns N' Roses song, launching into a melodic query about existential direction.

Everyone joins in. The bartenders stop moving and sing along. It's like being in a church and we are all hoping to be saved.

Afterwards, the three of us stand together at the top of the stairs at Bleecker St/Lafayette St station, trying to work out what to do next. We decide to take the subway to Alejandro's bakery in South Williamsburg. It's a few hours before dawn, we're already hungry. There are leftover cheese scones, he tells us. The bakery is a few minutes' walk down a short, unlit street from the Marcy Avenue stop. Alejandro leads us down to the basement, a low-ceilinged space cluttered with bags of organic unbleached wholemeal flour and large machinery. He takes a bag of scones from an industrial-sized freezer and fires up a small oven. We sit on top of the silver benchtops and chat about Alejandro's extended family back in Chile. They'll never make it in America in the new reality of the world. I'm not sure how to comfort him. His sadness dampens my appetite.

Alejandro uses a pair of tongs to take the scones out of the oven and peels off paper towels from a roll as plates. We eat in silence. Then he disappears, reappearing moments later with three glasses and a bottle of vodka. He pours us shots and we down them.

Tuba launches into a bitter attack on the clarinet. It is the most spineless instrument, he claims. It has absolutely nothing to say. 'At least the oboe is a bit abrasive—you know, cutting. But the clarinet? It's like that pretty, polite girl who is always in sensible shoes and smiles and laughs at everything but has absolutely no personality and no opinion about anything. I mean, Jesus, who the fuck even invented the clarinet?'

I'm laughing, the strain of muscles tightening around my abdomen, but I'm thinking about Noah.

'I dated a clarinet player once,' Tuba says. 'He broke my heart.'

The heat from the oven warms up the small space. I roll up the sleeves of my blouse, flap the hems of my skirt to fan myself.

The newness of the city has been replaced by something thick and heavy.

'I'm going outside,' I announce.

Tuba frowns. 'It's fucking zero degrees out there.'

They persuade me to stay. Tuba loosens his belt and takes off his shoes. I notice the whiteness of his socks, clean, unstained. One of them begins to help the other undress. Shirts are unbuttoned, fall to the concrete floor. I lean against the wall and watch silently, taking small sips of vodka, feeling its heat sear through my body. There is more hair on Tuba's chest than I expected.

'I hope you don't mind us doing this,' Alejandro says.

I watch Tuba. His eyes shut; mouth clamped. He doesn't want to be kissed. The two men sprawl across an open bench, unmoving at first, then they slide their hands across each other's bare torsos, pressing a cheek to a white stomach. I've never seen skin so white.

They stop and we chuckle. Alejandro puts on some tunes on his phone. Ella. Classic Ella.

He gets up and moves towards me. 'Is this okay?' he asks, touching my shoulders. I flinch, ruining the moment. But then he laughs. It's a high-pitched cackle. I don't mind. Tuba narrows his eyes, watching Alejandro, watching me.

One of them slides off his underwear. My head mixes them up. They look like the same person.

'Are you sure?' one of them asks.

I catch a glow of my reflection on a machine. My eyes are sad. My cheeks pale. I am invisible, even to myself.

'Come on. Loosen up, girl.'

I reach for my bag. Race past them towards the door.

'Jena!'

I don't know who calls out. Their voices, so distinctly different earlier, now sound the same.

I'm running through the night, dark pavement, feet crunching on dry snow. I can't seem to get my balance.

I see a taxi and wave wildly. It pulls over and I jump into it.

My phone pings. A text from Tuba. I throw my phone back into my bag without reading it.

When I reach the apartment, a single beam of gold traces the side of the building. It's 7 am when I open the door. Rehearsal is in one hour.

I undress and shower quickly. If I fall into bed now, I might never wake up.

Rehearsals are long and tiring. We work on a program of Copland, Strauss and Marsalis. I find them exhausting because there is so much to learn in such a short space of time. Maestro makes us repeat a two-bar passage twelve times. Each time, the sound is slightly altered, but then the twelfth time sounds exactly like the first. His black turtleneck collects the sweat from his head.

I focus on the back of Frank's head to stop myself from screaming. At one point I will myself to look over at Tuba, who does not look back at me.

I turn my eyes back to the front.

Frank is always in a T-shirt. The back of today's T-shirt lists the concert dates of a bluegrass band, Gerry's Gone Outta Town. Toronto. Atlantic City. San Antonio. El Paso. During sectionals, he points his bow at each desk before asking us to play individually. Everyone gets used to it. I snap upright when he calls on me to play a few bars of an especially difficult passage in the Copland. I play it and he rewards me with a nod of the head, no eye contact.

The sectionals are combined. I look across the orchestra and find a place to rest my eyes as Frank targets other musicians. I meet Tuba's grey eyes. They're staring back, penetrating my skull. Then he smiles. A short, quick twitch of the lips. I stare at him because I want to test his boundaries. He does not look away.

Frank calls on Tuba. Tells him to play the opening of the second movement.

Tuba sits forward, straightens his back, aligns his shoulders to the music stand in front of him. I watch his face change as he blows into his mouthpiece, eyes flashing. I don't recognise him as the man who undressed in front of me and another man only hours earlier. I do not recognise him at all. He holds the last note longer than needed. Maestro smiles. 'Good.'

We catch each other's eyes again. And then we look away, as if we've seen something we weren't meant to.

For a week, App-man is tied to family events. His mother is very religious; he goes to church with her each day leading up to Christmas. Tuba has gone back to Austin for the week. It feels like the worst time to be left alone in this big city. I wedge my body at the foot of the couch in the lounge and stare out the window at the spires of the First Presbyterian Church, phone pressed to my chest; the long days stretched out—in my mind, an infinite void of nothingness. I reach for Monkey as I've always done, but even his sad, kind face cannot console the needy child in me. I want attention and I want it all the time. The urge feels like a hunger I can't contain, an illness without remedy; for the first time in a long time, I close my eyes and think about Mark, his violent hands, his reckless mouth, and the ways I'd reach for him like a limitless reservoir of love. In this city, as families are reuniting, I rock myself to sleep on the floor, Monkey pressed to my shins; wondering how I can get myself out of this unlivable, dullish hell. Seven days, alone. I reach for my open case. Get up, Jena. Get up and play.

44

In the final days of the year, we work on perfecting Copland's 'The Quiet City'. It's so lonely, so maniacal. The trumpet, like the military bugle. On Friday evening, we play a concert for a visiting guest from Monaco. A member of the royal family, with a name that's hard to commit to memory. He sits in the sixth row beside his wife and two children, twin girls. They're dressed in Disney-princess gowns with silver lace draped across their skulls. During rests and in between movements, I see one of the girls sneak a hand into a pocket to play with her phone.

We're introduced to each of them at the cocktail party. They have gloved hands. I bend down and try to squeeze softly. Gloved hands remind me of Banks. He used to put them on before touching the bare parts of my shoulder. Leather gloves. Cold.

We stay for an hour, and then I retreat backstage for my violin and jacket and bag. As I'm strapping on my case, my phone buzzes in my bag.

My mother. She asks about the program. What the other musicians are like. All her questions sound scripted, as if she is reading from a book for parents who no longer know how to hold a conversation with their children. Hmm. Hmmmm? Hmm.

'And how's the hall?' she asks.

'The hall is the hall. It doesn't change.'

I massage my jaw with my hand, hoping she won't launch into an old grief involving Banks.

'The hall sounds good,' I add.

'Well, take a few videos, won't you?'

When I return to the apartment, I text App-man. The anticipation of his arrival is schoolgirl excitement. When he finally shows up, I am impatient. I push him against the wall and pin my mouth to his, gorging on his tongue like I'm trying to choke him. Everything feels balanced in the universe. He pushes me back gently. 'Give me a moment.'

I watch him move to the sink in the bathroom to splash his face with water. I follow him, bend over him, bury my face against the back of his neck. He flips me round, pushes me against the bathroom vanity and steps behind me. In the mirror, I see the colour of my own naked body, the dull yolk of my stomach, my small breasts. He unbuckles his belt and we have sex standing up. I stare at his hands. The smooth clamp of them. The way they cover my breasts, squeezing them. In the mirror, I watch the way my body shifts with each thrust from behind, the way my agile flesh adjusts, moves to the strokes of his fingers, his limbs entangled with mine. He is skilled in a way that feels entirely new and frightening. Being with him is like discovering a new planet. I feel his tempo increase; his breath quickens, coarse and wild. As he is about to come, I can barely see my flesh in the mirror. He is consuming me. I panic, suddenly realising I might not have brought the morning-after pills with me from home. I pull away.

'Go get a condom.'

He rushes to his backpack and takes one out, tearing the sleeve open and rolling the condom on calmly. He steps behind me again and clasps my body with his hands, pressing his mouth hard against my upper back, neck, face, mouth. I swallow him and he swallows me. He thrusts with a mechanic virility, a pushing that is rhythmic and vigorous, moving in time to my own quickened heartbeat. He pushes himself inside me and pushes and pushes like he wants to break open a shell with his whole body. He stops after a while.

'What happened?' I turn my head to face him.

'I came,' he says, looking at me with tired eyes.

We move to the bed.

He tells me about the man in the subway who harasses him constantly.

'He tries to give me the Bible, says I need saving.'

'Just take it and he'll stop bothering you.'

'I don't want to give him that satisfaction.'

'You don't believe in God?'

'I do.'

'Really?'

'Yes. The god that's between your clit and asshole.'

'Oh, right.'

'When I'm pounding you from behind, I see God reach out and touch me as I'm about to come. And then I see the face of God as I'm coming. God kisses me on the lips. Sometimes he sticks his tongue inside my mouth.'

'I think I might know God too.'

45

On the last day of the year, the streets are still lined with red and green banners, tinsel flickering against the bright white of the falling snow. In a few days, the decorations will be taken down. Christmas comes, goes.

After rehearsals one morning, Maestro makes an announcement to those of us on exchange. We are in the players' lounge; Tuba, Anne, Katie and I stand with our cases on our backs, waiting. He tells us the sectional leaders will be paying close attention to each of us during performances over the next few weeks.

'Just to get a sense of how you bond with the music, the crowds, and so on.' For the first time I realise he has a striking and uncomfortable resemblance to my father.

'That's pretty vague, if you don't mind me saying,' Tuba remarks.

Maestro shrugs. 'I'm afraid I don't make the rules around here. It just means we'll be looking at things like your fit for the culture. We'll be talking to other people in the orchestra. You know, all that jazz. And Jena, Frank will obviously be watching you closely.'

We thank him. He waves as he walks away.

'I feel like a kid,' Tuba says, picking up his bag.

That night, during the concert, I feel myself making persistent eye contact with Tuba and the other members of the exchange. We look stiffer than usual. Our postures erect.

After the concert, we disperse. Everyone to their own New Year's Eve plans. Nobody invites me to their celebrations. Tuba follows me out and walks beside me as I head back to the apartment.

'You don't know how to celebrate, do you?'

I blink away his glare. 'Big celebrations are a toll on my mental health.'

'How about a film then?' he suggests. 'They're showing indie films at the Spectacle. It's *Frances Ha* tonight, I think.'

'*Frances Ha*?'

'I've never seen it.'

We decide to meet at 10 pm at my apartment.

By the time Tuba arrives, I am two shots of vodka in, have brushed my teeth and wiped the sheets clean of sex and male scent.

We sit on the couch. I pour us vodka. We lean back and listen to the sounds of the city.

The blare of engines and horns on Fifth Avenue. The motor hum of the building's heating pipes.

We arrive at the cinema just before the film begins. There are half-a-dozen couples. A few solos scattered on the aisles. I lean over to Tuba during an ad. 'You're going to be a changed person in two hours' time.'

He rolls his eyes. 'God, I hate it when people say that. It just completely lowers my expectations.'

'I'm not people. I'm an expert.'

The film is so much a part of who I am, I want him to like it. I need him to like it. During the long monologue where Frances pours her heart out to strangers at a dinner party, I feel my heart racing, wild.

I think Tuba must be able to see the fabric of my sweater pulsing up and down with its beating.

At 2 am, we buy bagels from a food truck on the way back to my place. I put them on plates and pour us glasses of red wine and we carry everything to the couch.

'Well? Are you a changed man now?'

He smiles. 'Sure, why not.'

'A toast to you then—a changed man.'

We raise our glasses.

As we eat, he tells me the city's magic is lost on him because his parents struggled in their student days here.

'I'm sick of all the love letters to this place. There are more interesting cities in the world.'

He finishes his bagel in three bites. Leans back and stares at me, his gaze trailing down my body.

I get up to pee, leaving the bathroom door open.

He calls out from the couch, 'Tell me, what was it like?'

'What?'

'Being so famous?'

I flush the toilet, come out, leaving my hands unwashed.

'I wasn't.'

'Yes you were.'

'It didn't feel that way.'

'You were famous.'

'I was a kid.'

I sit down next to him.

'Yeah, but—'

'I didn't really notice all that.'

'I thought you'd have loved it,' he says.

'The attention?'

'Yeah.'

'What makes you say that?' I pick up my glass of red wine and swirl it around, drop my head back for a moment.

'I don't know. You seem like someone who is shy, but you actually crave attention.'

I take another sip of wine to stop myself from saying something I might regret. 'It's actually hard being so different.'

'Fuck off.' He laughs, shoving me gently.

'I think when I was younger, I just loved playing, but the love was something I didn't understand. There used to be so much meaning when I touched my violin. Like, something a bit crazy and magical. When I touched it, I felt my brain fire up with so many different emotions, and it was so overwhelming that the only way to deal with it was to keep playing, even when my shoulders felt like they were being stabbed by knives. I knew I had to keep going, keep performing that role. That privileged role, as my mother kept reminding me. I performed and broke through the pain because the attention from adults gave me fuel, maybe. I always felt loved. And that would be enough to carry me through to the following evening—and so it went for years and years.'

He reaches over and strokes my forearm. I adjust my posture; he retracts.

'The worst was when I had long flights. Monkey kept me slightly distracted. I couldn't even be without him for more than a few hours before I started to panic. There was a lot of congestion in my head, I think.'

'Monkey?'

I jump off the couch to retrieve him from my violin case.

'You're not serious?' He smiles, grabbing Monkey from me and squeezing his large head.

'He's my good luck charm.'

We continue taking sporadic sips from our wine.

'Nobody tells you that,' he says after a while.

What?'

'I've never heard it expressed that way before.'

'Brains exploding?'

'Well, no. That it's, like, painful.'

'That's because none of your friends were child prodigies.'

He taps his left eye.

'Look,' he says, pointing to his eye. 'It's pulsing.'

'And?'

'My left eyelid throbs when I'm around snobs.'

'You know, mothers had their sons castrated in Renaissance Italy to give them a musical career. I feel as though the psychological mutilation I went through was a bit like that.'

'Mutilation? It wasn't that bad, was it?'

'When I was younger, I saw success, but I couldn't really touch it. Then I got older and got closer to it, so close I could touch it, but then I began to see the cracks in this idea of success, and I didn't like it. It's like the closer I got to it, the less I liked it. The uglier it appeared. And the closer I got to this power, the less appeal it seemed to have. But because so many people were invested in me—I had to keep going. It would have been harder to turn around than it was to simply keep at it. I had such a strong connection to my violin, nothing else mattered. That sort of obsession is not healthy. If I ever have a kid, I hope they're not a prodigy. It's like a mental illness.' I hug my knees at the memory.

'We forgot to drink to the New Year.'

'Oh. 2017.'

'To mental illness.'

'To mental illness.'

46

People talk. They express their gratitude of the year finally gone. Cohen dead. Bowie dead. A racist becomes a president. Something happened over in the UK. The world is changing into something nobody recognises.

We're invited to a fundraiser at a gallery on the Upper East Side on the first day of the year. We are entrusted to preserve the orchestra's prestige when we're offstage, without our instruments. In fact, Tuba tells me this is perhaps of greater importance.

'What's of greater importance?' I ask.

We are striding through Central Park towards the gallery, our shoulders hunched beneath heavy coats. I tell him to slow down. The strap on my heel comes undone. I find a bench and sit to readjust it. An old man is reading the *New York Post* opposite us. Tuba nods at him.

'You kids off to some ball, huh?' The old man has a low, gruff voice. Throat cancer or asthma, or old age.

'Yes, sir.' Tuba smiles.

I fix my strap and leap up. I link my arm through Tuba's and pull him on.

Tuba continues, 'What you do offstage and how you chat to the patrons. That's more important than whatever you do onstage.'

'I know how to do that.'

'But New Yorkers are different. They're pretty toxic socialisers.'

'I've heard that before.'

'Have you?'

'Well, my parents hated parties, so we never had any ourselves growing up. Plus, we didn't have a large circle of friends in Sydney. When my mother and I toured, though, she had to pretend to like them.'

We stop at a set of lights. I look up to read the street sign. Seventy-seventh street. Ten more blocks of this conversation. As we cross the street, I feel Tuba's soft tread, his modest slouch, like he is embarrassed about his height. His height is what makes him commanding, but he doesn't want that sort of power. I feel a protectiveness towards him rise in my chest, glancing sideways every now and then to examine his posture, his expression. I catch him adjusting his stride to match my steps, though my legs are half the length of his. Occasionally, he catches me watching him. 'What?' he says, exasperated.

'Nothing.'

There's a poster at the entrance to the gallery, the word GALA printed in large block capitals. The benefit seeks to raise funds for an African-American dance troupe. The host is the great-niece of Herbert Hoover. Tuba tells me she was rumoured to have been romantically linked to JFK.

'So was every other person who had a cunt in America at that time,' I say.

At the end of a narrow corridor, a woman in a caterer's uniform asks for our coats. We strip off our coats, then another layer, and another. The woman is patient, collecting each piece we offer.

I pat down my blouse and straighten my pencil skirt. Check my hair in a mirror on the wall, tucking loose strands into my high ponytail.

'You look fine,' Tuba says. 'Stop fussing.'

He brushes his fingers across the back of my hand and hooks his thumb around my pinkie, pulling me behind him. My heels clack on the wooden floorboards. The room is large, the ceiling high. Beside me, Tuba loosens his grip on my finger and puts a hand on the small of my back. He is good at this performance. Proprietorial.

The crowd is mostly white. A few black women who look like magazine models.

Waiters circle the room with large silver trays; bowls of olives and glasses of champagne and white wine. Tuba and I each take a glass of pink champagne, sip carefully, waiting for people to make eye contact with us. In the corner by the coat rack, a small food stall has been set up. People mill in front of it. We move in for a closer look. A trio of kids, no more than ten years old, performing a cooking demonstration on a makeshift stove.

'Who are they?' Tuba asks a man standing beside him.

The man attempts a grin. He has a bow tie secured too high up his neck.

'Contestants from Rachael Ray's show.'

'Who?'

'*Kids Cook-Off.*'

We nod.

'It's a good show,' says the man.

'I wonder if they're getting paid,' Tuba whispers.

All three kids are boys, all of them like dolls in their little white aprons, glossy mops of pre-teen hair and high-pitched voices. Their doting mothers flutter about and take pictures on their iPhones, carefully arranging the boys' hair with manicured fingers. This is what it feels like to be in New York. You are part of the show whether you like it or not.

From our corner of the gallery, we alternate between looking at the backs of people's heads, kids showing us how to mix cake batter, and the art on the walls. Most of the works have price tags next to them that are beyond anything I will ever be able to afford. Perhaps Val's parents could.

I cross the room to find another place to stand for a while, looking occupied. I stare at a painting near the entrance. It's a picture of a woman crouching on a chair at the edge of a cliff. The painting is the size of my hand. I can't tell if she's dancing, having a seizure, or about to end her life. She is dressed in an orange cape, barefoot. I think she wants to fly away. I bend down to read the small tag: $54,550.

Tuba comes up beside me, narrows his eyes at the painting. 'How do they work out the price?'

I tell him I don't know.

The answer must be someplace, hanging above our heads. We move on to another painting. The price is again in the five figures.

'I suspect reputation has a lot to do with it,' he says, taking another glass of champagne from a roaming silver tray. 'The metric is there. Reputation and style and popularity, and perhaps even background.'

'You mean white?' I look up at him.

'I didn't say that.'

'But you agree with me.'

'I didn't say I agree with you.'

'There's colour in everything.'

'When I said background, I meant if they went to art school or studied with someone great.'

'There are plenty of artists who didn't go to art school and became successful.'

'Who?'

He leans his arm on the wall in front of me and obstructs my view of the room, eyes laughing.

He knows I won't be able to answer his question.

'My friend in Sydney went to art school and she's really good. But she's not making a lot of money. She thinks it's because she's Asian.'

'Do you have to racialise everything?'

'Of course you'd say that. You're white.'

'Anyway, my point is Monet, Matisse, Gauguin, van Gogh, they all studied art. Their paintings cost more because they went to school for it. They were disciplined.'

'They were old white misogynists and paedophiles.'

'They weren't always old.'

'Yeah, but their credibility and status grew with age.'

'So did Georgia O'Keeffe's.'

'How do you know so much about art?'

'My mother teaches art history.'

'Well, this conversation was entirely uncalled for. You entered it knowing I'd lose.'

We continue on around the gallery and pass a row of tables displaying bottles of wine and hampers with hair products, spa vouchers, gym memberships, less expensive paintings from local artists and cigars from Colombia. There is an auction at the end of the evening where the items will be sold off.

We eat food made by the TV kids. We go back for seconds and thirds.

Finally, late in the evening, the dancers emerge. Their silk slips glimmer like pearls in morning light. Music plays through the speakers, an inoffensive blend of slow jazz and pepped-up Afro-Cuban, and the dancers move around us, their limbs slender, perfectly proportioned.

It feels like we're on the streets, or at a festival. Tuba leans over and attempts to whisper profound and intelligent things into my ear, though they're really only comments about the dancers' bodies, how beautiful they are. I am not convinced a beautiful body warrants such ardent admiration.

When the dancers have finished, the host makes a speech and then, a few minutes before midnight, the auction takes place.

Afterwards, the host circulates. She introduces us to her grandson, who is twenty-seven years old and a banker. He is handsome, though vertically challenged, with dark eyes and a smile that looks like it's been taken from a Tommy Hilfiger ad circa 1995. He has a sensible name, Joel, and is affectionate with his grandmother, who calls him Joely.

'A banker?'

'You sound surprised,' the young man replies.

'I thought everyone under thirty in New York City was some sort of struggling artist.' Tuba pinches my arm.

Joel laughs. 'I'm also in a band but that's just a weekend thing.'

He uses his hands when he talks and laughs at his own jokes. It must be a New York brand of humour. I don't understand it, but laugh along anyway, because it seems like the right thing to do.

'There's a party in Brooklyn tonight,' Joel says. 'My friend Alex Wilson is launching his album. Why don't you guys come?'

Tuba and I exchange looks. He glances at his watch.

'You guys go ahead. I'm going to call it a night.'

I put a hand on his arm. 'Are you sure?'

He smiles and yawns. 'Of course. I'll see you later.'

As Joel starts to tell me about his friend's music, Tuba recedes into the gathering crowd near the coat stands.

I hang around and wait for Joel to finish his farewells. We stop at a liquor store for a tray of beer and a pack of Natural American Spirit. The man behind the counter asks for ID.

'I don't think I'll ever stop being carded,' Joel says.

'You look very young.'

'That always helps on the dating scene.'

'Yeah? How's that going?'

He grins, a shy teenager. 'Nothing serious.'

On the train he asks me about my music, whether I'd ever be interested in branching out into other genres. 'Hip hop? House or FemDom?'

I shake my head, rock against the metal pole. 'I'm a classical violinist. I think that's enough.'

'But that's like a writer saying they'll only ever write in one genre.'

'Most writers do only write in one genre.'

The carriage is crowded, filled with New Yorkers going about their nocturnal adventures.

'Anyway, what's FemDom?' I ask.

'All-female bands. Feminine dominant.'

'Do they sound different from all-male bands?'

'They sound angry.'

'Boy bands can be angry.'

He considers this for a moment, then says, 'It's a different sort of anger.'

He looks ahead while talking.

I feel a new kind of invisibility.

New York City. The centre of the world. Bushwick. The centre of the world of cool. The mecca. A bracelet of girls at the foot of an apartment block. They are smoking, they are cool. They are wearing large coats with frilled edges, and they wear too much eye make-up. They have flannel shirts tied around their waists, and they have wild, uncombed hair tamed into order by paisley-patterned headbands. They are white, they are flawless. They know they are flawless.

When they see Joel, they open their arms to him, no smiles. Joel introduces me and they shake my hand like good middle-class girls. They have names like Scout and Jazz and Mieka and Whitney. Another girl emerges from the building. She has a big nose, sweet-looking in the way Britney Spears looked sweet in 'Baby One More Time'. She is also wearing an excess of eye make-up. Behind her, a tall boy with blond hair appears. He is clean-shaven, attractive, but not too much so; attractive in the way the boy from *Juno* is attractive.

I assume they are lovers. The girl kisses Joel on the lips. This must be the way New Yorkers greet each other now. The tall boy stares at me while I explain to the group what I am doing in the city. I feel his gaze like a piercing flash of light. I can't turn away. I want to turn away.

'Cool,' he says. 'A violinist.'

'Ever met one before?'

'You're the first.'

They finish their cigarettes. Decide it's getting cold. We go upstairs to the party.

Two flights high. Inside, it is loud and congested, people talking and drinking and laughing and vaping. The band have already played their set.

Joel brings me a bottle of beer and apologises. 'We came too late, but they have a CD on sale and a cassette.'

'A cassette?' I take a swig of beer. 'Who has a cassette player?'

'I have two Walkmans.'

He is pulled away by a girl, sleeve of tattoos on each arm. I look around, trying to engage with my surroundings. The walls are covered in giant Rothko-esque paintings, squares of deep purple and blue; I want to crawl through them then settle there, invisible, turn around to face the party, watch without being watched.

I find a corner in the kitchen to repose. After a few minutes, two girls join me, and we are deep in conversation on identity politics in art and music.

One of them is Haitian French, the other Iraqi Welsh. They are both performance artists working as cleaners to save up for grad school. We are all a mix of nations and histories and pre-invented social mysteries.

Eventually, one of the girls cups her hands around her mouth and shouts a name then walks off into the abyss. The remaining girl and

I labour through a few more questions and answers. She seems older and more comfortable in her skin. A gush of cool wind rushes through the open window and ruffles her collared shirt. 'Jesus.' She walks off towards the window, perhaps to close it. She doesn't come back.

I finish my third beer and pour myself a cup of red wine, the size of a juice box; nobody is drinking from glasses. I feel my body loosen, my head lighter. The tall boy from downstairs comes over, offering shots.

'Thanks.'

As he pours, I stare at his face because it's so symmetrical and pleasurable to look at. He tells me he is an actor, currently making money as a set-hand.

'New York is the place to be,' he says, pouring another shot. 'Not LA.'

We tap our plastic cups together and toast to the city. We talk for a while about bad real estate decisions, and how warm it is in Sydney. He tells me his place is a few blocks away and he looks at me for a response.

Out on the street, he puts an arm around my waist and sticks his tongue inside my mouth. I can taste the alcohol in his saliva, distinguish it from my own. He prods his tongue awkwardly into the crevices of my mouth.

He calls an Uber and continues plunging his urgency into my mouth. The ride takes all of one minute.

His apartment is a fourth-floor walk-up. Inside, it is clean, spacious, bare. A velvet couch. Khon masks hang above a television set.

In his room, the bed fills most of the floor space. On his bedside table is a single book, Elizabeth Gilbert's *Big Magic*. I'm suspicious of people who read self-help books.

'It's a gift from my mom,' he says.

'Sure it is.'

There's a framed picture of him and his father in the woods. He looks about fourteen. They're looking at the camera, eyes squinting into the sun, arms laced around each other's backs, posing in front of a row of giant oak trees.

'So *American*,' I say.

He doesn't appear offended.

I don't know how the sex begins. It is like we are late for something and have to do it fast. We slide into bed and push our mouths together, clothes coming off. He climbs on top of me, shifting his legs awkwardly over mine. I can feel his hardness graze my thighs. He pants into my face like a dog.

'Do you have a condom?'

He peels himself off me, reaching underneath the bed, hands rummaging inside a box. He pulls out a condom, opens it, puts it on.

Then he climbs on top of me again and jams his cock inside me, elbows locked on either side of my ribs, staring into my eyes as if challenging me to look away. I am being fucked by a motor.

He keeps his elbows locked, torso pressing down against my navel. He angles his chest away from my breasts and maintains a good ruler-length distance for the entire time.

I don't like that he can look at my face and grunt. I look away and pretend to enjoy it. It feels like I am outside my body, like being locked out of a room.

When he comes, I almost laugh at the intensity of his expression, the explosion of ecstasy so excessive that I think he must have rehearsed it. 'Fuck. Fuck. Oh, FUUUUUCK.'

At dawn, I begin the silent dance of reapplying last night's tobacco-reeking clothes; skirt and shirt, stained underwear.

The boy stirs and asks for my number. I tell him I'll call him.

'Do you want my number?' he asks.

'I'll just get it from Joel.'

He smiles.

I strap on my heels and walk over to where his head rests on a blue pillow.

'See you later,' I whisper, kissing his temple.

How tender and easy this is. I am so good at this kind of love.

47

I order an Uber as I walk out of the apartment, wallet clasped between my fingers. In the car, I scroll through the contacts list on my phone. I don't have Joel's number. When I get back to the apartment, I take a quick shower. I play a few old tunes on my violin, simple melodies from my student days. Mozart. Bach. Haydn. Good. Easy. Predictable melodies. A commercial composer once told me that the most popular melodies go down in pitch. When I asked him why, he said, 'Gravity.'

Down, down, down we all fall. We want things resolved. Down, down, down. Like things that plummet, the release of tension. Maybe this is my descent. Maybe I have more in common with Mark than I realise. I've always thought my aloneness was some irreparable failure. Maybe it was not a failure to acquire friends, lovers, company, companionship. I had all that. I have some still. But then I see a couple holding each other on the street and I'm reminded of what I've failed to accomplish as a woman.

I practise the Brahms backwards, the third movement first, first movement last. The second movement is always the least technically challenging but the most emotionally taxing. My wrists feel bruised, tight, but I keep playing. I push through the pain.

Midway through my practice, I go into the kitchen and I run my hands under warm water to soften them. The water stings my dry skin, as though I'm putting my hands under a stream of warm acid. I turn off the tap and dry my hands with a towel. My fingertips are deep red, the top layer of skin is peeling off, blistering.

At 3 pm on Sunday, I find Tuba walking into the Kaufman Music Center alone, pulling off his beanie. I call out to him through the shuffling crowd. He moves swiftly towards the coat check counter; unbuckling his coat and separating his Beats around his neck. When he emerges from the line, phone in hand, I step in front of him, eyes wild with delight.

'I didn't know you'd be here.'

He moves his mouth, a lazy, mandatory smile. 'Oh, hey.'

'You've vanished so soon after every rehearsal and concert this week. Everything okay?'

He moves towards the opening of the Merkin Concert Hall and I trail behind, eager to catch what he has to say. Instead, at the entrance, the usher checks our tickets and so it's another two or three minutes before we're seated in the audience stalls and he can't ignore my question.

'Is everything okay?' I ask again.

'Yeah. I'm just tired.'

'Well, this concert's not exactly going to wake you up.'

We're here for the Philharmonic's ensemble, a matinee of Ravel's Piano Trio and Brahms' Piano Quintet in C minor. The pieces are searing, despairing, slow. Between movements, I stare up at the square panels of timber hovering above our heads like large pieces of Arnott's Nice biscuits. Revolving square plates on rotation. Tuba is quiet. He is not interested in talking.

•

Afterwards we take the number 2 down to The Grey Dog near our apartments.

We sit at a table by the window, catching filtered conversations from NYU students. Young crowd. Beautiful girls with small faces and huge scarfs wrapped around their necks. They have straight brown hair, half covered by knitted beanies. Beautiful boys who are tall and polite. Part-time dog owners. Parents who own houses in the Hamptons.

'We might spot James Franco,' I say. 'I've heard he comes here.'

Tuba eyes me while we sip bad coffee.

'Who'd you meet at Joel's party?' he asks.

'Why do you want to know?'

'I know Joel's friends. They're all assholes.'

'Is that why you bailed on me?'

'I didn't bail on you.'

'You didn't come.'

'I didn't want to.'

'You bailed on me.'

He looks away, posture tensing, resetting his jaw.

'I can't believe you slept with Alex Wilson.'

'Who?'

'Alex WILSON!'

'I don't know the names of the men I sleep with. Stop yelling at me.'

'I'm not yelling!' He taps the side of his coffee cup, looking at me with anticipation, like there's a question I'm meant to answer. I lift my shoulders, lips stilled; language clammed in some involuntary state of paralysis.

He grabs his coffee and stands.

'Where are you going?'

There should be a name for that feeling when a question you ask goes unanswered. He walks off towards the door and when he reaches the door, he pushes it open and walks through it and I'm still sitting there, hands shaking, wondering what the word for this feeling is.

48

The week leading up to the inauguration, a group of musicians plan a trip down to DC for the women's march. I text Tuba and ask if he wants to come. He does not respond. I redistribute my efforts to someone else; someone who is not interested in playing games. I spend time with App-man. I respond to emails from Val, Mike and Jacob, Banks. My mother, too. She tells me she live-streamed Stephen Hough's performance of Beethoven's Emperor on the Saturday night just past, and I said, 'That's nice, did you enjoy it?' She said she didn't like his physical gestures but he contemplated the emotional acuity of the piece well.

Val tells me the Museum of Contemporary Art has offered her an exhibition, a huge deal for someone so early in her career. She doesn't like living alone. She writes in short sentences. Clipped speech. Like she can't decide what she wants to share. I write a few words of encouragement, support, congratulations. Generic lines that I wouldn't be able to say out loud, if I were standing in front of her. At times like these, I think that on paper—or, rather, digitally—I can be a more expressive and caring human being. I think, I can be a better version of Jena through the internet. Huzzah!

Katie and Anne get me details about where to meet for the bus ride down to DC. On the morning of the march, I decide not to go. I want to make a good impression. Show Maestro that I choose my music above everything else.

I find Tuba at his locker in the green room before the evening's concert. He turns as if he doesn't see me, greets somebody else across the room.

At the end of the night, the orchestra receives a standing ovation that extends past our usual performance time. I look back and try to catch his eye from where I am sitting but several heads are in the way. I wait for him backstage. I wait ten, fifteen minutes.

Finally, he emerges at the same time as Maestro, who is clutching his folder of sheet music and his baton to his chest. 'Jena, can I have a word, please?'

I look over at Tuba, who is pulling a jacket out of his locker.

'Okay, sure.'

In the corner, Maestro asks me how I'd feel about staying in the Philharmonic.

I'm cautious, not quite sure what he's offering; if he's offering any-thing. There must be a more formal process than this to be considered for a permanent position.

'I guess I'd be happy,' I say.

I rush over to Tuba, who is scrolling through his phone on the couch as though he is waiting for someone.

'Hi.'

He looks up. 'What?'

'Are you waiting for me?'

'I'm waiting for Oboe.'

He stands, puts his phone into his jacket pocket. Keeps his hands inside them.

'Listen, I'm sorry,' he says. 'I didn't mean to act like such an asshole.' He drops his gaze. 'Alex Wilson was my best friend back in college. We were sort of into the same things.'

'You knew Joel?'

He sits back on the couch and shakes his head.

'No, I didn't know Joel. I guess Alex has a lot of friends.'

'You didn't say anything when Joel mentioned his name.'

'I didn't see the point in that.'

'That's not fair.'

He runs a hand through his hair. 'Sorry. What I mean is, that's not something you need to know. I mean, Alex and I were once—'

He lifts his gaze. 'Sorry. I just don't want to talk about it. Anyway, I'm not angry with you. I mean, I was, but I'm not now. I heard that Alex had slept with someone, an Australian, and of course I knew it was you. It's a pretty small group. Large city, sure, but the clans talk. Alex and I—it didn't end well. I didn't want to tell you because, well, I don't know. It was late in the evening.'

'What's this got to do with me?'

'Nothing. Well, everything. Of all the people at that party, you had to sleep with him.' He sighs.

'What do you want me to say?'

He drops his gaze to the floor. 'Look, I'd better go.'

When he walks away, the side of his case brushes the sleeve of my coat. My heart lurches forward. There is so much I want to say. I want to tell him how dull the last week has been without him. How I yearned for his company like thirst yearns for water. I don't know whether I want his company because I enjoy it, or just because I am lonely. My barometer for such things has been off for so long.

49

I message App-man, and he comes over. I tell him about Mark and his girlfriend, and about the end of my friendship with Olivia. I tell him about the tall boy, whose name is as plain as his sexual temperament, and I tell him about the sex I have back home in Sydney, the time, frequency, consistency, shape. I don't tell him about Tuba or Beethoven or Mozart or Maestro. He does not occupy that world.

App-man is not possessive, nor jealous, not even when I tell him how other men treat me in bed.

We share our fantasies. I tell him I'd like to be raped, though by someone I trust.

'Would you like me to rape you?' he asks.

'Well, no. Because you're not capable of that.'

'Why not?'

'Rape is sex without consent. You always have my consent.'

'Even when you're asleep?'

I nod slowly.

'No, thanks,' he says.

'Is it because you're black?'

'No. I just don't want to.'

App-man looks like a Greek god, Zeus, Hercules. Because he is black, I don't tell him he has the perfect proportions of a Greek statue. He might be offended.

I don't want to hurt him. There is no point.

I convince him to stay over. He says that since the election he's been wary about catching the subway, careful not to ride too late or too early.

In the morning, his mouth skates down my breasts to my cunt while I'm sprawled across the bed. When he has grown tired of my vagina, he flips me over and spreads my arse apart, slamming his mouth against the opening of my arsehole. An avalanche of ecstasy washes over me. I have never been rimmed like this. He adjusts, sometimes slow, tender. I can feel the tip of his tongue circle the most private part of me, the most disgusting part of me, I can feel his inhalation and exhalation, his teeth pressed against the soft skin and then, finally, his tongue wedging inside. I wonder if he can taste my shit.

I open my legs wide for him. He puts himself inside me and lifts my torso. I feel so wholesome. So monumentally *loved*.

Later, he says, 'I've got something for you.'

He holds a palm-sized mirror and guides my fingers down to where his tongue had been moments before. I watch my fingers tangle in his, the yellow and black knuckles spreading the lips of my vagina open. He is slow, gentle. An expert. Careful.

I fall asleep and dream about being raped by two strangers. They are aggressive, they are blunt, they don't care what I think or feel. In the dream, I can feel my clitoris throbbing. Sometimes, I want the sort of callousness I see in films. I want to no longer be so conscious of my own desires to please. I want a man to degrade me. Maybe that's the only way I can become a woman, because haven't women always been degraded by powerful men? Isn't that how men rise to the top? It has always required someone else's submission. Women let men do whatever they please to them, don't they? I want to assume this role. Play the part.

App-man takes a small black object from his bag. It looks like the duster cleaner that Val uses on her SLR camera. A small rubber ball with a nozzle which you squeeze for air to come out.

'What's that?'

He lies down next to me and kisses the skin below my breasts.

'Remember my fantasy?'

App-man's fantasy. He'd never tried it with anyone. 'I want a girl to fart in my mouth.'

He squeezes the toy in front of my face. The puff of rubbery air blows against my temple, sends a few strands of hair flying up.

'I don't know.'

'You don't have to if you don't want to.'

I reach for the end of the sheet and pull it up under my chin.

'I don't think I can.'

'That's cool.'

He tosses the rubber toy back into his bag, lies down next to me and strokes my stomach. 'Do you want to have a shower?'

I nod and follow him into the bathroom. Under the showerhead, he smooths my hair back and takes my face between his hands. When he kisses me under the water it feels dizzying. I want to bottle him up and carry him with me everywhere I go.

Afterwards, I walk him to the door.

'See you later,' he says, leaning over to press his lips over mine.

I tell myself I am empowered because I get men to do what I want them to do and it feels good. It's an achievement to have men like App-man try to please me. Sex with him feels like an especially sweet accomplishment. An adult accomplishment. This is what they talk about when they talk about sex without love.

50

When I'd landed in New York City three months earlier, the air had been brittle and cold. I'd felt an anticipation I didn't know how to hold in my hand. The promise of something I had no name for, something to change my life. Throughout February; with less than a month until I return to Sydney, a rising panic sets in and finds a home at the base of my throat. Each morning, I dread the inevitable return to that place, that world, that world that rejects my hunger; a hunger that goes unacknowledged.

The conversation with Maestro had felt promising, but I also know he's spoken to other players too.

In the second week of February, the sun makes a triumphant return one morning for a few hours, breaking through a thick grey sky. I slip on my sneakers and decide to walk around the neighbourhood. My body responds to the warmth, exposed skin clinging to each morsel of sunlight, and adjusts quickly. I walk through Washington Square Park and then down Fourth Street, all the way towards East River. I turn at Columbia Street, take the East River Promenade. For a few moments, the light stretches out, a golden bar shimmering across the rippling water. The sweat builds up around my thin sweater, staining the collar, the underarms, the upper back and chest. I reach under to readjust my bra. The air smells of coconut and diesel. It's the first time I have felt the breeze on my face in days. With my sunglasses on, I can look up at the bright sun for a few seconds, pretend I am back in Sydney. This is what it will feel like, I tell myself. And you will be okay.

Rumours skip from desk to desk, then from bar to bar outside Geffen Hall. In the final weeks of the exchange, we tackle mainstream canonical works. Mahler's 1st, Beethoven's 7th and 8th. After a concert on Saturday night, four of us head to The Smith on Broadway to talk about what we've heard.

'They're only giving away one position,' Tuba says.

'One for each section?' Katie, the flautist, sits back on her bar stool, arms folded, legs crossed at the ankle.

'One in total,' Tuba says.

'That's ridiculous.'

'Why?' I lean in so my voice carries across the noisy space. 'It's the New York Philharmonic. That they're opening up a spot at all is unusual.'

Nobody knows about the brief conversation I had with Maestro. Perhaps he has had a private word with each of us, and they're all pretending too.

We have another round and speculate some more but it's clear that none of us knows very much. They make plans to return, though they're also aware they have options. Europe is more conducive to such activities than Australia. They tell me I have options too. I was world famous once. Why can't I leverage that history? I smile when I'm offered such dimmed advice. I smile and then move on. The girls head to a party in Bed-Stuy.

Tuba lingers while I strap my case to my back.

'Can I go with you?' he asks.

•

During sectionals on Monday, Frank pulls me aside and tells me about the position. He's vague though warm, generally answering the questions I ask with the attention and care of an invested supervisor. In the lounge, we exchange violins and giggle like kids exchanging cards. He doesn't ask me about Taiwan and I don't ask him about China.

And then I continue to play as I always do—as though my life depended on it.

Our last concert falls on a Friday night. It is unremarkable, save for a man in the audience who has a heart attack during the last movement of Mahler's 4th. He later dies in hospital. These things happen more often than people expect, but even in my time playing with orchestras, I can count the number of concert fatalities on my hands. The afterparty is a mandatory inconvenience. I am anxious about the twenty-four-hour flight home. The music is too loud. The crowd, too polished. I'd have enjoyed a gathering with fewer people. Good, meaningful conversation. Instead, there are five hundred guests in the foyer of the hall. We're still in our performance blacks. Everyone is shouting to be heard, faces leaning close to each other. A live band is playing old jazz numbers. The musicians congregate in small groups.

Waiters weave through the throng with bottles of champagne, topping up glasses. I find myself shaking my head at each proffered bottle. They seem to think I want what everyone else wants.

Maestro pulls me into his conversation as I'm walking to the bathroom. He's talking to a suit. 'Jena, I want you to meet our new board member.' To the board member, he says, 'Jena thinks she might return to us next season as a permanent member of the orchestra.'

I look at him, startled. This is news to me.

'Of course, we still have much to discuss,' he adds. 'You're leaving when?'

The two men peer at me with expressions of paternal concern.

'Tomorrow.'

The board member shakes my hand, congratulates me. 'Stay here in New York. You won't ever be bored.'

They resume their discussion. I excuse myself. In the bathroom, I close my eyes and see Banks's face, his eyes, his disappointment souring everything I touch. He was part of every success. I want to be able to share this good news with him. But what does that mean? That I need his approval? Why should I need that now when I've done this all by myself?

Tuba and I leave the party together. We stroll along Amsterdam and then Fifty-Ninth and then the Hudson River Greenway to look out over the black river, the lights of New Jersey.

'When does your flight leave?'

'Noon.'

'Will you come back?'

He talks to the ground. The path is empty, save for a few late-night joggers in their long-sleeved thermals, puffer vests and beanies. I clutch the ends of my coat together and peer up.

'I don't know. It's pretty competitive.'

He stops by a ledge and leans over. We look across to the New Jersey skyline, which looks so small and tame compared with Manhattan's.

'You'll probably get it. You're the only one who was a child prodigy.'

'I'm beginning to think that matters very little.'

At the turn into my corner, he leans forward, his mouth moving towards mine. I apologise, though I'm not sure what for.

'Don't try to kiss me.'

He pulls back and looks at his shoes. 'I wasn't going to.'

He opens his arms wide and I step into them.

A text from App-man. He tells me to get in contact if I return. It's inevitable. After New York City, nothing will be the same. Or enough.

The city is always pulsating, floods of light and people and traffic. This is the only place where I can be myself completely and not itch. It's an existence that demands I am on all the time. The molecular energy in the air feeds me in a way I've not felt in any other city.

Like this city, I cannot stay still. At any hour of the day, someone in New York is making love, making art, making a historical account of what it feels like to be living, pouring their blood out somewhere publicly, and I have to be here to see it. To be part of its continuum. The stories are endless, and I will never want to stop being inside its wilderness. Its temperament. Its density. Its cruelty.

51

I spend the first few nights back in my room, watching videos of the performances we gave; Dvorak's 9th, Brahms' 3rd, Mahler's 1st, Beethoven's 9th.

There are close-ups of my face. I look coltish, unaware of the world. The camera zooms in on my bow hand, fades out of focus on my face. I have seen my face in magazines, on television, in books and newspapers. But I was a child, all those years ago. Looking at myself now feels disorientating. Like I am looking at somebody else. A less attractive version of myself.

There's an interview of me talking about the exchange. The merits of living in New York. How we survived the winter. I go on and on about the ensemble, how much I love chamber music.

I am speaking to a young woman with red hair, around my age. She holds the microphone to my mouth as I'm answering the questions. I sound nervous. I don't remember being nervous. My eyes dart from left to right. I look as though I don't know where I am.

'If you love chamber music so much, why are you not more active in quartets?' she asks.

My face cracks open. 'I love playing in big orchestras too.'

My door swings open and Val sticks her head in. 'What are you doing?'

I shift to make space for her on the bed beside me. 'Do I look a bit dull?'

She comes inside and leans over to look at the screen.

'That's you?'

'Yeah, what?'

'No, you just look so . . . pale.'

'As in, white?'

'You look starved. Like a child. They didn't give you a make-up artist or something?'

'It was just an interview for their website.'

'Exactly. So many people will watch it. Hey, you ready for my opening tomorrow?'

I've returned just in time for Val's solo exhibition at the Museum of Contemporary Art. An important American art dealer will be there. She reminds me to google him beforehand so I can appear informed when I meet him. He is a New Yorker. She wants to impress him with her entourage. Her exhibition is called 'Adultphobia | Again', a homage to her favourite artist, Yoshie Sakai, an American artist of Japanese descent who examines patriarchal society in Asian families. On my laptop, I read Val's show notes.

> Li uses the female naked body as the archetype of the 'victim', the used-up, washed-up Asian female body representing the immorality of human labour in China and other second world countries.

> Washed-up Asian female body. Washed-up Asian. Washed up.

Art people are hunched together on the third level of the gallery, drinking red wine, looking at their phones. There are a few press people. Art writers. I recognise a man from *The Guardian* and a woman who once interviewed me for the *Herald*. They are crossing their arms and one of them is nodding at something the other is saying. There are eighty, maybe a hundred people, flitting around the relatively large space, pausing idly to study the works on the walls. Mostly, they're interested in talking. Mike and Jacob arrive ten minutes before the speeches. They're wide-eyed, polished, a little breathless. They'd just raced back from a wedding in Newcastle. They're still in their suits. They look handsome, sleek hair oiled flat. We talk about their new works and they ask me about the US. It's been a week since I've returned, but that life has quickly faded into a vestigial memory.

The curator of Val's show makes a long and tangled introduction about the exhibition, the new trajectory the art gallery is taking, the new talent it aims to nurture. Val is a pioneer, and the museum will be the birthplace of a movement spurred on by artists including her. I want her to use the word 'genius', because I want the expression to circulate more widely among women, but she doesn't. I believe my friend is a genius, but I have not told her.

Jacob clutches a glass of white wine and leans against the wall beside me, pressing his hip against mine every now and then. 'It's nice to see you again,' he whispers. We clink glasses very softly.

When Val gets up to speak, we whoop and holler. Strangers glance back at us with tight, formal smiles. She makes a brief speech about the themes of her work.

'What I want,' she says, 'is for all of you to see that we exist. And that we are just as complex and complicated as you are.'

The Asian woman.

When the crowd shrinks, the light from the ceiling falls across in blue, triangular shapes. Val approaches us, finally. We throw ourselves at her. We're so proud. We're prouder than her parents could ever be.

'You relieved?' Mike asks.

'Not really,' she mutters.

I hand her my wine and I take a champagne from a passing waiter.

'It's another white affair. Nobody's going to take me seriously.'

'The art will speak for itself.'

'I'm deluding myself.'

'It's not something to spend your energy thinking about,' Jacob says. 'You've done something most twenty-somethings could never do.'

The boys leave soon after.

I turn to Val, whose baby blue jumpsuit glitters sadly against the gallery lights.

'No one here tonight will write about my work with the seriousness given to a man. Or somebody older. Or somebody white.'

'Have faith.'

'I'm a woman artist. We are put into boxes that are hard to climb out of. The man is the norm, the rule, the universal.'

I want to roll my eyes. She gets all angst-filled when she's nervous.

'Yeah, but you're more than that. You're so much more interesting than a cis white middle-aged male.'

'Pathetic comparison. Of course I'm better.'

I laugh into my champagne as she says this. 'I know, Val. Everyone will see your work for what it is.'

The American dealer is making the rounds. People are circling him. Moths around a flame. He is older. Fifty, fifty-five. Maybe more. Dark chocolate skin. Thick neck. Imposing height. He is wearing a bow tie; bright yellow with pink spots. If his face has wrinkles, I cannot see them. I tell him about the exchange with the Philharmonic, and he nods, half engaged.

At ten, the gallery staff start making signals. Val, the American and I decide to have a few more drinks together. I notice he has a limp as we walk up the road to the Glenmore Hotel. While he goes to the bar, Val and I take a high table by the window.

I extract my phone from my bag and check my emails, hoping to hear something from New York.

Nothing yet. I put my phone on the table, face down and glance at Val, who is looking nervously in the direction of the dealer.

'Is he trying to fuck us?' I ask Val, who is watching him at the bar. There's a wet patch on the table. I lift the sleeves of my cardigan off the surface and slide my phone back into my pants pocket.

'I don't think so,' she says. 'He's just trying to impress some young Asian girls.'

The dealer returns with three beers. I sip mine and stay quiet, careful not to disturb any connection forming between them. They discuss post-postmodernism and the growing trend of political anti-establishment art.

'You ought to move to the States,' he says. 'There's much more happening there.'

I am tempted to check my phone again.

When we finish our beers we exchange numbers. That is, the dealer gives Val his number and tells her to call him. Then he says to me, 'And you should give me a call if you're in New York again. It's good for musicians to be around artists.'

As we're walking out, I compliment his bow tie. 'You know why I wear it?'

I shake my head.

'So I don't get shot.'

I raise my eyebrows in query.

'So I don't appear threatening. I'm tall. I'm black. Tell me you don't see a criminal when you first see me.'

There is nothing I can say. I don't say anything.

The thought of sleeping with the dealer does not cross my mind until the weekend, when we are sitting next to him in the Drama Theatre at the Opera House. Val is to my right. He is to my left. He rests his hands close to mine on the armrest. He'd been given free tickets and invited us.

The play is about paedophilia in the age of virtual reality. Twenty small screens hang above the stage, replaying footage of the audience as we filed in. There are a few seconds of me staring catatonically into space. Then one of Val as she's furiously typing a text on her phone. The dealer chuckles into my ear, puts a hand over mine. It feels heavy, damp. I pull my hand away and tuck it underneath my thighs. It stays there throughout the show.

While sharing a pizza after the play, he tells us he is divorced. His wife has custody of the children. The court systems in New York favour the mother. It's unfair. There's no such thing as justice. We nod like sullen schoolgirls.

He has a few too many wines, and then he's pressing his face too close to ours. Val and I glance at each other.

'So, we'd better be going.' I am not good at leaving. The announcement startles him.

I stand up and take Val's hand, pulling her to her feet.

He frowns and stands too, grabs Val's other arm, teeters unsteadily. For a moment, I think he might collapse on top of her. He leans against the table, steadies himself.

'You should get to bed,' says Val. 'You look pretty wasted.' She looks half frightened, half concerned.

His jaw juts out. 'Here.' He takes out his wallet and slides out a card.

Val looks at me, her expression confused at first, though this quickly fades when she sees the hotel key.

I put a hand on the dealer's arm. 'We're going to catch a taxi home now.'

His eyes pinch small. He's examining me.

'I don't want you,' he says.

I clear my throat. 'Well, it was nice to meet you.'

I pick up my handbag and walk out. Val follows.

Outside, she pulls on my hand.

'Wait.'

'You're not seriously thinking about fucking that man.'

She crosses her arms, looks at her feet. 'He could show my art in New York.'

The old panic rises. It curls from the bottom of my ribs. Automatically, I reach for my phone. Still no email.

'Will you stop looking at your phone? You didn't get the position, okay? You'd have heard from them by now.'

'Don't attack me just because I can't give you what you want. And seriously, is this worth your dignity?'

She raises her eyes. '*Dignity*? Since when did you care about that for yourself?'

A group of people walking past slow to watch, drawn by the spectacle. Two Asian girls arguing on the streets on a Saturday night. Val's face is indignant. She's repulsed. I am the thing she is repulsed by.

'Val, I'm not trying to—'

'What, tell me what to do?'

'I'm just saying think about it.'

'I am thinking! And I'm asking you not judge me while I think.'

I hold out my hand, wait for her to take it.

She turns and walks back into the bar.

52

The thought of seeing Mark hangs over me like a chore. I run out of excuses not to see him. It's been more than ten days since I got back. I'm holding out. For what, I don't know.

He texts a few days after the scene outside the Drama Theatre restaurant, right when I happen to be looking at my phone, flicking my thumb over the screen, refreshing my emails and refreshing again to see whether new ones have come in. I've become an addict, a mouse inside a box, pressing the lever over and over and over, waiting for a treat.

Perhaps Val is right. If I got the position, they'd have told me by now, wouldn't they?

The morning after our argument, I knocked on her bedroom door until she opened it. I knew she'd returned home alone the previous night; I'd heard her come in. I apologised for being arrogant and hypocritical. I beat myself up verbally, so she'd know how awful I felt. Mostly, I don't want to lose her. I cannot lose her. I'd been careless and no longer wished to be.

She stood at her door, arms crossed, barely looking at me as I spoke. When I finished, she said, 'I would never have thought you were someone who would judge me or tell me what to do.'

I stepped into her space and put my arms around her.

I didn't want to think about how close I'd come to losing another friend.

I don't answer Mark's first text. I don't like this limbo state. Over the next few days he texts again, and again, and then he calls and calls before I finally agree to see him.

We arrange to meet on a weeknight. I cite my busy schedule; the concerts from Wednesday to Saturday, other commitments that I am vague about. Cleaning my room, going for long walks.

On the evening I'm due to see him, I throw on a pair of jeans and a T-shirt and pull my hair back into a bun. I arrive at the bar where we'd decided to meet on York Street a few minutes before seven. He's already there.

When he sees me, he smiles, big, whole face changing the air around him. His suit looks a bit loose around his shoulders. I am impressed again by his height, his strong hands. He is happy. I can see it in the way he moves his mouth, and his gaze, steady. I've never seen him so happy. He is jubilant. How did I make an adult man happy?

'Do you want to get out of here?' I'm already turning to walk out the door.

Outside, he picks me up and swings me around. I don't know what to do with my legs. We must look like two lovers reuniting after a long separation, which I suppose we are, but I'm not feeling what he feels.

We walk to another bar, smaller, quieter, frequented by young white women with ringed fingers and leather jackets and frameless glasses. EDM music pours out onto the street.

At the bar, he orders a jug of sangria and we sit at a table on leather-topped stools. I take out my phone and check my emails.

'It's good to see you,' he says. 'Come on, put that away.' He reaches over and caresses my left cheek.

I love the feeling of being claimed in public.

The bartender carries over the jug of sangria and two tall glasses. Mark pours our drinks. He hands me a glass and we clink loudly. 'To our beautiful reunion.'

I scull the drink. He laughs. 'Impressive!'

I want to ask after his girlfriend. He does not mention her, just talks about his work; new clients he's taken on, the cities he'll need to visit in the next few months. He might be promoted to deputy chair by the end of the year.

I sip my drink, gaze at him.

He orders another jug of sangria and two shots of tequila.

'Why are you drinking so much?'

He lifts his glass. 'I feel good. Anything wrong with that? Anyway, we're celebrating your return.' He leans forward and presses his lips against mine.

I pull away. 'Can we go now?'

'Wait, you haven't heard my news.'

I lean back.

'Dresden and I broke up.'

He is watching me eagerly, waiting for some reaction. He reaches across the table and runs his thumb along my wrist.

I flinch. Suddenly, everything feels unctuous. Being here with this sad, unwanted toy of a man. I'm not sure what to say, so I give him the smile he's hoping for. He thinks I'm happy. And I let him think what he wants to think. Is that not the definition of kindness?

Back at his place we lie in bed, exhaustion stilling our bodies. He rests his head on my stomach, puts his chin on my breast.

'I'm so happy to see you,' he says.

'I know.'

We fall asleep, his arm my pillow.

At some stage during the night, I wake to feel his torso, bare, pressing against me from behind, rocking backwards and forwards.

I turn around and give him my mouth. We move our bodies in opposite directions. I can see the red lines on his back and along the sides of his body where the white flesh has loosened its grip on the bones. The red marks are clear and distinctive. Some girl's sharp, manicured nails. I run my blunt fingers along the red welts, tracing their perfect clawed curves.

He rolls over and turns his face to me. He says something. A murmur.

He reaches over and grips my chin with two fingers, turning my face to his.

'What?'

He sighs and turns his head.

'Where are you?' he asks.

'I'm here.'

'You're a million miles away.'

'I was just thinking.' I rub my eyes.

After a pause, I look at him. 'I want to go back.'

'Back where?'

'To New York.'

'Well.'

I nod. I might be able to nod my way through this entire conversation. I roll across the bed and reach for my phone.

Still no email.

'Stop worrying,' he whispers. 'You'll get what you want.'

I throw my phone back onto the bedside table.

After a while, he shuffles a few inches away to get a better look at me, then asks, 'Why?'

'Why what?'

'Why New York?'

I arrange my mouth into a polite grin. 'It's just people, they've found their solace there. It's a refuge for all the lonely people.'

'You're not lonely.'

He looks at me intensely, waiting for an answer. He does not blink. He is studying me in a way I've never felt from him.

I half shrug, half smile.

He stands and heads to the bathroom to piss, doesn't close the door.

When he comes back, he tells me he'll need to head into the office soon. His voice fills the room like white noise. He keeps talking and talking and I find it comforting, reassuring.

I decide this must be love after all. Quiet, dull, still.

This is love, and it is enough. At the bar, I hadn't wanted him at all. It was exciting, for a moment, to be the other woman. Now, there is no other woman.

He bends forward to meet my lips. We kiss, slowly first, then deeply and with feverish hunger. I lace my arms around his neck.

What a pathetic man. Useless, unwanted, lonely.

53

Sydney is wrapped in a smothering blanket of heat throughout April. I play at a lunchtime concert and fill in for the concertmaster. The orchestra members applaud as I take my seat before the rehearsal in the morning, and then everything is back to as it was before. I feel the rumble stirring inside. It is growing into a new sort of violence. I hide it behind my face and perfect technique. My deskie, a new girl, leans over and tells me I play with great fury and passion. We are doing Mahler's 5th. There is no other way to play Mahler.

Since returning, I've found it difficult to readjust to the routine; four daytime rehearsals during the week, four evening concerts. My senses are dulled by the beautiful harbour and the perfect weather. The 9 pm closing times. The quietness of everything. The stupid conversations about heels in rehearsal breaks. The women in my section are always talking about heels. I am so bored.

Finally, in the first week of May, I hear from New York—an email from the manager of the Philharmonic to arrange a time for a call. We settle for noon. After rehearsal, I race to the green room and lock myself in a private studio, my hand quivering. I have a good feeling.

If they didn't want me, they'd let me down with an email. It must be good news.

I dial the number. The manager picks up after the third ring. I can barely breathe. My heart is pushing hard against my chest. I gasp a greeting, the 'hi' catching in my throat.

'I'm afraid I've got disappointing news.' His voice is bureaucratic, dry. Quiet. As though he is in a library and he is trying to keep his voice down. 'On reflection, we feel you might have more of a future as a soloist, not as an orchestral player.'

After a few more empty words we hang up. I sit there, motionless, heaving, then steadying my breath. I've entered a new reality, one whose operations I don't know how to navigate.

I want to call someone who will commiserate, but I am ashamed. I text Val. She texts back a few seconds later. Something about fate. Ships.

I throw myself into things, expecting always to get what I want. And I always get what I want. Now it feels like I've failed all over again. Only this time, there's no motivation behind it. I've just failed myself, and it hurts in a strange, unfamiliar way. The wound is deeper than anything I've ever felt.

54

The following Saturday, I drive to my parents' place in the afternoon. On the radio, I listen to a man talk about overcoming the grief of his father's suicide by learning to free-dive.

'Are you trying to face death?' the interviewer asks.

The man replies that despite what people think, free divers aren't toying with death. They learn to be patient in the face of danger and risk. It's okay to be vulnerable, he says. I remind myself to look into free-diving lessons the moment I get home. I want to learn to be patient when things fall apart.

My mother greets me in the driveway as I park the car. She's wearing a faded baseball cap and a pink windbreaker. I think I recall seeing a photo of her wearing this in the newspaper once; we were on tour. Somewhere in Europe. I open my arms for a hug, but she leans in sideways and pats my shoulder with one arm. She suggests a quick stroll before we go in.

'Where's Dad?' I ask.

'Inside. Sleeping.'

We walk through the local park, where children play on the mini zip-line. They fling their heads back, laughing wildly.

I want to run to them, ask them to trade places with me.

'It must be nice to be five,' I say.

My mother looks over to where the children are being called to a picnic table.

'You were hard to control,' she says.

'I've never liked to be controlled.'

'I thought children were supposed to listen to their parents.'

'Rebecca did.'

'She was a good girl.'

We turn into a small street lined with apartment blocks and Moreton Bay figs. At the end of the street is a bush track. There's a council sign; the rules—*No Dogs, No Fire, No Camping*—partly obscured by bird shit.

I let her lead. From behind, I notice the dry skin on the back of her legs. My mother has always had dry skin, especially her hands, which are always chapped and sore-looking. She frequently picks at the edge of her nails and sides of her knuckles. Every Christmas Rebecca buys her the most expensive hand cream, and every year she leaves them unopened on the bathroom vanity. I wonder why my mother refuses to make herself nice to touch.

We walk in a silence broken only by the crack of sticks underneath our sneakers and the calls of birds above our heads. Down a steep set of stairs. At the bottom, she pauses, steadies her breath. I put a hand on her arm.

She points to a picnic table nearby. 'Let's sit for a while.'

She walks slowly to the table, takes a seat on the edge. I sit opposite and try to read her face, wondering if she has brought me here for a reason. My mother has never been good at telling me what she's thinking.

'Do you remember how I came to be with your father?' she asks. I shake my head, curiosity clicked open like a purse.

'You've never told me.'

'I thought it didn't matter. It was such a long time ago. He was such a different person. Such a beauty. I didn't care about anything else. I barely even knew if he had hobbies, anything like that. It didn't matter, I just wanted him to be my husband. I wanted to possess him.'

She looks down at her hands resting on the table. Her fingers are slightly bent, knuckles pink.

'I see now that was a stupid thing to do,' she says, taking a deep breath and releasing it. 'I might have done wrong by him. We are such different people.'

'Is everything okay?' I ask.

'It's fine. I'm just thinking out loud.'

I lean back in my seat. 'You fell in love,' I say.

'The older I get, the more I'm convinced I know nothing about love.'

The light from the sky changes colour in an instant. The clouds part to allow columns of white onto the backs of our hands, like paint stripes. I raise my eyes to see the sky split, the thin grey separating like double doors opening to expose blue light. I look over at my mother, whose mouth seems to be lingering between thoughts.

'I always thought the older you get the more certain you are about things like that.'

'No,' she says quietly. 'I think it's the opposite.'

My mother comes into my old room after dinner. I'm folding some clothes into a garbage bag for donation.

Leaning against the doorframe, her face shadowed by the lamp in the hallway, she watches me move about the room, then glances around at the trophies on the shelves, the framed certificates. Things that seem to belong to someone else.

'Did I ever tell you that you took part in a research project when you were a baby?'

She steps forward and takes a hoodie from the wardrobe, begins folding it. She can't keep still.

'When you were growing up, your father had friends who worked at National Taipei University. Sociologists. They used to describe their research to us. We had many friends. We entertained a lot. That was before you got so busy.'

She keeps her eyes on her hands, straightening the corners of some towels.

'We,' I say, glancing over at her.

'What's that?'

'*We* got busy.'

'Right, I suppose so. Yes. Before you started the violin, our lives were full in other ways. We had a lot of friends who worked at the university. Researchers, academics. They talked about new studies that were changing the way we saw the world. New theories, that sort of thing.'

I kneel down to readjust the pile of clothes inside the garbage bag. My mother continues.

'One of our friends was a woman who worked in immunology. Often, she told me that touching your own child could stunt their development.'

She pauses, as though waiting for a sneeze, holding her cupped hands ready in front of her face. The sneeze doesn't come. She glances at me, then continues folding a T-shirt.

'It's ludicrous to think that now. But this was more than twenty years ago. It was such a different world. In Taipei, everything we consumed was from America and the researchers at these American colleges said that touching your child could contaminate them with diseases, could ruin them. We believed everything they said.'

I hold a pair of torn jeans between my hands. 'I rarely believe what other people tell me.'

Her eyes expand, flowers opening up. 'What are you talking about? Of course you do. That's what you've always done. That's why you were so good at the violin. You were brilliant because you were a good listener. You always did what the teachers told you to do.'

I put the jeans in the bag and straighten up to fold my arms. 'That's different. I was learning skills. I was trying to be better.'

'As was I. But I was so angry at your father. And my father, who was always so far away. I didn't want you to turn out like him. You know that. Your grandpapa was consumed by his music. He let his family rot. He was not a good husband and he was not a good father because he neglected his obligations. I didn't want a child like him. I don't think I was cared for very well by either parent. I think my mother suffered a lot for it. It seems so obvious now, but I don't think I was asking the right questions back then, when they were still alive. Your grandpapa, I can see it now. He suffered too. He craved the attention from the world. And that, of course, was never enough. The world was too small for him and I didn't want that to happen to you. But then . . .'

She puts the T-shirt she has been clutching into the bag, then reaches for another item of clothing. She does not meet my gaze.

'These friends, they told me I could earn a bit of money by participating in research. Your father was working all the time and I hardly saw him. I wanted to be more useful, not just to look after you and Rebecca.'

'What about your accounting job?'

'This was before I got that job. Your father didn't want me to work when you girls were small. Anyway, when you were about two, a friend from Taiwan returned from Boston with a research assignment. He asked if I wanted to be involved and I said yes. They wanted children under the age of three.'

She moves slowly towards the single bed and sits on the edge, hands assuming the choreography of a tired labourer.

'They recorded how long it would take babies to start crying after their mothers left the room. I took you in. We were all put into a waiting room together, about fifty mothers with their babies. They gave us biscuits wrapped in plastic. You know the sort. And tea and coffee.'

I nod, not sure what kind of response she wants.

'I was nervous. The other women were very chatty. We were at the end of the list, so I waited all day.'

I tie the top of the bag together slowly.

'You were such a good baby. You were always so patient.' She looks up at me, her eyes soft. 'They saw us finally at six or seven at night. Late. A man told us to go into the room they had set up and play with the toys. Fancy toys. You liked them. You took to them very quickly. Then they said we had to look out for a blue light above the door, and when that blue light went on I was to stop playing with you immediately and leave the room. I was so worried. I kept asking the researcher what they were going to do with you, and they kept saying, "Nothing, nothing, nothing," and I was even more confused. I didn't believe them. To reassure me, they let me watch the mother before me go in and do it. I saw her sit by her baby, and they were playing with some Lego. And then a light came on above the door, and the mother got up to leave. Her baby started crying even before she'd reached the door. The researcher told me that this was what had happened all day. The babies immediately started crying when their mothers left. So I assumed that you'd do the same.'

She stops talking.

'And?' I say. 'Did I cry?'

She drops her gaze to the floor.

'I didn't cry, did I?'

After a while, I feel her stare, but I can't look at her. I am too afraid of what I might see. The disappointment in her eyes. The trauma of a need, a love, an expectation, unfulfilled.

I stare down at my socked feet. Those feet she massaged before concerts in my hotel room, to calm me.

'You didn't cry.'

I open my mouth to say something but the words disintegrate somewhere between my stomach and throat. I press my lips together tightly, wondering what I can say to change history.

'You were a baby,' she says. 'Babies cry. Most do. Most babies cry. But you didn't. You didn't need me.'

I bring a hand to the back of my neck.

'Anyway,' she continues, 'this experiment went on for about a year. I'd take you in about once a month. I don't know why I kept going. Maybe I hoped you would change. That one day you would actually notice when I left you alone. But you never did.'

We look around the empty room, avoiding eye contact, the bag of old clothes sitting between us.

'I think I wanted some time apart from you after all that playing,' she confesses. 'I wanted my own space. After all those years of touring, I think I just needed to stop for a while. I craved a bit of my own identity, maybe. You understand that now, I hope?'

Sometimes, I don't know where my body is. Space, relation, distance. There are moments when I'm playing the violin onstage and feel as if my heart has transcended the physical world, and I find that I can't join the body with my consciousness. Of being utterly detached from flesh and thoughts.

'When you told me you were ready to come home from Wayne, I knew you'd want to play the violin again. I was nervous. I didn't want you to fall into the trap your grandpapa did. I didn't want you to neglect every other part of your life. And you are a girl. I knew that you would probably face harsher penalties for not doing those ordinary things. But of course, selfishly, part of me wanted you to play again because at least I'd know what sort of role I could play in your life. I was useful to you when you were playing. Without that, I didn't know who I was.'

I stand to twist the string of the bag around my fingers.

'So I'm going to drop this in the donation bin on my way home. Do you have anything you want me to take?'

Her face flushes into a mortified droop. It's such a terrifying expression I don't know what to do. So I walk out the door, gripping tightly to the bag. I don't look back.

55

A call wakes me mid-afternoon while I'm in a shallow nap. Banks wants to know why I haven't made the effort to see him. I've been back for three months now. He'd been looking forward to a debrief but he never heard from me. His voice is accusatory. He tells me he's been lingering around the Conservatorium hoping I might drop in after a concert or rehearsal.

I run out of excuses. I cannot lie, so I don't. I tell him I'm tired. I'm busy. I put my body and its wellbeing above cultivating his sense of worthiness. Then we hang up. A golf ball stuck in my throat. I delete his contact from my phone, though I know his number by heart.

Banks. Will I hurt for the rest of my life? Is that my burden to bear?

I wonder if my mother ever told him about the experiments. The university research. This must be what she felt all her life: that the child who was born of her womb might as well have been a stranger from another universe. I wonder if I'd have still been a violinist had I been the firstborn instead of Rebecca. Would I be the pretty one?

My mother's story doesn't feel like a story about me. I remember always being desperate for her to touch me, but feeling I could never reach out to her. I had always thought the distance came from her side. But maybe my mother needed the touch as much as I did.

Perhaps my mother had desires of her own, desires outside of my existence, outside of her role as mother and manager. Maybe she was too good at hiding it. But she did it because she believed at the time, and for all those years, that my hunger was more important, that my life was worth more than hers. That my talent meant more to the world, and to me, than anything she desired for herself. She knew that our hearts could not compete; that for one to be fulfilled, the other had to break. She broke her own heart for me. And then I went ahead and destroyed everything.

On the weekend, I receive an email from Tuba. My chest constricts. The two-second wait for the email to load. Three. Four. Five.

I scroll through it quickly to see how long it is. It's long. I scroll back up to the beginning and start reading.

He is setting up a new ensemble called the New York Chamber Group. Most players he has approached are Curtis and Juilliard graduates.

> It'll be one of the best groups in the world. Forget the Philharmonic. They're outdated. The repertoire will be diverse. Each concert will include at least one work by a female composer. We'll collaborate with dance groups and artists from Brooklyn and hold monthly funks, which are performances based on improvised ideas. I've already been offered funding by that rich woman we met at the New Year's Day Gala. Do you remember her? She's willing to sponsor your visa too. You can stay with me until you find a place. She has lots of money. Good to know people with a lot of money.

I read the email twice, then put my phone down and go into the bathroom to look at my eyebrows. I pick up the tweezers and pluck at a few stray hairs. I stand back and look at the symmetry again. Then

I go back to my phone and read the email again, this time focusing on the line:

We want you to lead the group.

Is this the silver lining? A second chance? Something always catches me on my way down. If I don't take this, what else will come my way? I had returned to playing for a reason. The reason is crystallising now. I have to believe that everything happens for a reason. That I can be someone again.

I pick up my phone and call my mother. I read her the email.

She is silent until I'm done, then she asks, 'Do you remember what I told you about the experiment?'

'Of course.'

'You know, I've carried that story with me for all these years. I've wanted to tell you for so long, but I knew you'd be too young to understand. It was a burden, you see. You do see that now, don't you?'

'Yes.'

'I felt ashamed, too. To let a baby affect me so much.'

We listen to the grey noise at the other end of the line. The cackle of a wavering bird on her end. The thrum of a buzzing motorcycle coasting in my ear.

'Everything was crazy. I held on to you because I was scared that the universe didn't think I was worthy to be your mother. Or enough. I needed to prove that I could nurture something great.'

I want to hold her hand. Open my arms to her. I imagine my body meeting hers in an embrace. But I stay there, motionless, phone pressed against my ear, speechless. There is nothing to say. I don't say anything at all.

Two nights later, Tuba calls while I'm eating a sandwich. When I see his name flash on my screen, I panic; the same panic I used to feel as a child, when, on the rare occasion I was home, someone would ring the doorbell, and I'd feel the panic of indecision erupt in my chest. Answer the door? Or don't answer the door? Acknowledge, or pretend nobody is home?

'What are you doing?' he asks.

I have to put the plate down on the sink because my hands are shaking. 'Nice to speak to you too.'

He laughs into the phone. 'It's getting really warm here. I think I prefer winter.'

I crack open my mouth to laugh along, but nothing comes out.

'What are you doing?' I ask him.

'I want to chat about the email. Have you thought about it?'

I walk out onto the balcony.

'It's only been two days.'

'Exactly. Two days too long.'

I wait for him to fill the silence.

'Are you only calling me because of the job?' he asks.

'What? You called me.'

In my ear, I hear his voice, clear and low and strong; police sirens in the background.

'Tell me about the city,' I say. 'Where are you?'

We talk for over an hour: about his new housemate, the rats, the congested bathroom drain and the condom packets lying around the apartment. The concert he saw the previous night. A Japanese tuba player. Jazz. 'Out of this world,' he says excitedly. A new concert series with the local conservatorium. The long meetings with the rich woman from the gallery. A new lover, who has, since last night, become his ex. The subway strikes. The terror his black and brown friends feel, and their families. The uncertainty of the future. We talk about my dream of living in New York.

'Don't you want this?' he asks. 'To make something of yourself over here? You said there's nothing in Sydney worth waking up for. Nothing worth bettering yourself for.'

'I have no interest in being virtuous.'

'That's exactly why New York City is perfect for you.'

Val enters the kitchen, keys dangling between her fingers. She opens the fridge and extracts a bottle of orange juice. I wave at her as she mouths something, which I miss; and leaves through the back door.

'Why are you being so nice now?' I ask. 'It wasn't strange? That I slept with that ex of yours?'

He doesn't say anything for a moment. Clicks his tongue. 'Yeah, sorry if I was an asshole. I don't care anymore about all that, frankly. I care about this. Our music. This ensemble is really something I've been thinking about a lot. I mean, why not? Why not now?'

56

Like a prized secret, I carry the decision in my heart for as long as I can without announcing it to the world. I defer it until I absolutely need to let those around me know. For seven days, I tell no one. It was an easy decision to make, in the end, because I'd known Sydney was never going to enliven my spirit; my hunger, my discontent.

When I do eventually tell others—my mother first, then Val, then Banks—they each express their pleasure. On hearing that I am moving to New York, Banks says, 'Well, that's to be expected. Perhaps you can still make it to Juilliard?'

'Very funny. You were the one who said I didn't need to go.'

I call him on a Monday morning. He sounds happy to hear from me.

'I was right. You were so much better than anyone else.'

Finally, one evening in the shower, I tell Mark.

He is lathering shampoo into my hair and rubbing foam into my scalp.

'I've taken it.'

'What?'

His hands stop moving.

I turn around, eyes still closed. 'I said I'm moving to New York.'

The sound of water splashing against tiles. There's never been a lonelier sound.

I palm my face and open my eyes. Mark's expression is flat and colourless. For the first time since I've known him, he looks his age.

'When?' he asks.

'August.'

He looks defeated, wounded. I know that look. It's the look Banks used to give me when I didn't do what he asked. If I overplayed a phrase or took the third movement of a concerto faster than he suggested.

A look of defeat, disappointment.

'Good for you,' Mark says. He places his hand on one of my shoulders and turns me around, continues rubbing my scalp, his fingers massaging the top of my skull more softly than before.

'Good for you,' he says again, his voice softer.

A few weeks later, after dinner at Mark's, I run the kitchen tap and pour dishwashing liquid into a bowl. I soak the cutlery in the water and leave the plates in the sink. Mark moves behind me and tugs on the edge of my shirt. I nudge him with a strong hand, and he counters with a bent arm just as I dip my head. His elbow knocks hard into my nose. Blood pours, a warm trail moving into my mouth and gums.

He brings me tissues, rubs my back while I lean back, pinching the bridge of my nose.

'Shit.'

'I'm fine.'

I walk to the bathroom, lift my chin and peer up my nose to survey the damage. He follows me, then kneels, pressing his face into my crotch. I can feel the tip of his nose.

'You smell so good.' He rubs his cheek against my thigh. Tries to lift my skirt.

'You've injured me enough.' I put my hand over my skirt and grip his head, hard, hoping he'll get up. Release me.

He looks up at me from the floor. 'Marry me.'

I put a hand on his shoulder, steady myself.

'What?'

He does not move. Instead he repeats the question. Slides his hand to the small of my back. I am frightened of what might happen. Frightened by my own desires and where that might lead me.

'Please get up.'

His eyes widen. 'You have to say yes.'

'What? What is this?'

I shift my balance away from him but his grip is tight.

'Let go of me.'

He grips even tighter. 'Do you love me?'

I try to arrange my features into an expression that matches his, but I can't read his face. Is it defiance? Humiliation?

Yes. Yes, I do love you. Perhaps if I say this, he will let go of me. *Don't leave. Don't let me be alone.*

Something inside me is always moving.

'Do you love me?' he asks again.

When did love became a threat?

I want for him to not look at my face, because I am scared the truth will be too obvious. I don't know how to arrange my lips, my cheeks, the muscles in my forehead.

I go to cover my face with both hands, but my nose is still bleeding, and my hands are full of bloodied tissues. I know I do not love him, I have never loved him, but it feels like such an admission might now be dangerous.

I stand with my eyes locked on his and wait for him to say more. But then I realise he is waiting on me.

My father once told me that deception is actually a kindness. Hide the truth, because the truth always hurts. Did this man deserve my truth?

I know that whatever I do now will change everything.

He is patient, waiting for a response. I pull him to his feet and hold him. I kiss him because it buys me more time to think. But he draws away, takes my face in his hands—those hands which I have come to love because they are large and strong but which now feel oppressive.

Maybe we'd been too busy to notice the absence of love. I thought he'd shown me indifference more than anything else, and now I am confused. I hadn't thought he cared for me at all.

'Don't go to New York,' he says. 'Stay here. I think we can make each other happy.'

'What are you talking about?'

'Stay here. Make me happy.'

A weight drops onto my chest. His expression twists into something else. Maybe he is just as confused as I am. Maybe that's why he'd suddenly started drinking a lot.

'Marry me. Stay here in Sydney.'

He drops to his knees again.

I pull his arm. Nothing shifts. I'm a small body trying to move a car.

'Stop it. You need to get up.'

'I mean it. I don't want you to go. Don't I make you happy? Don't you think we can be married?'

'Why are you asking me? This is wrong. I'm twenty-three.'

'Because I just broke your nose and I told myself I'd propose to you if I ever hurt you accidentally.'

'Stop lying.'

'I love you. Do you want me to ask you again?'

'No, please don't. It hurts.'

'*You* are hurting?'

A pained expression struggles for release behind his face.

'No, I mean, I don't want to hurt you.' My voice is quivering.

He removes his hand from my waist and stands up.

'What do you mean?' His voice is soft, wounded.

My mouth is dry. What comes out is a small croak.

'I don't know.'

Three lines crease along his forehead. I press my arms to my chest, steel myself.

'I don't think we should see each other anymore.'

Intuitively, I bow my head, expecting what, I'm not sure. I wait, study his reaction. His face twists into an expression I don't recognise. His eyes flit around the room; he doesn't want to look at me because he knows he will find something he doesn't want to see. Something resembling the truth.

'What are you talking about? We've been in love for months now, haven't we?' A pink warmth collects at his cheeks. He could be talking to anyone. I just happen to be the object right in front of him.

'Have *you*?' I ask.

'You make me happy.'

'That's not the same as love.'

I lunge for the tap. My hands nervously reaching for something to move.

He slaps my hand away.

'I want to spend my life with you.'

'Mark, did you even hear what I said? I don't think we should see each other anymore.' I extract my phone from my pocket. He reaches out and grabs it.

I hold my hand out. 'Please give me my phone back.'

'I want to marry you.'

He's gripping my phone in his right hand.

I ask again.

He folds his arms across his chest, clutching my phone.

I walk towards the bedroom. 'I don't want this.'

'How can you say that?' He laughs, a short manic burst. 'I can't believe I'm hearing this.'

He follows me into the bedroom.

'You never loved me?' he asks.

I don't know where to look. I stop in my place, halted by the frank, unexpected void he's opened.

I shake my head.

Everything is still in the apartment. For a moment, I think I hear the rattle of keys, someone to come and save me. But the sound fades; a neighbour, perhaps.

I look up at Mark's face, finally brave enough to take what is coming my way.

But at that moment, he walks to the door. Before he leaves, he half turns and whispers, just loud enough for me to hear, 'Fucking cunt.'

I realise later it is one of the few times I have ever heard him whisper.

That night, back home, I dream of Olivia. She has come back to me. She arrives at my apartment with a Tupperware container of brownies. She holds me in her arms and buries her face in my neck, repeating sorry, sorry, sorry. I run my hand over her long soft hair. She tells me secrets about Noah. She says she knows what I did with him, but that she's not angry. I forgive you, she says, I forgive you. I forgive you. She is sorry she has abandoned everyone she loves. Then her body metamorphoses into a giant snake and I step back to look at my hands, which are now scaly and clasping flakes of dried skin. The snake has shed its skin. The snake slithers away. I try to run after it, but then Banks appears. He's got a walking stick. He seems to have aged at least a decade. He's wearing an expensive coat and a grey beret. I ask him where the snake has gone. He strikes me across the head with the stick.

I wake up, shaking.

I am alone and, in this aloneness, paralysed by a fear that feels strangely comforting. I wonder whether Olivia knows I am still dreaming about her, that she still exists in my mind, more powerful than when she was part of my life in the flesh. I can't seem to draw a bridge across to the other side of this hurt.

My greatest fears are realised in my other life, during my sleeping hours. I dream about Banks committing violence against me because I believe he dreams of this too. He must still be angry with me for what I did. For walking offstage and deciding my own fate, without consulting him or my mother. If I let myself think about it, return to that time, I see, finally, that it must have been shattering for him. Of course it would have been. He didn't speak to me when I was in the States. The touring put cracks into his life. Thinned out his marriage. Of course it was all my fault. I destroyed the lives of the two people who cared about me the most. And tonight, it feels like this. A man I never loved wants to destroy mine.

57

The following week the orchestra begins a new concert series of works by Argentinian composers of the nineteenth and twentieth centuries: Bacalov, Panizza and Ginastera. It's my final season with the SSO. I'd spoken to Bryce eventually and told him of my decision. He seemed happy for me. He makes a comment about the program I will finish with. 'Good, don't you think? Adventurous.'

I nod. 'They're still all men though.'

What lasts in art is what the general consensus declares to be 'good'. The general consensus has always been old white men. Rich old white men. If your art does not speak to them and their narrow set of experiences it will be lost in the universe of abandoned things, erased from history. At times, I think about all those lost songs; melodies that were written at the beginning of a break-up, a breakdown; all the lines written and then unwritten because 'the general consensus' did not believe they were worth preserving. I wonder why none of the music I play has been created by a woman and whether that exclusion was deliberate. What is the point of being any kind of artist if your skin colour or gender excludes you from the choices of old white men, just because you don't look like them and they don't see themselves in you?

During the performance, I look out onto the sea of bodies sheathed in night-time gowns sparkling in the stage lights. I see the women's faces, their long dresses. I wonder if they think about our own cultural erasure.

'Meg Ryan and Tom Hanks are such an annoying classic white couple,' Val says.

On a free evening, we're sitting on the couch with a blanket across our legs watching *You've Got Mail*.

'I'm trying to fantasise my way into a better, nicer life.'

'Don't be stupid. You only ever watch films set in New York. Have you noticed that?'

I think for a moment, eyes fixed on the screen, watching Meg Ryan flirt with Tom Hanks in her bookshop. 'I suppose.'

'Her hair's always kind of perfect, huh?'

'Why don't we watch *Frances Ha* after this?' she suggests.

'I saw that in New York with a guy.'

'Which guy?'

'Just someone in the orchestra.'

After a while, she pats my hand.

'Are you okay? Has he tried to call?'

I shake my head.

Val knows that since I broke up with Mark a week ago he's been sending texts. I deleted the first few and then, when they kept coming, I blocked his number.

Val lifts my hand to her cheek and squeezes it.

'What did you want from him?' she asks.

'I'm not sure.'

She puts her arm around me.

'Do you think it would help to write this all down? Perhaps in a letter? You don't have to send it.'

'Write a letter? You mean, to him?'

'Well, to him, yeah. Or to whoever.'

'F–O–X.'

Meg Ryan is flashing her teeth, impressed by a five-year-old's spelling.

I recall my dream about Olivia. I want to talk to her again. Tell her about the dream.

'What would I say to Mark? "Dear Mark, you're a cunt. Stay away from me."'

She laughs, a short, muffled burst. 'Yeah, sure.'

'I guess he deserves it.'

'He deserves so much of your contempt.'

We sit for a while. I tell her about the other thing that's been gnawing at me: the research project. My mother's betrayal. No. My mother did not betray me. My mother opened herself; all her efforts for a life of her own were ravaged. When I was young, I felt this great love to be stifling because, at that age, there is no other way to feel love.

For the first time in years, I feel a wariness unfurl inside me. I bury my face in my hands.

'I've heard people talk about this stuff, experiments like this,' Val says quietly. 'I think attachment theories were popular when our parents were young. I mean, their parents grew up with that shit and they probably inhaled it from them. You know what they were about, right?'

I can see she's trying to distract me, and I nod to indicate for her to continue.

'Baby monkeys were locked up in tiny cages and given the choice to go to two fake 'mother' monkeys—one was just this piece of metal with a cartoon face but it had a bottle of milk attached while the other had nothing but it was wrapped in a blanket. Guess which one the monkeys went to?'

'The one with the milk?'

'The blanketed one.'

'Well, I'd rather not starve than be touched if I had a choice.'

'That's the thing. These experiments proved that our need for physical touch is just as strong, if not stronger, than our need for food.'

'By *our* you mean monkeys, which we're not.'

'Sure, okay, it *suggested*. The researchers made up these crazy monkeys, models that looked nothing like monkeys, made out of metal, they looked like robots, basic kid stuff, with electronic arms attached and stuff that could fling the baby monkeys off, even punch them and shit. And the monkeys just kept going back. They liked the blanket so much.'

'I thought they were just random pieces of metal put together.'

'They were. But they were also wrapped in blankets.'

'How can you want a blanket that's uncomfortable?'

'If I made you sit on a chair made of ten knives, I mean, it's sharp and impossible, but the surface might feel good.'

I'm not convinced. 'So they made some grand statement about love based on these monkeys getting tortured in a lab?'

'Something like that.'

'It's just biology.'

'It's pretty cool.'

I put a hand on her arm for apology. Desire, discomfort.

'You're saying the researchers thought this showed something about children and mothers and love? But it was done decades ago. You know how fast things change. Today they say one thing and tomorrow there's something that'll totally contradict what was said. I mean, is it love? Or is it infatuation? Maybe it's just all in the language. It's just some other kind of need. Calling it love is just a way to make more money. People love love.'

Val moves strands of hair off her face. 'Well, yeah. Love always sounds better.'

I'd always known that desiring is harder than being desirable. I'd known that my mother told me once, before a big competition, that wanting was tremendous and powerful, but that if she got to choose, she'd choose to be the desired one, not the desiring. 'There's less to do being desirable.'

I saw that she was virtuous, and good, but also that being virtuous and good made her unhappy. There were moments in the last few months, thinking about my mother and realising that perhaps I'd been too close to her all those years, when I saw that she'd given up so much of her life for my achievements. Achievements that now feel thin. I saw that those reasons came to bind her, too, and when she lost her husband, and then me, well, I couldn't imagine how she found the resolve to keep herself steady. I will always be too afraid to ask her about Banks.

'Anyway.'

Before bed that night, I sneak a look at my phone. An email from Olivia. The light from the phone illuminates my room. I read the message with my heart in my throat.

I'll be in Sydney next week. How are you?

Val takes me out for breakfast the next morning. We drink our soy lattes in silence. My mind is preoccupied with the image of Mark chewing his bottom lip—he called it his 'love face'; when he punctured my body he'd put on this face; like a little boy in the playground who was concentrating on smashing something.

'Can I say something?' Val leans forward. 'Remember that time I quit my shitty studio job and I rang you right after? Do you remember what you said to me?'

I roll my eyes and give her a weak smile.

'Are you seriously giving me the cheesy post-break-up talk?'

A tan pug strolls by, sniffs around my feet. I bend over, caress its neck. 'I don't know. Maybe I was lazy. Sometimes he made me happy. I don't know. I don't know if I was happy or if I was deluded or if I was feeling really powerful in bed, and you know, that felt good.'

The pug nuzzles my ankles and then moves on to the woman at the next table.

'You didn't love him?'

'I think I would have told you if we ever started using that word.'

I play with the sourdough on my plate.

'He never left his girlfriend,' I say sombrely.

'What does that have to do with anything?'

I take a pinch of salt from the small bowl in the centre of the table, rubbing it between my fingertips. Val's eyes are fixed on my face. Her penetrating stare like huge flashlights.

'Maybe I never wanted him, in that way. I don't know.'

'You never seemed all that bothered by Dresden.' Val shakes her head and leans back in her chair. 'Did you ever think he'd fall in love with you?'

I sip my water. She looks at me, waiting. How can I explain something I don't even understand? How can this all mean something now, in light of everything that has happened?

'I used to walk on this track near my parents' place in Willoughby. There was one month when I walked there every day at around the same time, just before sunset. Some nights the cicadas would scream like crazy, and the next night it would be silent. Totally silent. Then the following night the noise would be back again, louder than ever. I thought maybe it had something to do with the weather, or a rise in humidity or air pressure. But I couldn't come up with one reason why the noise was sometimes there and sometimes not. Maybe that's how I feel about Mark.'

A waitress comes by to collect our plates. 'How was everything, girls?'

'Great!' we snap like automated machines.

'Would you like anything else?' she asks.

Val looks over at me. 'You want anything Jena?'

I smile instinctively and shake my head. 'I think I'm good.'

That night, we watch *Frances Ha*. Val promises it will cheer me up. I have long wanted to be part of Frances's world. Black and white. She occupies the space of the other world, one where everyone is brave. Where young people are able to lie in bed and think about which anxieties to focus on for the day.

When Frances runs through the streets full of joy, her smile filling everything, Val claps her hands. 'You do know this scene is plagiarised? It's taken from a scene in a French film. Here, look.'

She presses the space button on her laptop and opens up YouTube. A man is staggering along a street. It's night-time, and there's no one around. The soundtrack is David Bowie's 'Modern Love', the same tune Frances runs to. The man starts running when the music picks up, leaping and cartwheeling, a strange mix of despair and elation on his face. It feels both exhilarating and painful to watch.

'This is so beautiful.'

Later, I think about the ways classical musicians have plagiarised all the players who've ever come before them. Doesn't great art derive from other great art? We are the con artists. Some people are just better at pretending it's all new. The better the deception, the better the artist.

If I'd known this when I was six years old, would I have practised as hard as I did? I must have seen some meaning in it. I must have enjoyed it.

I think about this as I'm washing my hair in the shower, feeling the old comfort of the familiar return to me. And it's then, while rubbing conditioner in my hair, that I feel resolved—of course this is the right decision. Of course I must be in New York. There is no other alternative for this life I want. This life, I understand, could not have worked out any other way.

58

I spend the next few weeks packing, arraging things in order. In my occasional breaks from sorting boxes and bags and other junk, I scroll through Facebook, mindlessly passing hours. I pause on a new post from Olivia. A picture of Mark. He is in a suit, holding the hand of a woman dressed in a bridal gown. She holds a bouquet of pink roses. They are smiling. They are beautiful. Something cracks between my ribs.

I call my mother, wanting a place to deposit my confusion. Wanting someone to analyse my strange despair. She knows nothing about Mark because I have never told her. I still wasn't prepared to tell her the entire story. Perhaps in the future, but not now. Not when I am about to leave for another country.

She's tending to her garden when I call.

I ask her what to do about Banks. Should I go see him? I reach for something when I call her but then something else surfaces instead. Was my confusion about Mark or Banks?

'He's a stubborn man, Jena,' she says. 'But he'll always want to see you.'

'But I'm not a child anymore. Maybe he won't be so quick to forgive me.'

She sighs into the phone. 'Have a little faith. You'll be surprised.'

•

On the weekend, I am lying in bed, rereading Virginia Woolf's *To the Lighthouse*. The rain drums against the windows. Val returns from her studio. She stands in the doorway and tells me she'd bumped into Olivia on King Street.

'She had news.'

'What?'

'Mark and Dresden got married in Melbourne. It was a last-minute thing, apparently.'

I knew this already, of course. I'd seen the pictures on Facebook.

I close the book in my hand.

'How was Olivia?' I ask. The last time I'd seen her was—I don't remember. I'd left her last email unanswered. The last time I'd seen Noah was the concert at Newington. The yacht.

'Didn't you hear?' Val asks.

'What?'

'She broke up with Noah.'

I hear the neighbours' cackling laughs. A chorus of adult voices. The sharp clicking of bats beginning their nocturnal flight.

Through the window, I see them silhouetted against the blue-black sky like pieces of ash above a fire, flickering, floating.

I pull on a thread of my jumper. A sleeve is unravelling.

Val leans against the doorframe, waiting for me to say something. My silence is supposed to encourage her to say more.

I touch my stomach, the flesh above my belly button. Then I rush to the bathroom sink and retch. Nothing comes out. I feel like emptying my heart, everything inside my body.

I type a message to Olivia.

I'm sorry about Noah.

59

Banks calls mid-week. He has texted a handful of times since I got back from New York, updates about performance opportunities, most of which I turn down. He doesn't mind texting; short, quick, like medical appointment notifications. Each time I write back, I tell myself to visit him. The dream of him striking me with a walking stick still haunts me at unusual hours of the day. Sometimes, I lie awake at night, unable to relax into sleep for fear of meeting him in my other life. He doesn't try to call, until a Wednesday, a week before I leave for New York.

'Can you do a concert tomorrow?' he asks. 'The Willoughby Symphony need someone to step in to do the Bach Concerto. One of the soloists has food poisoning.'

A community orchestra.

'It's the Bach double.'

'Who's the other violinist?'

'Olivia Gregory.'

Olivia. Olivia. Olivia.

'Oh.'

'A problem?' He waits for me to make a sound.

'No, no problem. I'll do it. I'll definitely do it.'

•

On the train to the Concourse in Chatswood, I rehearse what I'll say to her. Single words. Nothing fully formed. Maybe she will only want to focus on the music.

I walk inside the building and fold my umbrella. It smells like wet carpet and cheap cologne. The lights are dimmed in the green room. I hear the shuffle of bass stools on the stage. Rehearsal has started. I unpack my violin and pull out my bow, rosining rapidly. There is something missing in my case. Monkey. I'd pulled him out for a wash over the weekend and forgot to place him back inside my case.

The stage door is right behind the second violin section. I slip through in a half-crouch to make my entrance unobtrusive. There is no subtle way of doing this when the stage lights are on. I can feel the heat of the orange light spread along my spine. The other musicians are still. Some turn their heads as I creep past.

I see Olivia. She is standing in front of the first violins, holding her violin at its neck, swinging her bow gently. I look away. From where I am, I can see the conductor, the edge of his shirt, a dark patch under his arm.

I make a sound, like a greeting. Wave.

A sea of heads turns to gaze. I do my best to walk gracefully to the empty seat, weaving through the chairs and stands and bows poking in all directions, violin scrolls inhibiting my path.

'Everyone, please welcome our other soloist, Jena Lin.'

The bows tap stands and hands slap thighs.

'We'll just be another few minutes before we run through the Bach.'

I nod and sit on a chair in the front row. I stare at the back of the concertmaster's head and begin counting the strands of grey hair on his head. The stage lights are so bright they illuminate the silvery tones; a sunset scattered with silver clouds.

I look over at Olivia, who catches my eye and gives me a nervous grin. I look away.

The conductor lifts his baton and fifty-nine spines straighten, reeds to mouths and neck rests under chins. He drops his arm to his side.

'Good, you're all paying attention.'

I glance over to Olivia who catches my eye.

'You ready?' I ask.

She nods. 'You?'

After the concert, we walk side by side to the station like we used to, talking about our plans.

'Noah says hi.'

'What's he doing now?' I ask.

'He's going overseas to study with some clarinet player for a few months. I think he's sick of Sydney too.'

I tell her about New York, about Tuba, about Banks.

'Oh, you know Banks was there at the concert?' She stops walking for a moment. 'He was sitting at the back. I saw him while we were playing.'

'Why didn't he come say hi?'

She shrugs. 'Maybe he had someplace else to go.'

I reach over. Put a hand on her shoulder. 'You're always so good, aren't you?'

60

My parents drive me to the airport, insisting I ask a friend to come along. Val sits in the back seat, peering over every few seconds.

I've spent the last few days on the phone with Tuba, arranging meeting times. Logistics. Administrative tasks. His voice on the phone sounds lower, though at times it breaks into a squeal when he gets excited and talks about the opening season's program.

'I knew you'd never stay in Sydney,' my mother says in the car.

My father is driving, silent, eyes on the road.

'You did?'

'Of course. You were born in the wrong country.'

At the airport, my father drops us off then goes to park the car. My mother and Val stand beside me at the departure gates. I fiddle with the zip of my backpack to distract myself from speeches. I have nothing planned.

'So,' Val takes me into her arms and squeezes too hard. 'You'll be back, won't you?'

'Or, we can come visit you,' my mother says. She turns to Val and signals something with her eyes.

Val retreats. Her eyes are moist.

'Your friend told me about an older man you were seeing.' I can't believe she's bringing this up now. 'Why didn't you ever tell me?'

'I was ashamed, I guess.'

She rests her hand on my shoulder. 'Don't forget, I'm your mother. I will always be here when you need me.'

I look at the mole on her neck so I don't have to look her in the eye.

'I was lonely,' I mutter.

She sighs. 'Maybe you need to stop using that word as an excuse to mistreat yourself.'

'But it's the truth. I was just . . . lonely.'

She pats my back. 'To be lonely is to want too much. And that's fine. But it doesn't mean you should let people hurt you. You know that now, right?'

She holds out her arms, opening like an infinite gesture.

'Don't worry. You couldn't fit into Sydney even if you tried. Your hunger is what makes you special, even though some days, most days, it won't feel like that at all. That's when you need to believe the hardest, that hunger is what makes you who you are. Don't be ashamed of it.'

In my heart, I feel the promise of a love so deep and secure expand into a full, round star, burning and pulsating with each breath.

Only afterwards, as I'm waiting in line to pass through customs, do I realise my face is wet with tears.

I stroll around the shops and spray perfume on my collar at the cosmetics counter. I find my face reflected on each mirror and decide to submit to the heavy weight of this new life.

My phone rings. An unidentified number. I wait for it to ring out. A text comes in—someone has left a voicemail message. I put the phone to my ear.

A sharp jolt of adrenaline snaps behind my ribs at the sound of Mark's voice.

ACKNOWLEDGEMENTS

Thanks to Alice Pung, Lex Hirst, Michelle Cahill, Tiffany Tsao, Rachel Cruz, Angela Savage, Alice Grundy, Yen-Rong Wong, Emily Maguire, Grace Heifetz, Mieke Eerkens, Shu-Ling Chua, Melanie Thorne, Tony Tulathimutte, Nam Le, Christos Tsiolkas and Iain Giblin for your support and advice. Thanks to my agent Melanie Ostell, for your wisdom, clarity, charm and general pizzaz. Thanks to my publisher Jane Palfreyman for your commitment and unwavering support. Thanks to Ali Lavau for your extraordinary and peerless editorial talent. To Tessa Feggans, Pamela Dunne, Jennifer Thurgate and all the team at Allen & Unwin. Thanks to the Australia Council for the Arts for their grant which allowed me to study writing in the US. Thanks to the Altantic Center for the Arts, for the most productive and sublime three weeks of my writing career so far.

Thanks to Judy Banki, Susan Banki, Emma Bryant, Annie Bryant, Kyle Caputo, Yiannis Chambers, Adam Chen, Elizabeth Cooney, Jessica Davis, Risa Denenberg, Martha Kate Dos Santos, Frances Doyle, Ernesto Escaler, Stephen Finch, Spencer Grubbs, Louise Giovanelli, Suha Gunti, Dimitra Harvey, Ally Havas, Beth Hilberding, Georgina Horsburgh, Shona Lee, Sally Lewis, Iannie Liu, Kristen Luong, Barbara Robinson, Milena Roglic, Thea Soutar, Kellie Southan, Billy Stevenson and Lily

Tao for your conversations and friendships. Thank you Helen, Kevin, Lisa, Luke, Sion, Kumiko, Alan, Arya, Bruce, Russell, Evie, Paddy and Jake for all the joys of being in a loving family. Thank you Eli Tapuchi for your gentle, quiet love. You are my eyes, ears, breath and pulse when I'm away from New York City.

Finally, thanks to my parents, who are the beginning and end of everything I do. 媽媽, 爸爸 謝謝您為我所做的一切。我永遠, 永遠感激。永遠。

ABOUT THE AUTHOR

Jessie Tu was born in Taiwan and immigrated to Sydney at age five. She has written for *The Guardian, LA Review of Books* and many literary journals. She trained as a classical violinist for more than fifteen years, has taught at numerous secondary schools and now works as a journalist. Her first collection of poems, *You Should Have Told Me We Had Nothing Left*, was published in 2018. This is her debut novel.